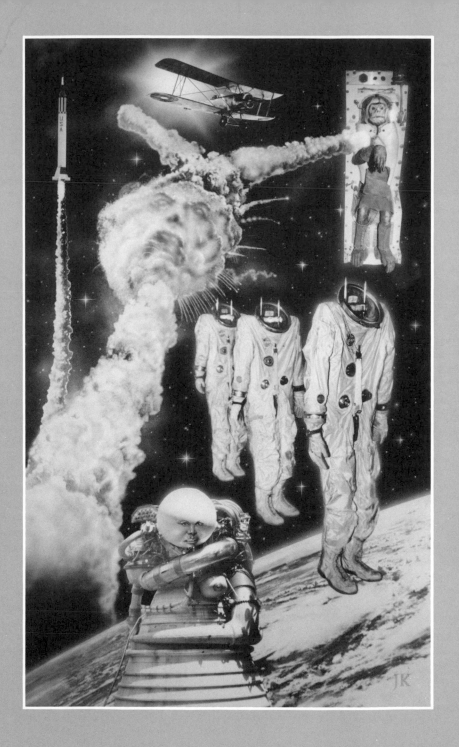

MEMORIES OF THE SPACE AGE

J. G. BALLARD

ARTWORK BY JEFFREY K. POTTER

ARKHAM HOUSE PUBLISHERS, INC.

$F I c$

Library of Congress Cataloging-in-Publication Data

Ballard, J. G., 1930–
   Memories of the space age / J. G. Ballard; with illustrations
by Jeffrey K. Potter.—1st ed.
      p.   cm.
   Eight stories originally published between 1962 and 1985.
   ISBN 0-87054-157-9 (alk. paper)
   1. Science fiction, English.   I. Title.
PR6052.A46M46   1988
823′.914—dc19   88-15075

The stories in this collection were first published in the
following magazines: *Ambit, Fantastic Stories, Fantasy and
Science Fiction, Interzone, New Worlds,* and *Playboy.*
Printed in the United States of America
First Edition

R00661 19540

Φράζεο, Τυδείδη, καὶ χάζεο, μηδὲ θεοῖσιν
Ἶσ' ἔθελε φρονέειν, ἐπεὶ οὔ ποτε φῦλον ὁμοῖον
Ἀθανάτων τε θεῶν χαμαὶ ἐρχομένων τ' ἀνθρώπων.

—HOMER

Denn mit Göttern
Soll sich nicht messen
Irgendein Mensch.
Hebt er sich aufwärts
Und berührt
Mit dem Scheitel die Sterne,
Nirgends haften dann
Die unsichern Sohlen,
Und mit ihm spielen
Wolken und Winde.

—GOETHE

By leaving his planet and setting off into outer space
man had committed an evolutionary crime, a
breach of the rules governing his tenancy of the
universe, and of the laws of time and space.
Perhaps the right to travel through space belonged
to another order of beings, but his crime was being
punished just as surely as would be any attempt
to ignore the laws of gravity.

—BALLARD

CONTENTS

THE CAGE OF SAND

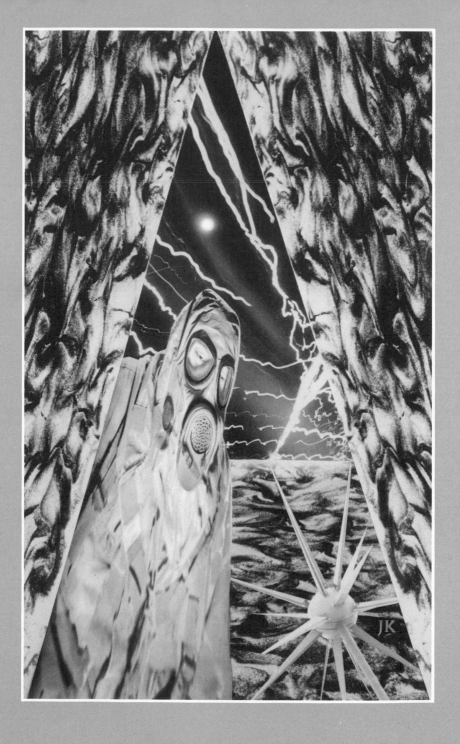

AT SUNSET, WHEN THE VERMILION GLOW REFLECTED FROM THE dunes along the horizon fitfully illuminated the white faces of the abandoned hotels, Bridgman stepped onto his balcony and looked out over the long stretches of cooling sand as the tides of purple shadow seeped across them. Slowly, extending their slender fingers through the shallow saddles and depressions, the shadows massed together like gigantic combs, a few phosphorescing spurs of obsidian isolated for a moment between the tines, and then finally coalesced and flooded in a solid wave across the half-submerged hotels. Behind the silent façades, in the tilting sand-filled streets which had once glittered with cocktail bars and restaurants, it was already night. Haloes of moonlight beaded the lamp-standards with silver dew, and draped the shuttered windows and slipping cornices like a frost of frozen gas.

As Bridgman watched, his lean bronzed arms propped against the rusting rail, the last whorls of light sank away into the cerise funnel withdrawing below the horizon, and the first wind stirred across the dead Martian sand. Here and there miniature cyclones whirled about a sand-spur, drawing off swirling feathers of moon-washed spray, and a nimbus of white dust swept across the dunes and settled in the dips and hollows. Gradually the drifts accumulated, edging towards the former shoreline below the hotels. Already the first four floors had been inundated and the sand now reached up to within two feet of Bridgman's balcony. After the next sandstorm he would be forced yet again to move to the floor above.

"Bridgman!"

The voice cleft the darkness like a spear. Fifty yards to his right, at the edge of the derelict sand-break he had once attempted to build below the hotel, a square stocky figure wearing a pair of frayed cotton shorts waved up at him. The moonlight etched the broad sinewy muscles of his chest, the powerful bowed legs sinking almost to their calves in the soft Martian sand. He was about forty-five years old, his thinning hair close-cropped so that he seemed almost bald. In his right hand he carried a large canvas holdall.

Bridgman smiled to himself. Standing there patiently in the moonlight below the derelict hotel, Travis reminded him of some long-delayed tourist arriving at a ghost resort years after its extinction.

"Bridgman, are you coming?" When the latter still leaned on his balcony rail, Travis added: "The next conjunction is tomorrow."

Bridgman shook his head, a rictus of annoyance twisting his mouth. He hated the bimonthly conjunctions, when all seven of the derelict satellite capsules still orbiting the Earth crossed the sky together. Invariably on these nights he remained in his room, playing over the old memo-tapes he had salvaged from the submerged chalets and motels further along the beach (the hysterical "This is Mamie Goldberg, 62955 Cocoa Boulevard, I really wanna protest against this crazy evacuation . . ." or resigned "Sam Snade here, the Pontiac convertible in the black garage belongs to anyone who can dig it out"). Travis and Louise Woodward always came to the hotel on the conjunction nights—it was the highest building in the resort, with an unrestricted view from horizon to horizon—and would follow the seven converging stars as they pursued their endless courses around the globe. Both would be oblivious of everything else, which the wardens knew only too well, and they reserved their most careful searches of the sand-sea for these bimonthly occasions. Invariably Bridgman found himself forced to act as lookout for the other two.

"I was out last night," he called down to Travis. "Keep away from the northeast perimeter fence by the Cape. They'll be busy repairing the track."

Most nights Bridgman divided his time between excavating the buried motels for caches of supplies (the former inhabitants of the resort area had assumed the government would soon rescind its evacuation order) and disconnecting the sections of metal roadway laid across the desert for the wardens' jeeps. Each of the squares of wire mesh was about five yards wide and weighed over three hundred pounds. After he had snapped the lines of rivets, dragged the sections away, and buried them among the dunes he would be exhausted, and spend most of the next day nursing his strained hands and shoulders. Some sections of the track were now permanently anchored with heavy steel stakes, and he knew that sooner or later they would be unable to delay the wardens by sabotaging the roadway.

Travis hesitated, and with a noncommittal shrug disappeared among the dunes, the heavy tool-bag swinging easily from one powerful arm. Despite the meagre diet which sustained him, his energy and determination seemed undiminished—in a single night Bridgman had watched him dismantle twenty sections of track and then loop together the adjacent limbs of a crossroad, sending an entire convoy of six vehicles off into the wastelands to the south.

Bridgman turned from the balcony, then stopped when a faint tang of brine touched the cool air. Ten miles away, hidden by the lines of dunes, was the sea, the long green rollers of the middle Atlantic breaking against the red Martian strand. When he had first come to the beach five years earlier there had never been the faintest scent of brine across the intervening miles of sand. Slowly, however, the Atlantic was driving the shore back to its former margins. The tireless shoulder of the Gulf Stream drummed against the soft Martian dust and piled the dunes into grotesque rococo reefs which the wind carried away into the sand-sea. Gradually the ocean was returning, reclaiming its great smooth basin, sifting out the black quartz and Martian obsidian which would never be wind-borne and drawing these down into its deeps. More and more often the stain of brine would hang on the evening air, reminding Bridgman why he had first come to the beach and removing any inclination to leave.

Three years earlier he had attempted to measure the rate of approach, by driving a series of stakes into the sand at the water's edge, but the shifting contours of the dunes carried away the coloured poles. Later, using the promontory at Cape Canaveral, where the old launching gantries and landing ramps reared up into the sky like derelict pieces of giant sculpture, he had calculated by triangulation that the advance was little more than thirty yards per year. At this rate—without wanting to, he had automatically made the calculation—it would be well over five hundred years before the Atlantic reached its former littoral at Cocoa Beach. Though discouragingly slow, the movement was nonetheless in a forward direction, and Bridgman was happy to remain in his hotel ten miles away across the dunes, conceding towards its time of arrival the few years he had at his disposal.

Later, shortly after Louise Woodward's arrival, he had thought of dismantling one of the motel cabins and building himself a small chalet by the water's edge. But the shoreline had been too dismal and forbidding. The great red dunes rolled on for miles, cutting off half the sky, dissolving slowly under the impact of the slate-green water. There was no formal tide-line, but only a steep shelf littered with nodes of quartz and rusting fragments of Mars rockets brought back with the ballast. He spent a few days in a cave below a towering sand-reef, watching the long galleries of compacted red dust crumble and dissolve as the cold Atlantic stream sluiced through them, collapsing like the decorated colonnades of a baroque cathedral. In the summer the heat reverberated from the hot sand as from the slag of some molten sun, burning the rubber soles from his boots, and the light from the scattered flints of washed quartz flickered with diamond hardness. Bridgman had returned to the hotel grateful for his room overlooking the silent dunes.

Leaving the balcony, the sweet smell of brine still in his nostrils, he went over to the desk. A small cone of shielded light shone down over the tape-recorder and rack of spools. The rumble of the wardens' unsilenced engines always gave him at least five minutes' warning of their arrival, and it would have been safe to install another lamp in the room— there were no roadways between the hotel and the sea, and from a distance any light reflected onto the balcony was indistinguishable from the corona of glimmering phosphors which hung over the sand like myriads of fireflies. However,

Bridgman preferred to sit in the darkened suite, enclosed by the circle of books on the makeshift shelves, the shadow-filled air playing over his shoulders through the long night as he toyed with the memo-tapes, fragments of a vanished and unregretted past. By day he always drew the blinds, immolating himself in a world of perpetual twilight.

Bridgman had easily adapted himself to his self-isolation, soon evolved a system of daily routines that gave him the maximum of time to spend on his private reveries. Pinned to the walls around him were a series of huge whiteprints and architectural drawings, depicting various elevations of a fantastic Martian city he had once designed, its glass spires and curtain walls rising like heliotropic jewels from the ver-milion desert. In fact, the whole city was a vast piece of jewellery, each elevation brilliantly visualised but as sym-metrical, and ultimately as lifeless, as a crown. Bridgman continually retouched the drawings, inserting more and more details, so that they almost seemed to be photographs of an original.

Most of the hotels in the town—one of a dozen similar resorts buried by the sand which had once formed an un-broken strip of motels, chalets, and five-star hotels thirty miles to the south of Cape Canaveral—were well stocked with supplies of canned food abandoned when the area was evacuated and wired off. There were ample reservoirs and cisterns filled with water, apart from a thousand intact cocktail bars six feet below the surface of the sand. Travis had excavated a dozen of these in search of his favourite vin-tage bourbon. Walking out across the desert behind the town one would suddenly find a short flight of steps cut into the annealed sand and crawl below an occluded sign announcing THE SATELLITE BAR or THE ORBIT ROOM into the in-ner sanctum, where the jutting deck of a chromium bar had been cleared as far as the diamond-paned mirror freighted with its rows of bottles and figurines. Bridgman would have been glad to see them left undisturbed.

The whole trash of amusement arcades and cheap bars on the outskirts of the beach resorts were a depressing com-mentary on the original spaceflights, reducing them to the level of monster sideshows at a carnival.

Outside his room, steps sounded along the corridor, then

slowly climbed the stairway, pausing for a few seconds at every landing. Bridgman lowered the memo-tape in his hand, listening to the familiar tired footsteps. This was Louise Woodward, making her invariable evening ascent to the roof ten storeys above. Bridgman glanced at the time-table pinned to the wall. Only two of the satellites would be visible, between 12:25 and 12:35 A.M., at an elevation of sixty-two degrees in the southwest, passing through Cetus and Eridanus, neither of them containing her husband. Although the siting was two hours away, she was already taking up her position, and would remain there until dawn.

Bridgman listened wanly to the feet recede slowly up the stairwell. All through the night the slim, pale-faced woman would sit out under the moonlit sky, as the soft Martian sand her husband had given his life to reach sifted around her in the dark wind, stroking her faded hair like some mourning mariner's wife waiting for the sea to surrender her husband's body. Travis usually joined her later, and the two of them sat side by side against the elevator house, the frosted letters of the hotel's neon sign strewn around their feet like the fragments of a dismembered zodiac, then at dawn made their way down into the shadow-filled streets to their eyries in the nearby hotels.

Initially Bridgman often joined their nocturnal vigil, but after a few nights he began to feel something repellent, if not actually ghoulish, about their mindless contemplation of the stars. This was not so much because of the macabre spectacle of the dead astronauts orbiting the planet in their capsules, but because of the curious sense of unspoken communion between Travis and Louise Woodward, almost as if they were celebrating a private rite to which Bridgman could never be initiated. Whatever their original motives, Bridgman sometimes suspected that these had been overlaid by other, more personal ones.

Ostensibly, Louise Woodward was watching her husband's satellite in order to keep alive his memory, but Bridgman guessed that the memories she unconsciously wished to perpetuate were those of herself twenty years earlier, when her husband had been a celebrity and she herself courted by magazine columnists and TV reporters. For fifteen years after his death—Woodward had been killed testing a new lightweight launching platform—she had lived a nomadic existence, driving restlessly in her cheap car from motel to motel across the continent, following her husband's star as it disappeared into the eastern night, and had at last made her home at Cocoa Beach in sight of the rusting gantries across the bay.

Travis's real motives were probably more complex. To Bridgman, after they had known each other for a couple of years, he had confided that he felt himself bound by a debt of honour to maintain a watch over the dead astronauts for the example of courage and sacrifice they had set him as a child (although most of them had been piloting their wrecked capsules for fifty years before Travis's birth), and that now they were virtually forgotten he must singlehandedly keep alive the fading flame of their memory. Bridgman was convinced of his sincerity.

Yet later, going through a pile of old news magazines in the trunk of a car he excavated from a motel port, he came across a picture of Travis wearing an aluminium pressure suit and learned something more of his story. Apparently Travis had at one time himself been an astronaut—or rather, a would-be astronaut. A test pilot for one of the civilian agencies setting up orbital relay stations, his nerve had failed him a few seconds before the last "hold" of his countdown, a moment of pure unexpected funk that cost the company some five million dollars.

Obviously it was his inability to come to terms with this failure of character, unfortunately discovered lying flat on his back on a contour couch two hundred feet above the launching pad, which had brought Travis to Canaveral, the abandoned Mecca of the first heroes of astronautics.

Tactfully Bridgman had tried to explain that no one would blame him for this failure of nerve—less his responsibility than that of the selectors who had picked him for the flight, or at least the result of an unhappy concatenation of ambiguously worded multiple-choice questions (crosses in the wrong boxes, some heavier to bear and harder to open than others! Bridgman had joked sardonically to himself). But Travis seemed to have reached his own decision about himself. Night after night, he watched the brilliant funerary convoy weave its gilded pathway towards the dawn sun, salving his own failure by identifying it with the greater, but blameless, failure of the seven astronauts. Travis still wore his hair in the regulation "Mohican" cut of the spaceman, still kept himself in perfect physical trim by the vigorous routines he had practised before his abortive flight. Sustained by the personal myth he had created, he was now more or less unreachable.

"Dear Harry, I've taken the car and deposit box. Sorry it should end like—"

Irritably, Bridgman switched off the memo-tape and its recapitulation of some thirty-year-old private triviality. For some reason he seemed unable to accept Travis and Louise Woodward for what they were. He disliked this failure of compassion, a nagging compulsion to expose other people's motives and strip away the insulating sheaths around their naked nerve strings, particularly as his own motives for being at Cape Canaveral were so suspect. Why was *he* there, what failure was *he* trying to expiate? And why choose Cocoa Beach as his penitential shore? For three years he had asked himself these questions so often that they had ceased to have any meaning, like a fossilised catechism or the blunted self-recrimination of a paranoiac.

He had resigned his job as the chief architect of a big space development company after the large government contract on which the firm depended, for the design of the first Martian city-settlement, was awarded to a rival consortium. Secretly, however, he realised that his resignation had marked his unconscious acceptance that despite his great imaginative gifts he was unequal to the specialised and more prosaic tasks of designing the settlement. On the drawing board, as elsewhere, he would always remain earthbound.

His dreams of building a new Gothic architecture of launching ports and control gantries, of being the Frank Lloyd Wright and Le Corbusier of the first city to be raised outside Earth, faded forever, but leaving him unable to accept the alternative of turning out endless plans for low-cost hospitals in Ecuador and housing estates in Tokyo. For a year he had drifted aimlessly, but a few colour photographs of the vermilion sunsets at Cocoa Beach and a news story about the recluses living on in the submerged motels had provided a powerful compass.

He dropped the memo-tape into a drawer, making an effort to accept Louise Woodward and Travis on their own terms, a wife keeping watch over her dead husband and an old astronaut maintaining a solitary vigil over the memories of his lost comrades-in-arms.

The wind gusted against the balcony window, and a light spray of sand rained across the floor. At night dust-storms churned along the beach. Thermal pools isolated by the cooling desert would suddenly accrete like beads of quicksilver and erupt across the fluffy sand in miniature tornadoes.

Only fifty yards away, the dying cough of a heavy diesel cut through the shadows. Quickly Bridgman turned off the small desk light, grateful for his meanness over the battery packs plugged into the circuit, then stepped to the window.

At the leftward edge of the sand-break, half hidden in the long shadows cast by the hotel, was a large tracked vehicle with a low camouflaged hull. A narrow observation bridge had been built over the bumpers directly in front of the squat snout of the engine housing, and two of the beach wardens were craning up through the plexiglass windows at the balconies of the hotel, shifting their binoculars from room to room. Behind them, under the glass dome of the extended driving cabin, were three more wardens, controlling an outboard spotlight. In the centre of the bowl a thin mote of light pulsed with the rhythm of the engine, ready to throw its powerful beam into any of the open rooms.

Bridgman hid back behind the shutters as the binoculars focused upon the adjacent balcony, moved to his own, hesitated, and passed to the next. Exasperated by the sabotaging of the roadways, the wardens had evidently decided on a new type of vehicle. With their four broad tracks, the huge squat sand-cars would be free of the mesh roadways and able to rove at will through the dunes and sand-hills.

Bridgman watched the vehicle reverse slowly, its engine barely varying its deep bass growl, then move off along the line of hotels, almost indistinguishable in profile among the shifting dunes and hillocks. A hundred yards away, at the first intersection, it turned towards the main boulevard, wisps of dust streaming from the metal cleats like thin spumes of steam. The men in the observation bridge were still watching the hotel. Bridgman was certain that they had seen a reflected glimmer of light, or perhaps some movement of Louise Woodward's on the roof. However reluctant to leave the car and be contaminated by the poisonous dust, the wardens would not hesitate if the capture of one of the beachcombers warranted it.

Racing up the staircase, Bridgman made his way to the roof, crouching below the windows that overlooked the boulevard. Like a huge crab, the sand-car had parked under the jutting overhang of the big department store opposite. Once fifty feet from the ground, the concrete lip was now separated from it by little more than six or seven feet, and the sand-car was hidden in the shadows below it, engine silent. A single movement in a window, or the unexpected return of Travis, and the wardens would spring from the hatchways, their long-handled nets and lassoes pinioning them around the necks and ankles. Bridgman remembered one beachcomber he had seen flushed from his motel hideout and carried off like a huge twitching spider at the centre of a black rubber web, the wardens with their averted faces and masked mouths like devils in an abstract ballet.

Reaching the roof, Bridgman stepped out into the opaque white moonlight. Louise Woodward was leaning on the balcony, looking out towards the distant, unseen sea. At the faint sound of the door creaking she turned and began to walk listlessly around the roof, her pale face floating like a nimbus. She wore a freshly ironed print dress she had found in a rusty spin drier in one of the launderettes, and her streaked blonde hair floated out lightly behind her on the wind.

"Louise!"

Involuntarily she started, tripping over a fragment of the neon sign, then moved backwards towards the balcony overlooking the boulevard.

"Mrs. Woodward!" Bridgman held her by the elbow, raised a hand to her mouth before she could cry out. "The wardens are down below. They're watching the hotel. We must find Travis before he returns."

Louise hesitated, apparently recognising Bridgman only by an effort, and her eyes turned up to the black marble sky.

Bridgman looked at his watch; it was almost 12:25. He searched the stars in the southwest.

Louise murmured: "They're nearly here now, I must see them. Where is Travis, he should be here?"

Bridgman pulled at her arm. "Perhaps he saw the sand-car. Mrs. Woodward, we should leave."

Suddenly she pointed up at the sky, then wrenched away from him and ran to the rail. "There they are!"

Fretting, Bridgman waited until she had filled her eyes with the two companion points of light speeding from the western horizon. These were Merril and Pokrovski—like every schoolboy he knew the sequences perfectly, a second system of constellations with a more complex but far more tangible periodicity and precession—the Castor and Pollux of the orbiting zodiac, whose appearance always heralded a full conjunction the following night.

Louise Woodward gazed up at them from the rail, the rising wind lifting her hair off her shoulders and entraining it horizontally behind her head. Around her feet the red Martian dust swirled and rustled, silting over the fragments of the old neon sign, a brilliant pink spume streaming from her long fingers as they moved along the balcony edge. When the satellites finally disappeared among the stars along the horizon, she leaned forward, her face raised to the milk-blue moon as if to delay their departure, then turned back to Bridgman, a bright smile on her face.

His earlier suspicions vanishing, Bridgman smiled back at her encouragingly. "Roger will be here tomorrow night, Louise. We must be careful the wardens don't catch us before we see him."

He felt a sudden admiration for her, at the stoical way she had sustained herself during her long vigil. Perhaps she thought of Woodward as still alive, and in some way was patiently waiting for him to return? He remembered her saying once: "Roger was only a boy when he took off, you know, I feel more like his mother now," as if frightened how Woodward would react to her dry skin and fading hair, fearing that he might even have forgotten her. No doubt the death she visualised for him was of a different order from the mortal kind.

Hand in hand, they tiptoed carefully down the flaking

steps, jumped down from a terrace window into the soft sand below the windbreak. Bridgman sank to his knees in the fine silver moon-dust, then waded up to the firmer ground, pulling Louise after him. They climbed through a breach in the tilting palisades, then ran away from the line of dead hotels looming like skulls in the empty light.

"Paul, wait!" Her head still raised to the sky, Louise Woodward fell to her knees in a hollow between two dunes, with a laugh stumbled after Bridgman as he raced through the dips and saddles. The wind was now whipping the sand off the higher crests, flurries of dust spurting like excited wavelets. A hundred yards away, the town was a fading film set, projected by the camera obscura of the sinking moon. They were standing where the long Atlantic seas had once been ten fathoms deep, and Bridgman could scent again the tang of brine among the flickering whitecaps of dust, phosphorescing like shoals of animalcula. He waited for any signs of Travis.

"Louise, we'll have to go back to the town. The sandstorms are blowing up, we'll never see Travis here."

They moved back through the dunes, then worked their way among the narrow alleyways between the hotels to the northern gateway to the town. Bridgman found a vantage point in a small apartment block, and they lay down looking out below a window lintel into the sloping street, the warm sand forming a pleasant cushion. At the intersections the dust blew across the roadway in white clouds, obscuring the warden's beach-car parked a hundred yards down the boulevard.

Half an hour later an engine surged, and Bridgman began to pile sand into the interval in front of them. "They're going. Thank God!"

Louise Woodward held his arm. "Look!"

Fifty feet away, his white vinyl suit half hidden in the dust clouds, one of the wardens was advancing slowly towards them, his lasso twirling lightly in his hand. A few feet behind was a second warden, craning up at the windows of the apartment block with his binoculars.

Bridgman and Louise crawled back below the ceiling, then dug their way under a transom into the kitchen at the rear. A window opened onto a sand-filled yard, and they darted away through the lifting dust that whirled between the buildings.

Suddenly, around a corner, they saw the line of wardens moving down a side-street, the sand-car edging along behind them. Before Bridgman could steady himself a spasm of pain seized his right calf, contorting the gastrocnemius muscle, and he fell to one knee. Louise Woodward pulled him back against the wall, then pointed at a squat, bowlegged figure trudging towards them along the curving road into town.

"Travis—"

The tool-bag swung from his right hand, and his feet rang faintly on the wire-mesh roadway. Head down, he seemed unaware of the wardens hidden by a bend in the road.

"Come on!" Disregarding the negligible margin of safety, Bridgman clambered to his feet and impetuously ran out into the centre of the street. Louise tried to stop him, and they had covered only ten yards before the wardens saw them. There was a warning shout, and the spotlight flung its giant cone down the street. The sand-car surged forward, like a massive dust-covered bull, its tracks clawing at the sand.

"Travis!" As Bridgman reached the bend, Louise Woodward ten yards behind, Travis looked up from his reverie, then flung the tool-bag over one shoulder and raced ahead of them towards the clutter of motel roofs protruding from the other side of the street. Lagging behind the others, Bridgman again felt the cramp attack his leg, broke off into a painful shuffle. When Travis came back for him Bridgman tried to wave him away, but Travis pinioned his elbow and propelled him forward like an attendant straight-arming a patient.

The dust swirling around them, they disappeared through the fading streets and out into the desert, the shouts of the beach-wardens lost in the roar and clamour of the baying engine. Around them, like the strange metallic flora of some extraterrestrial garden, the old neon signs jutted from the red Martian sand—SATELLITE MOTEL, PLANET BAR, MERCURY MOTEL. Hiding behind them, they reached the scrub-covered dunes on the edge of the town, then picked up one of the trails that led away among the sand-reefs. There, in the deep grottoes of compacted sand which hung like inverted palaces, they waited until the storm subsided. Shortly before dawn the wardens abandoned their search, unable to bring the heavy sand-car onto the disintegrating reef.

Contemptuous of the wardens, Travis lit a small fire with his cigarette lighter, burning splinters of driftwood that had gathered in the gullies. Bridgman crouched beside it, warming his hands.

"This is the first time they've been prepared to leave the sand-car," he remarked to Travis. "It means they're under orders to catch us."

Travis shrugged. "Maybe. They're extending the fence along the beach. They probably intend to seal us in forever."

"What?" Bridgman stood up with a sudden feeling of uneasiness. "Why should they? Are you sure? I mean, what would be the point?"

Travis looked up at him, a flicker of dry amusement on his bleached face. Wisps of smoke wreathed his head, curled up past the serpentine columns of the grotto to the winding interval of sky a hundred feet above. "Bridgman, forgive me saying so, but if you want to leave here, you should leave now. In a month's time you won't be able to."

Bridgman ignored this, and searched the cleft of dark sky overhead, which framed the constellation Scorpio, as if hoping to see a reflection of the distant sea. "They must be crazy. How much of this fence did you see?"

"About eight hundred yards. It won't take them long to complete. The sections are prefabricated, about forty feet high." He smiled ironically at Bridgman's discomfort. "Relax, Bridgman. If you do want to get out, you'll always be able to tunnel underneath it."

"I don't want to get out," Bridgman said coldly. "Damn them, Travis, they're turning the place into a zoo. You know it won't be the same with a fence all the way around it."

"A corner of Earth that is forever Mars." Under the high forehead, Travis's eyes were sharp and watchful. "I see their point. There hasn't been a fatal casualty now"—he glanced at Louise Woodward, who was strolling about in the colonnades—"for nearly twenty years, and passenger rockets are supposed to be as safe as commuters' trains. They're quietly sealing off the past, Louise and I and you with it. I suppose it's pretty considerate of them not to burn the place down with flamethrowers. The virus would be a sufficient excuse. After all, we three are probably the only reservoirs left on the planet." He picked up a handful of red dust and examined the fine crystals with a sombre eye. "Well, Bridgman, what are you going to do?"

His thoughts discharging themselves through his mind like frantic signal flares, Bridgman walked away without answering.

Behind them, Louise Woodward wandered among the deep galleries of the grotto, crooning to herself in a low voice to the sighing rhythms of the whirling sand.

The next morning they returned to the town, wading through the deep drifts of sand that lay like a fresh fall of red snow between the hotels and stores, coruscating in the brilliant sunlight. Travis and Louise Woodward made their way towards their quarters in the motels further down the beach. Bridgman searched the still crystal air for any signs of the wardens, but the sand-car had gone, its tracks obliterated by the storm.

In his room he found their calling-card.

A huge tide of dust had flowed through the French windows and submerged the desk and bed, three feet deep against the rear wall. Outside the sand-break had been inundated, and the contours of the desert had completely altered, a few spires of obsidian marking its former perspectives like buoys on a shifting sea. Bridgman spent the morning digging out his books and equipment, dismantled the electrical system and its batteries, and carried everything to the room above. He would have moved to the penthouse on the top floor, but his lights would have been visible for miles.

Settling into his new quarters, he switched on the tape-recorder, heard a short, clipped message in the brisk voice which had shouted orders at the wardens the previous evening. "Bridgman, this is Major Webster, deputy commandant of Cocoa Beach Reservation. On the instructions of the Anti-Viral Subcommittee of the UN General Assembly we are now building a continuous fence around the beach area.

On completion no further egress will be allowed, and anyone escaping will be immediately returned to the reservation. Give yourself up now, Bridgman, before—''

Bridgman stopped the tape, then reversed the spool and erased the message, staring angrily at the instrument. Unable to settle down to the task of rewiring the room's circuits, he paced about, fiddling with the architectural drawings propped against the wall. He felt restless and hyperexcited, perhaps because he had been trying to repress, not very successfully, precisely those doubts of which Webster had now reminded him.

He stepped onto the balcony and looked out over the desert, at the red dunes rolling to the windows directly below. For the fourth time he had moved up a floor, and the sequence of identical rooms he had occupied was like displaced images of himself seen through a prism. Their common focus, that elusive final definition of himself which he had sought for so long, still remained to be found. Timelessly the sand swept towards him, its shifting contours, approximating more closely than any other landscape he had found to complete psychic zero, enveloping his past failures and uncertainties, masking them in its enigmatic canopy.

Bridgman watched the red sand flicker and fluoresce in the steepening sunlight. He would never see Mars now, and redress the implicit failure of talent, but a workable replica of the planet was contained within the beach area.

Several million tons of the Martian topsoil had been ferried in as ballast some fifty years earlier, when it was feared that the continuous firing of planetary probes and space vehicles, and the transportation of bulk stores and equipment to Mars, would fractionally lower the gravitational mass of the Earth and bring it into tighter orbit around the sun. Although the distance involved would be little more than a few millimetres, and barely raise the temperature of the atmosphere, its cumulative effects over an extended period might have resulted in a loss into space of the tenuous layers of the outer atmosphere, and of the radiological veil which alone made the biosphere habitable.

Over a twenty-year period a fleet of large freighters had shuttled to and from Mars, dumping the ballast into the sea near the landing-grounds of Cape Canaveral. Simultaneously the Russians were filling in a small section of the Caspian Sea. The intention had been that the ballast should be swallowed by the Atlantic and Caspian waters, but all too soon it was found that the microbiological analysis of the sand had been inadequate.

At the Martian polar caps, where the original water vapour in the atmosphere had condensed, a residue of ancient organic matter formed the topsoil, a fine sandy loess containing the fossilised spores of the giant lichens and mosses which had been the last living organisms on the planet millions of years earlier. Embedded in these spores were the crystal lattices of the viruses which had once preyed on the plants, and traces of these were carried back to Earth with the Canaveral and Caspian ballast.

A few years afterwards a drastic increase in a wide range of plant diseases was noticed in the southern states of America and in the Kazakhstan and Turkmenistan republics of the Soviet Union. All over Florida there were outbreaks of blight and mosaic disease, orange plantations withered and died, stunted palms split by the roadside like dried banana skins, saw grass stiffened into paper spears in the summer heat. Within a few years the entire peninsula was transformed into a desert. The swampy jungles of the Everglades became bleached and dry, the rivers' cracked husks strewn with the gleaming skeletons of crocodiles and birds, the forests petrified.

The former launching-ground at Canaveral was closed, and shortly afterwards the Cocoa Beach resorts were sealed off and evacuated, billions of dollars of real estate were abandoned to the virus. Fortunately never virulent to animal hosts, its influence was confined to within a small radius of the original loess which had borne it, unless ingested by the human organism, when it symbioted with the bacteria in the gut flora, benign and unknown to the host, but devastating to vegetation thousands of miles from Canaveral if returned to the soil.

Unable to rest despite his sleepless night, Bridgman played irritably with the tape-recorder. During their close escape from the wardens he had more than half hoped they would catch him. The mysterious leg cramp was obviously psycho-

genic. Although unable to accept consciously the logic of
Webster's argument, he would willingly have conceded to
the *fait accompli* of physical capture, gratefully submitted
to a year's quarantine at the Parasitological Cleansing Unit
at Tampa, and then returned to his career as an architect,
chastened but accepting his failure.

As yet, however, the opportunity for surrender had failed
to offer itself. Travis appeared to be aware of his ambiva-
lent motives; Bridgman noticed that he and Louise Woodward had made no arrangements to meet him that evening
for the conjunction.

In the early afternoon he went down into the streets,
ploughed through the drifts of red sand, following the foot-
prints of Travis and Louise as they wound in and out of the
side-streets, finally saw them disappear into the coarser,
flintlike dunes among the submerged motels to the south
of the town. Giving up, he returned through the empty,
shadowless streets, now and then shouted up into the hot
air, listening to the echoes boom away among the dunes.

Later that afternoon he walked out towards the northeast,
picking his way carefully through the dips and hollows,
crouching in the pools of shadow whenever the distant
sounds of the construction gangs along the perimeter were
carried across to him by the wind. Around him, in the great
dust basins, the grains of red sand glittered like diamonds.
Barbs of rusting metal protruded from the slopes, remnants
of Mars satellites and launching stages which had fallen onto
the Martian deserts and then been carried back again to
Earth. One fragment which he passed, a complete section
of hull plate like a concave shield, still carried part of an iden-
tification numeral, and stood upright in the dissolving sand
like a door into nowhere.

Just before dusk he reached a tall spur of obsidian that
reared up into the tinted cerise sky like the spire of a ruined
church, climbed up among its jutting cornices and looked
out across the intervening two or three miles of dunes to the
perimeter. Illuminated by the last light, the metal grilles
shone with a roseate glow like fairy portcullises on the edge
of an enchanted sea. At least half a mile of the fence had
been completed, and as he watched another of the giant
prefabricated sections was cantilevered into the air and

staked to the ground. Already the eastern horizon was cut off by the encroaching fence, the enclosed Martian sand like the gravel scattered at the bottom of a cage.

Perched on the spur, Bridgman felt a warning tremor of pain in his calf. He leapt down in a flurry of dust, without looking back made off among the dunes and reefs.

Later, as the last baroque whorls of the sunset faded below the horizon, he waited on the roof for Travis and Louise Woodward, peering impatiently into the empty moon-filled streets.

Shortly after midnight, at an elevation of thirty-five degrees in the southwest, between Aquila and Ophiuchus, the conjunction began. Bridgman continued to search the streets, and ignored the seven points of speeding light as they raced towards him from the horizon like an invasion from deep space. There was no indication of their convergent orbital pathways, which would soon scatter them thousands of miles apart, and the satellites moved as if they were always together in the tight configuration Bridgman had known since childhood, like a lost zodiacal emblem, a constellation detached from the celestial sphere and forever frantically searching to return to its place.

"Travis! Confound you!" With a snarl, Bridgman swung away from the balcony and moved along to the exposed section of rail behind the elevator head. To be avoided like a pariah by Travis and Louise Woodward forced him to accept that he was no longer a true resident of the beach and now existed in a no-man's-land between them and the wardens.

The seven satellites drew nearer, and Bridgman glanced up at them cursorily. They were disposed in a distinctive but unusual pattern resembling the Greek letter X, a limp cross, a straight lateral member containing four capsules more or less in line ahead—Connolly, Tkachev, Merril, and Maiakovski—bisected by three others forming with Tkachev an elongated Z—Pokrovski, Woodward, and Brodisnek. The pattern had been variously identified as a hammer and sickle, an eagle, a swastika, and a dove, as well as a variety of religious and runic emblems, but all these were being defeated by the advancing tendency of the older capsules to vaporise.

It was this slow disintegration of the aluminium shells that made them visible—it had often been pointed out that the observer on the ground was looking, not at the actual capsule, but at a local field of vaporised aluminium and ionised hydrogen peroxide gas from the ruptured altitude jets now distributed within half a mile of each of the capsules. Woodward's, the most recently in orbit, was a barely perceptible point of light. The hulks of the capsules, with their perfectly preserved human cargoes, were continually dissolving, and a wide fan of silver spray opened out in a phantom wake behind Merril and Pokrovski (1998 and 1999), like a double star transforming itself into a nova in the centre of a constellation. As the mass of the capsules diminished they sank into a closer orbit around the Earth, would soon touch the denser layers of the atmosphere and plummet to the ground.

Bridgman watched the satellites as they moved towards him, his irritation with Travis forgotten. As always, he felt himself moved by the eerie but strangely serene spectacle of the ghostly convoy endlessly circling the dark sea of the midnight sky, the long-dead astronauts converging for the ten-thousandth time upon their brief rendezvous and then setting off upon their lonely flight-paths around the perimeter of the ionosphere, the tidal edge of the beachway into space which had reclaimed them.

How Louise Woodward could bear to look up at her husband he had never been able to understand. After her arrival he once invited her to the hotel, remarking that there was an excellent view of the beautiful sunsets, and she had snapped back bitterly: "Beautiful? Can you imagine what it's like looking up at a sunset when your husband's spinning through it in his coffin?"

This reaction had been a common one when the first astronauts had died after failing to make contact with the launching platforms in fixed orbit. When these new stars rose in the west an attempt had been made to shoot them down—there was the unsettling prospect of the skies a thousand years hence, littered with orbiting refuse—but later they were left in this natural graveyard, forming their own monument.

Obscured by the clouds of dust carried up into the air by the sandstorm, the satellites shone with little more than the intensity of second-magnitude stars, winking as the reflected light was interrupted by the lanes of stratocirrus. The wake of diffusing light behind Merril and Pokrovski which usually screened the other capsules seemed to have diminished in size, and he could see both Maiakovski and Brodisnek clearly for the first time in several months. Wondering whether Merril or Pokrovski would be the first to fall from orbit, he looked towards the centre of the cross as it passed overhead.

With a sharp intake of breath, he tilted his head back. In surprise he noticed that one of the familiar points of light was missing from the centre of the group. What he had assumed to be an occlusion of the conjoint vapour trails by dust clouds was simply due to the fact that one of the capsules—Merril's, he decided, the third of the line ahead—had fallen from its orbit.

Head raised, he sidestepped slowly across the roof, avoiding the pieces of rusting neon sign, following the convoy as it passed overhead and moved towards the eastern horizon. No longer overlaid by the wake of Merril's capsule, Woodward's shone with far greater clarity, and almost appeared to have taken the former's place, although he was not due to fall from orbit for at least a century.

In the distance somewhere an engine growled. A moment later, from a different quarter, a woman's voice cried out faintly. Bridgman moved to the rail, over the intervening rooftops saw two figures silhouetted against the sky on the elevator head of an apartment block, then heard Louise Woodward call out again. She was pointing up at the sky with both hands, her long hair blown about her face, Travis trying to restrain her. Bridgman realised that she had misconstrued Merril's descent, assuming that the fallen astronaut was her husband. He climbed onto the edge of the balcony, watching the pathetic tableau on the distant roof.

Again, somewhere among the dunes, an engine moaned. Before Bridgman could turn around, a brilliant blade of light cleft the sky in the southwest. Like a speeding comet, an immense train of vaporising particles stretching behind it to the horizon, it soared towards them, the downward curve of its pathway clearly visible. Detached from the rest of the capsules, which were now disappearing among the stars along the eastern horizon, it was little more than a few miles off the ground.

Bridgman watched it approach, apparently on a collision course with the hotel. The expanding corona of white light, like a gigantic signal flare, illuminated the rooftops, etching the letters of the neon signs over the submerged motels on the outskirts of the town. He ran for the doorway, and as he raced down the stairs saw the glow of the descending capsule fill the sombre streets like a hundred moons. When he reached his room, sheltered by the massive weight of the hotel, he watched the dunes in front of the hotel light up like a stage set. Three hundred yards away the low camouflaged hull of the warden's beach-car was revealed poised on a crest, its feeble spotlight drowned by the glare.

With a deep metallic sigh, the burning catafalque of the dead astronaut soared overhead, a cascade of vaporising metal pouring from its hull, filling the sky with incandescent light. Reflected below it, like an expressway illuminated by an aircraft's spotlights, a long lane of light several hundred yards in width raced out into the desert towards the sea. As Bridgman shielded his eyes, it suddenly erupted in a tremendous explosion of detonating sand. A huge curtain of white dust lifted into the air and fell slowly to the ground. The sounds of the impact rolled against the hotel, mounting in a sustained crescendo that drummed against the windows. A series of smaller explosions flared up like opalescent fountains. All over the desert fires flickered briefly where fragments of the capsule had been scattered. Then the noise subsided, and an immense glistening pall of phosphorescing gas hung in the air like a silver veil, particles within it beading and winking.

Two hundred yards away across the sand was the running figure of Louise Woodward, Travis twenty paces behind her. Bridgman watched them dart in and out of the dunes, then abruptly felt the cold spotlight of the beach-car hit his face and flood the room behind him. The vehicle was moving straight towards him, two of the wardens, nets and lassoes in hand, riding the outboard.

Quickly Bridgman straddled the balcony, jumped down into the sand, and raced towards the crest of the first dune. He crouched and ran on through the darkness as the beam probed the air. Above, the glistening pall was slowly fading, the particles of vaporised metal sifting towards the dark Martian sand. In the distance the last echoes of the impact were still reverberating among the hotels of the beach colonies further down the coast.

Five minutes later he caught up with Louise Woodward and Travis. The capsule's impact had flattened a number of the dunes, forming a shallow basin some quarter of a mile in diameter, and the surrounding slopes were scattered with the still glowing particles, sparkling like fading eyes. The beach-car growled somewhere four or five hundred yards behind him, and Bridgman broke off into an exhausted walk. He stopped beside Travis, who was kneeling on the ground, breath pumping into his lungs. Fifty yards away Louise Woodward was running up and down, distraughtly gazing at the fragments of smouldering metal. For a moment the spotlight of the approaching beach-car illuminated her, and she ran away among the dunes. Bridgman caught a glimpse of the inconsolable anguish in her face.

Travis was still on his knees. He had picked up a piece of the oxidised metal and was pressing it together in his hands.

"Travis, for God's sake tell her! This was Merril's capsule, there's no doubt about it! Woodward's still up there."

Travis looked up at him silently, his eyes searching Bridgman's face. A spasm of pain tore his mouth, and Bridgman realised that the barb of steel he clasped reverently in his hands was still glowing with heat.

"Travis!" He tried to pull the man's hands apart, the pungent stench of burning flesh gusting into his face, but Travis wrenched away from him. "Leave her alone, Bridgman! Go back with the wardens!"

Bridgman retreated from the approaching beach-car. Only thirty yards away, its spotlight filled the basin. Louise Woodward was still searching the dunes. Travis held his ground as the wardens jumped down from the car and advanced towards him with their nets, his bloodied hands raised at his sides, the steel barb flashing like a dagger. At the head of the wardens, the only one unmasked was a trim, neat-featured man with an intent, serious face. Bridgman guessed that this was Major Webster, and that the wardens had known of the impending impact and hoped to capture them, and Louise in particular, before it occurred.

Bridgman stumbled back towards the dunes at the edge of the basin. As he neared the crest he trapped his foot in a semicircular plate of metal, sat down and freed his heel. Unmistakably it was part of a control panel, the circular instrument housings still intact.

Overhead the pall of glistening vapour had moved off to the northeast, and the reflected light was directly over the rusting gantries of the former launching site at Cape Canaveral. For a few fleeting seconds the gantries seemed to be enveloped in a sheen of silver, transfigured by the vaporised body of the dead astronaut, diffusing over them in a farewell gesture, his final return to the site from which he had set off to his death a century earlier. Then the gantries sank again into their craggy shadows, and the pall moved off like an immense wraith towards the sea, barely distinguishable from the star glow.

Down below Travis was sitting on the ground surrounded by the wardens. He scuttled about on his hands like a frantic crab scooping handfuls of the virus-laden sand at them. Holding tight to their masks, the wardens manoeuvred around him, their nets and lassoes at the ready. Another group moved slowly towards Bridgman.

Bridgman picked up a handful of the dark Martian sand beside the instrument panel, felt the soft glowing crystals warm his palm. In his mind he could still see the silver-sheathed gantries of the launching site across the bay, by a curious illusion almost identical with the Martian city he had designed years earlier. He watched the pall disappear over the sea, then looked around at the other remnants of Merril's capsule scattered over the slopes. High in the western night, between Pegasus and Cygnus, shone the distant disc of the planet Mars, which for both himself and the dead astronaut had served for so long as a symbol of unattained ambition. The wind stirred softly through the sand, cooling this replica of the planet which lay passively around him, and at last he understood why he had come to the beach and been unable to leave it.

Twenty yards away Travis was being dragged off like a wild dog, his thrashing body pinioned in the centre of a web of lassoes. Louise Woodward had run away among the dunes towards the sea, following the vanished gas cloud.

In a sudden access of refound confidence, Bridgman drove his fist into the dark sand, buried his forearm like a foundation pillar. A flange of hot metal from Merril's capsule burned his wrist, bonding him to the spirit of the dead astronaut. Scattered around him on the Martian sand, in a sense Merril had reached Mars after all.

"Damn it!" he cried exultantly to himself as the wardens' lassoes stung his neck and shoulders. "We made it!"

A

QUESTION

OF

RE-ENTRY

ALL DAY THEY HAD MOVED STEADILY UPSTREAM, OCCASIONALLY pausing to raise the propeller and cut away the knots of weed, and by three o'clock had covered some seventy-five miles. Fifty yards away, on either side of the patrol launch, the high walls of the jungle river rose over the water, the unbroken massif of the Mato Grosso which swept across the Amazonas from Campos Buros to the delta of the Orinoco. Despite their progress—they had set off from the telegraph station at Trés Buritis at seven o'clock that morning— the river showed no inclination to narrow or alter its volume. Sombre and unchanging, the forest followed its course, the aerial canopy shutting off the sunlight and cloaking the water along the banks with a black velvet sheen. Now and then the channel would widen into a flat expanse of what appeared to be stationary water, the slow oily swells which disturbed its surface transforming it into a sluggish mirror of the distant, enigmatic sky, the islands of rotten balsa logs refracted by the layers of haze like the drifting archipelagoes of a dream. Then the channel would narrow again and the cooling jungle darkness enveloped the launch.

Although for the first few hours Connolly had joined Captain Pereira at the rail, he had become bored with the endless green banks of the forest sliding past them, and since noon had remained in the cabin, pretending to study the trajectory maps. The time might pass more slowly there, but at least it was cooler and less depressing. The fan hummed and pivoted, and the clicking of the cutwater and the whispering plaint of the current past the gliding hull soothed the slight headache induced by the tepid beer he and Pereira had shared after lunch.

This first encounter with the jungle had disappointed Connolly. His previous experience had been confined to the Dredging Project at Lake Maracaibo, where the only forests consisted of the abandoned oil rigs built out into the water. Their rusting hulks, and the huge draglines and pontoons of the dredging teams, were fauna of a man-made species. In the Amazonian jungle he had expected to see the full variety of nature in its richest and most colourful outpouring, but instead it was nothing more than a moribund tree-level swamp, unweeded and overgrown, if anything more dead than alive, an example of bad husbandry on a continental scale. The margins of the river were rarely well-defined; except where enough rotting trunks had gathered to form a firm parapet, there were no formal banks, and the shallows ran off among the undergrowth for a hundred yards, irrigating huge areas of vegetation that were already drowning in moisture.

Connolly had tried to convey his disenchantment to Pereira, who now sat under the awning on the deck, placidly smoking a cheroot, partly to repay the captain for his polite contempt for Connolly and everything his mission implied. Like all the officers of the Native Protection Missions whom Connolly had met, first in Venezuela and now in Brazil, Pereira maintained a proprietary outlook towards the jungle and its mystique, which would not be breached by any number of fresh-faced investigators in their crisp drill uniforms. Captain Pereira had not been impressed by the UN flashes on Connolly's shoulders with their orbital monogram, nor by the high-level request for assistance cabled to the Mission three weeks earlier from Brasilia. To Pereira, obviously, the office suites in the white towers at the capital were as far away as New York, London, or Babylon.

Superficially, the captain had been helpful enough, supervising the crew as they stowed Connolly's monitoring equipment aboard, checking his Smith & Wesson and exchanging a pair of defective mosquito boots. As long as Connolly had wanted to, he had conversed away amiably, pointing out this and that feature of the landscape, identifying an unusual bird or lizard on an overhead bough.

But his indifference to the real object of the mission—he had given a barely perceptible nod when Connolly described it—soon became obvious. It was this neutrality which irked Connolly, implying that Pereira spent all his time ferrying UN investigators up and down the rivers after their confounded lost space capsule like so many tourists in search of some nonexistent El Dorado. Above all there was the suggestion that Connolly and the hundreds of other investigators deployed around the continent were being too persistent. When all was said and done, Pereira implied, five years had elapsed since the returning lunar spacecraft, the *Goliath 7,* had plummeted into the South American landmass, and to prolong the search indefinitely was simply bad form, even, perhaps, necrophilic. There was not the faintest chance of the pilot's still being alive, so he should be decently forgotten, given a statue outside a railway station or airport car-park, and left to the pigeons.

Connolly would have been glad to explain the reasons for the indefinite duration of the search, the overwhelming moral reasons, apart from the political and technical ones. He would have liked to point out that the lost astronaut, Colonel Francis Spender, by accepting the immense risks of the flight to and from the moon, was owed the absolute discharge of any assistance that could be given him. He would have liked to remind Pereira that the successful landing on the moon, after some half-dozen fatal attempts—at least three of the luckless pilots were still orbiting the moon in their dead ships—was the culmination of an age-old ambition with profound psychological implications for mankind, and that the failure to find the astronaut after his return might induce unassuageable feelings of guilt and inadequacy. (If the sea was a symbol of the unconscious, was space perhaps an image of unfettered time, and the inability to penetrate it a tragic exile to one of the limbos of eternity, a symbolic death in life?)

But Captain Pereira was not interested. Calmly inhaling the scented aroma of his cheroot, he sat imperturbably at the rail, surveying the fetid swamps that moved past them.

Shortly before noon, when they had covered some forty miles, Connolly pointed to the remains of a bamboo landing-stage elevated on high poles above the bank. A threadbare rope bridge trailed off among the mangroves, and through an embrasure in the forest they could see a small clearing where a clutter of abandoned adobe huts dissolved like refuse heaps in the sunlight.

"Is this one of their camps?"

Pereira shook his head. "The Espirro tribe, closely related to the Nambikwaras. Three years ago one of them carried influenza back from the telegraph station, an epidemic broke out, turned into a form of pulmonary edema, within forty-eight hours three hundred Indians had died. The whole group disintegrated, only about fifteen of the men and their families are still alive. A great tragedy."

They moved forward to the bridge and stood beside the tall Negro helmsman as the two other members of the crew began to shackle sections of fine wire mesh into a cage over the deck. Pereira raised his binoculars and scanned the river ahead.

"Since the Espirros vacated the area the Nambas have begun to forage down this far. We won't see any of them, but it's as well to be on the safe side."

"Do you mean they're hostile?" Connolly asked.

"Not in a conscious sense. But the various groups which comprise the Nambikwaras are permanently feuding with each other, and this far from the settlement we might easily be involved in an opportunist attack. Once we get to the settlement we'll be all right—there's a sort of precarious equilibrium there. But even so, have your wits about you. As you'll see, they're as nervous as birds."

"How does Ryker manage to keep out of their way? Hasn't he been here for years?"

"About twelve." Pereira sat down on the gunwale and eased his peaked cap off his forehead. "Ryker is something of a special case. Temperamentally he's rather explosive— I meant to warn you to handle him carefully, he might easily whip up an incident—but he seems to have manoeuvred himself into a position of authority with the tribe. In some ways he's become an umpire, arbitrating in their various feuds. How he does it I haven't discovered yet; it's quite uncharacteristic of the Indians to regard a white man in that way. However, he's useful to us, we might eventually set up a mission here. Though that's next to impossible—we tried it once and the Indians just moved five hundred miles away."

Connolly looked back at the derelict landing-stage as it disappeared around a bend, barely distinguishable from the jungle, which was as dilapidated as this sole mournful artifact.

"What on Earth made Ryker come out here?" He had heard something in Brasilia of this strange figure, sometime journalist and man of action, the self-proclaimed world citizen who at the age of forty-two, after a life spent venting his spleen on civilisation and its gimcrack gods, had suddenly disappeared into the Amazonas and taken up residence with one of the aboriginal tribes. Most latter-day Gauguins were absconding confidence men or neurotics, but Ryker seemed to be a genuine character in his own right, the last of a race of true individualists retreating before the barbed-wire fences and regimentation of twentieth-century life. But his chosen paradise seemed pretty scruffy and degenerate, Connolly reflected, when one saw it at close quarters. However, as long as the man could organise the Indians into a few search-parties he would serve his purpose. "I can't understand why Ryker should pick the Amazon basin. The South Pacific yes, but from all I've heard—and you've confirmed just now—the Indians appear to be a pretty diseased and miserable lot, hardly the noble savage."

Captain Pereira shrugged, looking away across the oily water, his plump sallow face mottled by the lacelike shadow of the wire netting. He belched discreetly to himself, and then adjusted his holster belt. "I don't know the South Pacific, but I should guess it's also been oversentimentalised. Ryker didn't come here for a scenic tour. I suppose the Indians are diseased and, yes, reasonably miserable. Within fifty years they'll probably have died out. But for the time being they do represent a certain form of untamed, natural existence, which after all made us what we are. The hazards facing them are immense, and they survive." He gave Connolly a sly smile. "But you must argue it out with Ryker."

They lapsed into silence and sat by the rail, watching the river unfurl itself. Exhausted and collapsing, the great trees crowded the banks, the dying expiring among the living, jostling each other aside as if for a last despairing assault on the patrol boat and its passengers. For the next half an hour, until they opened their lunch packs, Connolly searched the treetops for the giant bifurcated parachute which should have carried the capsule to earth. Virtually impermeable to the atmosphere, it would still be visible, spreadeagled like an enormous bird over the canopy of leaves. Then, after drinking a can of Pereira's beer, he excused himself and went down to the cabin.

The two steel cases containing the monitoring equipment had been stowed under the chart table, and he pulled them out and checked that the moisture-proof seals were still intact. The chances of making visual contact with the capsule were infinitesimal, but as long as it was intact it would continue to transmit both a sonar and radio beacon, admittedly over little more than twenty miles, but sufficient to identify its whereabouts to anyone in the immediate neighbourhood. However, the entire northern half of the South Americas had been covered by successive aerial sweeps, and it seemed unlikely that the beacons were still operating. The disappearance of the capsule argued that it had sustained at least minor damage, and by now the batteries would have been corroded by the humid air.

Recently certain of the UN Space Department agencies had begun to circulate the unofficial view that Colonel Spender had failed to select the correct attitude for re-entry and that the capsule had been vaporised on its final descent, but Connolly guessed that this was merely an attempt to pacify world opinion and prepare the way for the resumption of the space programme. Not only the Lake Maracaibo Dredging Project, but his own presence on the patrol boat, indicated that the Department still believed Colonel Spender to be alive, or at least to have survived the landing. His final re-entry orbit should have brought him down into the landing zone five hundred miles to the east of Trinidad, but the last radio contact before the ionisation layers around the capsule severed transmission indicated that he had undershot his trajectory and come down somewhere on the South American landmass along a line linking Lake Maracaibo with Brasilia.

Footsteps sounded down the companionway, and Captain Pereira lowered himself into the cabin. He tossed his hat onto the chart table and sat with his back to the fan, letting the air blow across his fading hair, carrying across to Connolly a sweet unsavoury odour of garlic and cheap pomade.

"You're a sensible man, Lieutenant. Anyone who stays up on deck is crazy. However,"—he indicated Connolly's pallid face and hands, a memento of a long winter in New York—"in a way it's a pity you couldn't have put in some sunbathing. That metropolitan pallor will be quite a curiosity to the Indians." He smiled agreeably, showing the yellowing teeth which made his olive complexion even darker. "You may well be the first white man in the literal sense that the Indians have seen."

"What about Ryker? Isn't he white?"

"Black as a berry now. Almost indistinguishable from the Indians, apart from being seven feet tall." He pulled over a collection of cardboard boxes at the far end of the seat and began to rummage through them. Inside was a collection of miscellaneous oddments—balls of thread and raw cotton, lumps of wax and resin, urucu paste, tobacco and seed-beads. "These ought to assure them of your good intentions."

Connolly watched as he fastened the boxes together. "How many search-parties will they buy? Are you sure you brought enough? I have a fifty-dollar allocation for gifts."

"Good," Pereira said matter-of-factly. "We'll get some more beer. Don't worry, you can't buy these people, Lieutenant. You have to rely on their goodwill; this rubbish will put them in the right frame of mind to talk."

Connolly smiled dourly. "I'm more keen on getting them off their hunkers and out into the bush. How are you going to organise the search-parties?"

"They've already taken place."

"What?" Connolly sat forward. "How did that happen? But they should have waited"—he glanced at the heavy monitoring equipment—"they can't have known what—"

Pereira silenced him with a raised hand. "My dear Lieutenant. Relax, I was speaking figuratively. Can't you understand, these people are nomadic, they spend all their lives continually on the move. They must have covered every square foot of this forest a hundred times in the past five years. There's no need to send them out again. Your only hope is that they may have seen something and then persuade them to talk."

Connolly considered this as Pereira unwrapped another parcel. "All right, but I may want to do a few patrols. I can't just sit around for three days."

"Naturally. Don't worry, Lieutenant. If your astronaut came down anywhere within five hundred miles of here, they'll know about it." He unwrapped the parcel and removed a small teak cabinet. The front panel was slotted, and lifted to reveal the face of a large ormolu table clock, its Gothic hands and numerals below a gilded belldome. Captain Pereira compared its time with his wristwatch. "Good. Running perfectly, it hasn't lost a second in forty-eight hours. This should put us in Ryker's good books."

Connolly shook his head. "Why on Earth does he want a clock? I thought the man had turned his back on such things."

Pereira packed the tooled metal face away. "Ah, well, whenever we escape from anything we always carry a memento of it with us. Ryker collects clocks; this is the third I've bought for him. God knows what he does with them."

The launch had changed course, and was moving in a wide circle across the river, the current whispering in a tender rippling murmur across the hull. They made their way up onto the deck, where the helmsman was unshackling several sections of the wire mesh in order to give himself an uninterrupted view of the bows. The two sailors climbed through the aperture and took up their positions fore and aft, boat-hooks at the ready.

They had entered a large bow-shaped extension of the river, where the current had overflowed the bank and produced a series of low-lying mud flats. Some two or three hundred yards wide, the water seemed to be almost motionless, seeping away through the trees which defined its margins so that the exit and inlet of the river were barely perceptible. At the inner bend of the bow, on the only firm ground, a small cantonment of huts had been built on a series of wooden palisades jutting out over the water. A narrow promontory of forest reached to either side of the cantonment, but a small area behind it had been cleared to form an open campong. On its far side were a number of wattle storage-huts, a few dilapidated shacks and hovels of dried palm.

The entire area seemed deserted, but as they approached, the cutwater throwing a fine plume of white spray across the glassy swells, a few Indians appeared in the shadows below the creepers trailing over the jetty, watching them stonily. Connolly had expected to see a group of tall broad-shouldered warriors with white markings notched across their arms and cheeks, but these Indians were puny and degenerate, their pinched faces lowered beneath their squat bony skulls. They seemed undernourished and depressed, eyeing the visitors with a sort of sullen watchfulness, like pariah dogs from a gutter.

Pereira was shielding his eyes from the sun, across whose inclining path they were now moving, searching the ram-shackle bungalow built of woven rattan at the far end of the jetty.

"No signs of Ryker yet. He's probably asleep or drunk." He noticed Connolly's distasteful frown. "Not much of a place, I'm afraid."

As they moved towards the jetty, the wash from the launch slapping at the greasy bamboo poles and throwing a gust of foul air into their faces, Connolly looked back across the open disc of water, into which the curving wake of the launch was dissolving in a final summary of their long voyage upriver to the derelict settlement, fading into the slack brown water like a last tenuous thread linking him with the order and sanity of civilisation. A strange atmo-sphere of emptiness hung over this inland lagoon, a flat pall of dead air that in a curious way was as menacing as any overt signs of hostility, as if the crudity and violence of all the Amazonian jungles met here in a momentary balance which some untoward movement of his own might upset, unleashing appalling forces. Away in the distance, down-shore, the great trees leaned like corpses into the glazed air, and the haze over the water embalmed the jungle and the late afternoon in an uneasy stillness.

They bumped against the jetty, rocking lightly into the palisade of poles and dislodging a couple of waterlogged outriggers lashed together. The helmsman reversed the engine, waiting for the sailors to secure the lines. None of the Indians had come forward to assist them. Connolly caught a glimpse of one old simian face regarding him with a rheumy eye, riddled teeth nervously worrying a pouchlike lower lip.

He turned to Pereira, glad that the captain would be interceding between himself and the Indians. "Captain, I should have asked before, but—are these Indians cannibalistic?"

Pereira shook his head, steadying himself against a stanchion. "Not at all. Don't worry about that, they'd have been extinct years ago if they were."

"Not even—white men?" For some reason Connolly found himself placing a peculiarly indelicate emphasis upon the word "white."

Pereira laughed, straightening his uniform jacket. "For God's sake, Lieutenant, no. Are you worrying that your astronaut might have been eaten by them?"

"I suppose it's a possibility."

"I assure you, there have been no recorded cases. As a matter of interest, it's a rare practice on this continent. Much more typical of Africa—and Europe," he added with sly humour. Pausing to smile at Connolly, he said quietly, "Don't despise the Indians, Lieutenant. However diseased and dirty they may be, at least they are in equilibrium with their environment. And with themselves. You'll find no Christopher Columbuses or Colonel Spenders here, but no Belsens either. Perhaps one is as much a symptom of unease as the other?"

They had begun to drift down the jetty, overrunning one of the outriggers, whose bow creaked and disappeared under the stern of the launch, and Pereira shouted at the helmsman: "Ahead, Sancho! More ahead! Damn Ryker, where is the man?"

Churning out a Niagara of boiling brown water, the launch moved forward, driving its shoulder into the bamboo supports, and the entire jetty sprung lightly under the impact. As the motor was cut and the lines finally secured, Connolly looked up at the jetty above his head.

Scowling down at him, an expression of bilious irritability on his heavy-jawed face, was a tall bare-chested man wearing a pair of frayed cotton shorts and a sleeveless waistcoat of pleated raffia, his dark eyes almost hidden by a wide-brimmed straw hat. The heavy muscles of his exposed chest and arms were the colour of tropical teak, and the white scars on his lips and the fading traces of the heat ulcers which studded his shin bones provided the only lighter colouring. Standing there, arms akimbo with a sort of jaunty arrogance, he seemed to represent to Connolly that quality of untamed energy which he had so far found so conspicuously missing from the forest.

Completing his scrutiny of Connolly, the big man bellowed: "Pereira, for God's sake, what do you think you're doing? That's my bloody outrigger you've just run down! Tell that steersman of yours to get the cataracts out of his eyes or I'll put a bullet through his backside!"

Grinning good humouredly, Pereira pulled himself up onto the jetty. "My dear Ryker, contain yourself. Remember your blood-pressure." He peered down at the water-logged hulk of the derelict canoe which was now ejecting itself slowly from the river. "Anyway, what good is a canoe to you, you're not going anywhere."

Grudgingly, Ryker shook Pereira's hand. "That's what you like to think, Captain. You and your confounded Mission, you want me to do all the work. Next time you may find I've gone a thousand miles upriver. And taken the Nambas with me."

"What an epic prospect, Ryker. You'll need a Homer to celebrate it." Pereira turned and gestured Connolly onto the jetty. The Indians were still hanging about listlessly, like guilty intruders.

Ryker eyed Connolly's uniform suspiciously. "Who's this? Another so-called anthropologist, sniffing about for smut? I warned you last time, I will not have any more of those."

"No, Ryker. Can't you recognise the uniform? Let me introduce Lieutenant Connolly, of that brotherhood of latter-day saints, by whose courtesy and generosity we live in peace together—the United Nations."

"What? Don't tell me they've got a mandate here now? God above, I suppose he'll bore my head off about cereal/protein ratios!" His ironic groan revealed a concealed reserve of acid humour.

"Relax. The lieutenant is very charming and polite. He

works for the Space Department, Reclamation Division. You know, searching for lost aircraft and the like. There's a chance you may be able to help him." Pereira winked at Connolly and steered him forward. "Lieutenant, the Rajah Ryker."

"I doubt it," Ryker said dourly. They shook hands, the corded muscles of Ryker's fingers like a trap. Despite his thick-necked stoop, Ryker was a good six to ten inches taller than Connolly. For a moment he held on to Connolly's hand, a slight trace of wariness revealed below his mask of bad temper. "When did this plane come down?" he asked. Connolly guessed that he was already thinking of a profitable salvage operation.

"Some time ago," Pereira said mildly. He picked up the parcel containing the cabinet clock and began to stroll after Ryker towards the bungalow at the end of the jetty. A low-eaved dwelling of woven rattan, its single room was surrounded on all sides by a veranda, the overhanging roof shading it from the sunlight. Creepers trailed across from the surrounding foliage, involving it in the background of palms and fronds, so that the house seemed a momentary formalisation of the jungle.

"But the Indians might have heard something about it," Pereira went on. "Five years ago, as a matter of fact."

Ryker snorted. "My God, you've got a hope." They went up the steps onto the veranda, where a slim-shouldered Indian youth, his eyes like moist marbles, was watching from the shadows. With a snap of irritation, Ryker cupped his hand around the youth's pate and propelled him with a backward swing down the steps. Sprawling on his knees, the youth picked himself up, eyes still fixed on Connolly, then emitted what sounded like a high-pitched nasal hoot, compounded partly of fear and partly of excitement. Connolly looked back from the doorway, and noticed that several other Indians had stepped onto the pier and were watching him with the same expression of rapt curiosity.

Pereira patted Connolly's shoulder. "I told you they'd be impressed. Did you see that, Ryker?"

Ryker nodded curtly, as they entered his living-room pulled off his straw hat and tossed it onto a couch under the window. The room was dingy and cheerless. Crude bamboo shelves were strung around the walls, ornamented with a few primitive carvings of ivory and bamboo. A couple of rocking chairs and a card-table were in the centre of the room, dwarfed by an immense Victorian mahogany dresser standing against the rear wall. With its castellated mirrors and ornamental pediments it looked like an altarpiece stolen from a cathedral. At first glance it appeared to be leaning to one side, but then Connolly saw that its rear legs had been carefully raised from the tilting floor with a number of small wedges. In the centre of the dresser, its multiple reflections receding to infinity in a pair of small wing-mirrors, was a cheap three-dollar alarm clock, ticking away loudly. An over-and-under Winchester shotgun leaned against the wall beside it.

Gesturing Pereira and Connolly into the chairs, Ryker raised the blind over the rear window. Outside was the compound, the circle of huts around its perimeter. A few Indians squatted in the shadows, spears upright between their knees.

Connolly watched Ryker moving about in front of him, aware that the man's earlier impatience had given away to a faint but noticeable edginess. Ryker glanced irritably through the window, apparently annoyed to see the gradual gathering of the Indians before their huts.

There was a sweetly unsavoury smell in the room, and over his shoulder Connolly saw that the card-table was loaded with a large bale of miniature animal skins, those of a vole or some other forest rodent. A halfhearted attempt had been made to trim the skins, and tags of clotted blood clung to their margins.

Ryker jerked the table with his foot. "Well, here you are," he said to Pereira. "Twelve dozen. They took a hell of a lot of getting, I can tell you. You've brought the clock?"

Pereira nodded, still holding the parcel in his lap. He gazed distastefully at the dank scruffy skins. "Have you got some rats in there, Ryker? These don't look much good. Perhaps we should check through them outside. . . ."

"Dammit, Pereira, don't be a fool!" Ryker snapped. "They're as good as you'll get. I had to trim half the skins myself. Let's have a look at the clock."

"Wait a minute." The captain's jovial, easy-going manner had stiffened. Making the most of his temporary advantage, he reached out and touched one of the skins gingerly, shaking his head. "Pugh . . . Do you know how much I paid for this clock, Ryker? Seventy-five dollars. That's your credit for three years. I'm not so sure. And you're not very helpful, you know. Now about this aircraft that may have come down—"

Ryker snapped his fingers. "Forget it. Nothing did. The Nambas tell me everything." He turned to Connolly. "You can take it from me there's no trace of an aircraft around here. Any rescue mission would be wasting their time."

Pereira watched Ryker critically. "As a matter of fact it wasn't an aircraft." He tapped Connolly's shoulder flash. "It was a rocket capsule—with a man on board. A very important and valuable man. None other than the moon pilot, Colonel Francis Spender."

"Well . . ." Eyebrows raised in mock surprise, Ryker ambled to the window, stared out at a group of Indians who had advanced halfway across the compound. "My God, what next! The moon pilot. Do they really think he's around here? But what a place to roost." He leaned out of the window and bellowed at the Indians, who retreated a few paces and then held their ground. "Damn fools," he muttered, "this isn't a zoo."

Pereira handed him the parcel, watching the Indians. There were more than fifty around the compound now, squatting in their doorways, a few of the younger men honing their spears. "They are remarkably curious," he said to Ryker, who had taken the parcel over to the dresser and was unwrapping it carefully. "Surely they've seen a pale-skinned man before?"

"They've nothing better to do." Ryker lifted the clock out of the cabinet with his big hands, with great care placed it beside the alarm clock, the almost inaudible motion of its pendulum lost in the metallic chatter of the latter's escapement. For a moment he gazed at the ornamental hands and numerals. Then he picked up the alarm clock and with an almost valedictory pat, like an officer dismissing a faithful if stupid minion, locked it away in the cupboard below. His former buoyancy returning, he gave Pereira a playful slap on the shoulder. "Captain, if you want any more rat-skins just give me a shout!"

Backing away, Pereira's heel touched one of Connolly's feet, distracting Connolly from a problem he had been puzzling over since their entry into the hut. Like a concealed clue in a detective story, he was sure that he had noticed something of significance, but was unable to identify it.

"We won't worry about the skins," Pereira said. "What we'll do with your assistance, Ryker, is to hold a little parley with the chiefs, see whether they remember anything of this capsule."

Ryker stared out at the Indians now standing directly below the veranda. Irritably he slammed down the blind. "For God's sake, Pereira, they don't. Tell the lieutenant he isn't interviewing people on Park Avenue or Piccadilly. If the Indians had seen anything, I'd know."

"Perhaps." Pereira shrugged. "Still, I'm under instructions to assist Lieutenant Connolly and it won't do any harm to ask."

Connolly sat up. "Having come this far, Captain, I feel I should do two or three forays into the bush." To Ryker he explained: "They've recalculated the flight-path of the final trajectory, there's a chance he may have come down further along the landing-zone. Here, very possibly."

Shaking his head, Ryker slumped down onto the couch, and drove one fist angrily into the other. "I suppose this means they'll be landing here at any time with thousands of bulldozers and flamethrowers. Dammit, Lieutenant, if you have to send a man to the moon, why don't you do it in your own backyard?"

Pereira stood up. "We'll be gone in a couple of days, Ryker." He nodded judiciously at Connolly and moved towards the door.

As Connolly climbed to his feet Ryker called out suddenly: "Lieutenant. You can tell me something I've wondered." There was an unpleasant downward curve to his mouth, and his tone was belligerent and provocative. "Why did they really send a man to the moon?"

Connolly paused. He had remained silent during the conversation, not wanting to antagonise Ryker. The rudeness and complete self-immersion were pathetic rather than annoying. "Do you mean the military and political reasons?"

"No, I don't." Ryker stood up, arms akimbo again, measuring Connolly. "I mean the *real* reasons, Lieutenant."

Connolly gestured vaguely. For some reason formulating a satisfactory answer seemed more difficult than he had expected. "Well, I suppose you could say it was the natural spirit of exploration."

Ryker snorted derisively. "Do you seriously believe that, Lieutenant? 'The spirit of exploration'! My God! What a fantastic idea. Pereira doesn't believe that, do you, Captain?"

Before Connolly could reply, Pereira took his arm. "Come on, Lieutenant. This is no time for a metaphysical discussion." To Ryker he added: "It doesn't much matter what you and I believe, Ryker. A man went to the moon and came back. He needs our help."

Ryker frowned ruefully. "Poor chap. He must be feeling pretty unhappy by now. Though anyone who gets as far as the moon and is fool enough to come back deserves what he gets."

There was a scuffle of feet on the veranda, and as they stepped out into the sunlight a couple of Indians darted away along the jetty, watching Connolly with undiminished interest.

Ryker remained in the doorway, staring listlessly at the clock, but as they were about to climb into the launch he came after them. Now and then glancing over his shoulder at the encroaching semicircle of Indians, he gazed down at Connolly with sardonic contempt. "Lieutenant," he called out before they went below. "Has it occurred to you that if he had landed, Spender might have wanted to stay on here?"

"I doubt it, Ryker," Connolly said calmly. "Anyway, there's little chance that Colonel Spender is still alive. What we're interested in finding is the capsule."

Ryker was about to reply when a faint metallic buzz sounded from the direction of his hut. He looked around sharply, waiting for it to end, and for a moment the whole tableau, composed of the men on the launch, the gaunt outcast on the edge of the jetty, and the Indians behind him, was frozen in an absurdly motionless posture. The mechanism of the old alarm clock had obviously been fully wound, and the buzz sounded for thirty seconds, finally ending with a high-pitched ping.

Pereira grinned. He glanced at his watch. "It keeps good time, Ryker." But Ryker had stalked off back to the hut, scattering the Indians before him.

Connolly watched the group dissolve, then suddenly snapped his fingers. "You're right, Captain. It certainly does keep good time," he repeated as they entered the cabin.

Evidently tired by the encounter with Ryker, Pereira slumped down among Connolly's equipment and unbuttoned his tunic. "Sorry about Ryker, but I warned you. Frankly, Lieutenant, we might as well leave now. There's nothing here. Ryker knows that. However, he's no fool, and he's quite capable of faking all sorts of evidence just to get a retainer out of you. He wouldn't mind if the bulldozers came."

"I'm not so sure." Connolly glanced briefly through the porthole. "Captain, has Ryker got a radio?"

"Of course not. Why?"

"Are you certain?"

"Absolutely. It's the last thing the man would have. Anyway, there's no electrical supply here, and he has no batteries." He noticed Connolly's intent expression. "What's on your mind, Lieutenant?"

"You're his only contact? There are no other traders in the area?"

"None. The Indians are too dangerous, and there's nothing to trade. Why do you think Ryker has a radio?"

"He must have. Or something very similar. Captain, just now you remarked on the fact that his old alarm clock kept good time. Does it occur to you to ask *how*?"

Pereira sat up slowly. "Lieutenant, you have a valid point."

"Exactly. I knew there was something odd about those two clocks when they were standing side by side. That type of alarm clock is the cheapest obtainable, notoriously inaccurate. Often they lose two or three minutes in twenty-four hours. But that clock was telling the right time to within ten seconds. No optical instrument would give him that degree of accuracy.''

Pereira shrugged sceptically. "But I haven't been here for over four months. And even then he didn't check the time with me.''

"Of course not. He didn't need to. The only possible explanation for such a degree of accuracy is that he's getting a daily time fix, either on a radio or some long-range beacon.''

"Wait a moment, Lieutenant.'' Pereira watched the dusklight fall across the jungle. "It's a remarkable coincidence, but there must be an innocent explanation. Don't jump straight to the conclusion that Ryker has some instrument taken from the missing moon capsule. Other aircraft have crashed in the forest. And what would be the point? He's not running an airline or railway system. Why should he need to know the time, the *exact* time, to within ten seconds?''

Connolly tapped the lid of his monitoring case, controlling his growing exasperation at Pereira's reluctance to treat the matter seriously, at his whole permissive attitude of lazy tolerance towards Ryker, the Indians, and the forest. Obviously he unconsciously resented Connolly's sharp-eyed penetration of this private world.

"Clocks have become his *idée fixe,*'' Pereira continued. "Perhaps he's developed an amazing sensitivity to its mechanism. Knowing exactly the right time could be a substitute for the civilisation on which he turned his back.'' Thoughtfully, Pereira moistened the end of his cheroot. "But I agree that it's strange. Perhaps a little investigation would be worthwhile after all.''

After a cool jungle night in the air-conditioned cabin, the next day Connolly began discreetly to reconnoitre the area. Pereira took ashore two bottles of whiskey and a soda syphon, and was able to keep Ryker distracted while Connolly roved about the campong with his monitoring equipment. Once or twice he heard Ryker bellow jocularly at him from his window as he lolled back over the whiskey. At intervals, as Ryker slept, Pereira would come out into the sun, sweating like a drowsy pig in his stained uniform, and try to drive back the Indians.

"As long as you stay within earshot of Ryker you're safe," he told Connolly. Chopped-out pathways crisscrossed the bush at all angles, a new one added whenever one of the bands returned to the campong, irrespective of those already established. This maze extended for miles around them. "If you get lost, don't panic but stay where you are. Sooner or later we'll come out and find you."

Eventually giving up his attempt to monitor any of the signal beacons built into the lost capsule—both the sonar and radio meters remained at zero—Connolly tried to communicate with the Indians by sign language, but with the exception of one, the youth with the moist limpid eyes who had been hanging about on Ryker's veranda, they merely stared at him stonily. This youth Pereira identified as the son of the former witch-doctor ("Ryker's more or less usurped his role, for some reason the old boy lost the confidence of the tribe"). While the other Indians gazed at Connolly as if seeing some invisible numinous shadow, some extracorporeal nimbus which pervaded his body, the youth was obviously aware that Connolly possessed some special talent, perhaps not dissimilar from that which his father had once practised. However, Connolly's attempts to talk to the youth were handicapped by the fact that he was suffering from a purulent ophthalmia, gonococcic in origin and extremely contagious, which made his eyes water continuously. Many of the Indians suffered from this complaint, threatened by permanent blindness, and Connolly had seen them treating their eyes with water in which a certain type of fragrant bark had been dissolved.

Ryker's casual, offhand authority over the Indians puzzled Connolly. Slumped back in his chair against the mahogany dresser, one hand touching the ormolu clock, most of the time he and Pereira indulged in a lachrymose back-chat. Then, oblivious of any danger, Ryker would amble out into the dusty campong, push his way blurrily through the Indians and drum up a party to collect firewood for the water-still, jerking them bodily to their feet as they squatted about their huts. What interested Connolly was the Indians' reaction to this type of treatment. They seemed to be restrained, not by any belief in his strength of personality or primitive kingship, but by a grudging acceptance that for the time being, at any rate, Ryker possessed the whip-hand over them all. Obviously Ryker served certain useful roles for them as an intermediary with the Mission, but this alone would not explain the sources of his power. Beyond certain more or less defined limits—the perimeter of the campong—his authority was minimal.

A hint of explanation came on the second morning of their visit, when Connolly accidentally lost himself in the forest.

After breakfast Connolly sat under the awning on the deck of the patrol launch, gazing out over the brown jellylike surface of the river. The campong was silent. During the night the Indians had disappeared into the bush. Like lemmings they were apparently prone to these sudden irresistible urges. Occasionally the nomadic call would be strong enough to carry them two hundred miles away; at other times they would set off in high spirits and then lose interest after a few miles, returning dispiritedly to the campong in small groups.

Deciding to make the most of their absence, Connolly shouldered the monitoring equipment and climbed onto the pier. A few dying fires smoked plaintively among the huts, and abandoned utensils and smashed pottery lay about in the red dust. In the distance the morning haze over the forest had lifted, and Connolly could see what appeared to be a low hill—a shallow rise no more than a hundred feet in height which rose off the flat floor of the jungle a quarter of a mile away.

On his right, among the huts, someone moved. An old man sat alone among the refuse of pottery shards and raffia baskets, cross-legged under a small makeshift awning. Barely distinguishable from the dust, his moribund figure seemed to contain the whole futility of the Amazon forest.

Still musing on Ryker's motives for isolating himself in the jungle, Connolly made his way towards the distant rise.

Ryker's behaviour the previous evening had been curious. Shortly after dusk, when the sunset sank into the western forest, bathing the jungle in an immense ultramarine and golden light, the daylong chatter and movement of the Indians ceased abruptly. Connolly had been glad of the silence—the endless thwacks of the rattan canes and grating of the stone mills in which they mixed the Government-issue meal had become tiresome. Pereira made several cautious visits to the edge of the campong, and each time reported that the Indians were sitting in a huge circle outside their huts, watching Ryker's bungalow. The latter was lounging on his veranda in the moonlight, chin in hand, one boot upon the rail, morosely surveying the assembled tribe.

"They've got their spears and ceremonial feathers," Pereira whispered. "For a moment I almost believed they were preparing an attack."

After waiting half an hour, Connolly climbed up onto the pier, found the Indians squatting in their dark silent circle, Ryker glaring down at them. Only the witch-doctor's son made any attempt to approach Connolly, sidling tentatively through the shadows, a piece of what appeared to be blue obsidian in his hand, some talisman of his father's that had lost its potency.

Uneasily, Connolly returned to the launch. Shortly after 3:00 A.M. they were wakened in their bunks by a tremendous whoop, reached the deck to hear the stampede of feet through the dust, the hissing of overturned fires and cooking-pots. Apparently leading the pack, Ryker, emitting a series of re-echoed "Haroohs!" disappeared into the bush. Within a minute the campong was empty.

"What game is Ryker playing?" Pereira muttered as they stood on the creaking jetty in the dusty moonlight. "This must be the focus of his authority over the Nambas." Baffled, they went back to their bunks.

Reaching the margins of the rise, Connolly strolled through a small orchard which had returned to nature, hearing in his mind the exultant roar of Ryker's voice as it had cleaved the midnight jungle. Idly he picked a few of the barely ripe guavas and vividly coloured cajus with their astringent delicately flavoured juice. After spitting away the pith, he searched for a way out of the orchard, but within a few minutes realised that he was lost.

A continuous mound when seen from the distance, the rise was in fact a nexus of small hillocks that formed the residue of a onetime system of oxbow lakes, and the basins between the slopes were still treacherous with deep mire. Connolly rested his equipment at the foot of a tree. Withdrawing his pistol, he fired two shots into the air in the hope of attracting Ryker and Pereira. He sat down to await his rescue, taking the opportunity to unlatch his monitors and wipe the dials.

After ten minutes no one had appeared. Feeling slightly demoralised, and frightened that the Indians might return and find him, Connolly shouldered his equipment and set off towards the northwest, in the approximate direction of the campong. The ground rose before him. Suddenly, as he turned behind a palisade of wild magnolia trees, he stepped into an open clearing on the crest of the hill.

Squatting on their heels against the tree-trunks and among the tall grass was what seemed to be the entire tribe of the Nambikwaras. They were facing him, their expressions immobile and watchful, eyes like white beads among the sheaves. Presumably they had been sitting in the clearing, only fifty yards away, when he fired his shots, and Connolly had the uncanny feeling that they had been waiting for him to make his entrance exactly at the point he had chosen.

Hesitating, Connolly tightened his grip on the radio monitor. The Indians' faces were like burnished teak, their shoulders painted with a delicate mosaic of earth colours. Noticing the spears held among the grass, Connolly started to walk on across the clearing towards a breach in the palisade of trees.

For a dozen steps the Indians remained motionless. Then, with a chorus of yells, they leapt forward from the grass and surrounded Connolly in a jabbering pack. None of them were more than five feet tall, but their plump agile bodies buffeted him about, almost knocking him off his feet. Eventually the tumult steadied itself, and two or three of the leaders stepped from the cordon and began to scrutinise Connolly more closely, pinching and fingering him with curious positional movements of the thumb and forefinger, like connoisseurs examining some interesting taxidermic object.

Finally, with a series of high-pitched whines and grunts, the Indians moved off towards the centre of the clearing, propelling Connolly in front of them with sharp slaps on his legs and shoulders, like drovers goading on a large pig. They were all jabbering furiously to each other, some hacking at the grass with their machetes, gathering bundles of leaves in their arms.

Tripping over something in the grass, Connolly stumbled onto his knees. The catch slipped from the lid of the monitor, and as he stood up, fumbling with the heavy cabinet, the revolver slipped from his holster and was lost under his feet in the rush.

Giving way to his panic, he began to shout over the bobbing heads around him, to his surprise heard one of the Indians beside him bellow to the others. Instantly, as the refrain was taken up, the crowd stopped and re-formed its cordon around him. Gasping, Connolly steadied himself, and started to search the trampled grass for his revolver, when he realised that the Indians were now staring, not at himself, but at the exposed counters of the monitor. The six meters were swinging wildly after the stampede across the clearing, and the Indians craned forward, their machetes and spears lowered, gaping at the bobbing needles.

Then there was a roar from the edge of the clearing, and a huge wild-faced man in a straw hat, a shotgun held like a crowbar in his hands, stormed in among the Indians, driving them back. Dragging the monitor from his neck, Connolly felt the steadying hand of Captain Pereira take his elbow.

"Lieutenant, Lieutenant," Pereira murmured reprovingly as they recovered the pistol and made their way back to the campong, the uproar behind them fading among the undergrowth, "we were nearly in time to say grace."

Later that afternoon Connolly sat back in a canvas chair on the deck of the launch. About half the Indians had returned and were wandering about the huts in a desultory manner, kicking at the fires. Ryker, his authority re-asserted, had returned to his bungalow.

"I thought you said they weren't cannibal," Connolly reminded Pereira.

The captain snapped his fingers, as if thinking about something more important. "No, they're not. Stop worrying, Lieutenant, you're not going to end up in a pot." When Connolly demurred, he swung crisply on his heel. He had sharpened up his uniform, and wore his pistol belt and Sam Browne at their regulation position, his peaked cap jutting low over his eyes. Evidently Connolly's close escape had confirmed some private suspicion. "Look, they're not cannibal in the dietary sense of the term, as used by the Food & Agriculture Organisation in its classification of aboriginal peoples. They won't stalk and hunt human game in preference for any other. But"—here the captain stared fixedly at Connolly—"in certain circumstances, after a fertility ceremonial, for example, they will eat human flesh. Like all members of primitive communities which are small numerically, the Nambikwara never bury their dead. Instead, they eat them, as a means of conserving the loss and to perpetuate the corporeal identity of the departed. Now do you understand?"

Connolly grimaced. "I'm glad to know now that I was about to be perpetuated."

Pereira looked out at the campong. "Actually they would never eat a white man, to avoid defiling the tribe." He paused. "At least, so I've always believed. It's strange, something seems to have. . . . Listen, Lieutenant," he explained, "I can't quite piece it together, but I'm convinced we should stay here for a few days longer. Various elements make me suspicious, I'm sure Ryker is hiding something. That mound where you were lost is a sort of sacred tumulus, the way the Indians were looking at your instrument made me certain that they'd seen something like it before— perhaps a panel with many flickering dials . . . ?"

"The *Goliath 7*?" Connolly shook his head sceptically. He listened to the undertow of the river drumming dimly against the keel of the launch. "I doubt it, Captain. I'd like to believe you, but for some reason it doesn't seem very likely."

"I agree. Some other explanation is preferable. But what? The Indians were squatting on that hill, waiting for someone to arrive. What else could your monitor have reminded them of?"

"Ryker's clock?" Connolly suggested. "They may regard it as a sort of juju object, like a magical toy."

"No," Pereira said categorically. "These Indians are highly pragmatic, they're not impressed by useless toys. For them to be deterred from killing you means that the equipment you carried possessed some very real, down-to-earth power. Look, suppose the capsule did land here and was secretly buried by Ryker, and that in some way the clocks help him to identify its whereabouts"—here Pereira shrugged hopefully—"it's just possible."

"Hardly," Connolly said. "Besides, Ryker couldn't have buried the capsule himself, and if Colonel Spender had lived through re-entry Ryker would have helped him."

"I'm not so sure," Pereira said pensively. "It would probably strike our friend Mr. Ryker as very funny for a man to travel all the way to the moon and back just to be killed by savages. Much too good a joke to pass over."

"What religious beliefs do the Indians have?" Connolly asked.

"No religion in the formalised sense of a creed and dogma. They eat their dead, so they don't need to invent an afterlife in an attempt to re-animate them. In general they subscribe to one of the so-called cargo cults. As I said, they're very material. That's why they're so lazy. Sometime in the future they expect a magic galleon or giant bird to arrive carrying an everlasting cornucopia of worldly goods, so they just sit about waiting for the great day. Ryker encourages them in this idea. It's very dangerous—in some Melanesian islands the tribes with cargo cults have degenerated completely. They lie around all day on the beaches, waiting for the WHO flying boat, or. . . ." His voice trailed off.

Connolly nodded and supplied the unspoken thought. "Or —a space capsule?"

Despite Pereira's growing if muddled conviction that something associated with the missing spacecraft was to be found in the area, Connolly was still sceptical. His close escape had left him feeling curiously calm and emotionless, and he looked back on his possible death with fatalistic detachment, identifying it with the total ebb and flow of life in the Amazon forests, with its myriad unremembered deaths, and with the endless vistas of dead trees leaning across the jungle paths radiating from the campong. After only two days the jungle had begun to invest his mind with its own logic, and the possibility of the spacecraft landing there seemed more and more remote. The two elements belonged to different systems of natural order, and he found it increasingly difficult to visualise them overlapping. In addition there was a deeper reason for his scepticism, underlined by Ryker's reference to the "real" reasons for the spaceflights. The implication was that the entire space programme was a symptom of some inner unconscious malaise afflicting mankind, and in particular the Western technocracies, and that the spacecraft and satellites had been launched because their flights satisfied certain buried compulsions and desires. By contrast, in the jungle, where the unconscious was manifest and exposed, there was no need for these insane projections, and the likelihood of the Amazonas playing any part in the success or failure of the spaceflight became, by a sort of psychological parallax, increasingly blurred and distant, the missing capsule itself a fragment of a huge disintegrating fantasy.

However, he agreed to Pereira's request to borrow the monitors and follow Ryker and the Indians on their midnight romp through the forest.

Once again, after dusk, the same ritual silence descended over the campong, and the Indians took up their positions in the doors of their huts. Like some morose exiled princeling, Ryker sat sprawled on his veranda, one eye on the clock through the window behind him. In the moonlight the scores of moist dark eyes never wavered as they watched him.

At last, half an hour later, Ryker galvanised his great body into life, with a series of tremendous whoops raced off across the campong, leading the stampede into the bush. Away in the distance, faintly outlined by the quarter moon, the shallow hump of the tribal tumulus rose over the black canopy of the jungle. Pereira waited until the last heel-beats had subsided, then climbed onto the pier and disappeared among the shadows.

Far away Connolly could hear the faint cries of Ryker's pack as they made off through the bush, the sounds of machetes slashing at the undergrowth. An ember on the opposite side of the campong flared in the low wind, illuminating the abandoned old man, presumably the former witch-doctor, whom he had seen that morning. Beside him was another slimmer figure, the limpid-eyed youth who had followed Connolly about.

A door stirred on Ryker's veranda, providing Connolly with a distant image of the white moonlit back of the river reflected in the mirrors of the mahogany dresser. Connolly watched the door jump lightly against the latch, then walked quietly across the pier to the wooden steps.

A few empty tobacco tins lay about on the shelves around the room, and a stack of empty bottles cluttered one corner behind the door. The ormolu clock had been locked away in the mahogany dresser. After testing the doors, which had been secured with a stout padlock, Connolly noticed a dog-eared paperback book lying on the dresser beside a half-empty carton of cartridges.

On a faded red ground, the small black lettering on the cover was barely decipherable, blurred by the sweat from Ryker's fingers. At first glance it appeared to be a set of logarithm tables. Each of the eighty or so pages was covered with column after column of finely printed numerals and tabular material.

Curious, Connolly carried the manual over to the doorway. The title page was more explicit.

ECHO III
CONSOLIDATED TABLES OF CELESTIAL TRAVERSES
1965–1980

Published by the National Aeronautics and Space Administration, Washington, D.C., 1965. Part XV. Longitude 40-80 West, Latitude 10 North–35 South (South American Subcontinent) Price 35¢.

His interest quickening, Connolly turned the pages. The manual fell open at the section headed: Lat. 5 South, Long. 60 West. He remembered that this was the approximate position of Campos Buros. Tabulated by year, month, and day, the columns of figures listed the elevations and compass bearings for sightings of the *Echo III* satellite, the latest of the huge aluminium spheres which had been orbiting the Earth since *Echo I* was launched in 1960. Rough pencil lines had been drawn through all the entries up to the year 1968. At this point the markings became individual, each minuscule entry crossed off with a small blunt stroke. The pages were grey with the blurred graphite.

Guided by this careful patchwork of cross-hatching, Connolly found the latest entry: March 17, 1978. The time and sighting were: 1:22 A.M. Elevation forty-three degrees WNW, Capella–Eridanus. Below it was the entry for the next day, an hour later, its orientations differing slightly.

Ruefully shaking his head in admiration of Ryker's cleverness, Connolly looked at his watch. It was about 1:20, two minutes until the next traverse. He glanced at the sky, picking out the constellation Eridanus, from which the satellite would emerge.

So this explained Ryker's hold over the Indians! What more impressive means had a down-and-out white man of intimidating and astonishing a tribe of primitive savages? Armed with nothing more than a set of tables and a reliable clock, he could virtually pinpoint the appearance of the satellite at the first second of its visible traverse. The Indians would naturally be awed and bewildered by this phantom charioteer of the midnight sky, steadily pursuing its cosmic round, like a beacon traversing the profoundest deeps of their own minds. Any powers which Ryker cared to invest in the satellite would seem confirmed by his ability to control the time and place of its arrival.

Connolly realised now how the old alarm clock had told the correct time—by using his tables Ryker had read the exact time off the sky each night. A more accurate clock presumably freed him from the need to spend unnecessary time waiting for the satellite's arrival; he would now be able to set off for the tumulus only a few minutes beforehand.

Walking along the pier, he began to search the sky. Away in the distance a low cry sounded into the midnight air, diffusing like a wraith over the jungle. Beside him, sitting on the bows of the launch, Connolly heard the helmsman grunt and point at the sky above the opposite bank. Following the upraised arm, he quickly found the speeding dot of light.

It was moving directly towards the tumulus. Steadily the satellite crossed the sky, winking intermittently as it passed behind lanes of high-altitude cirrus, the conscripted ship of the Nambikwaras' cargo cult.

It was about to disappear among the stars in the southeast when a faint shuffling sound distracted Connolly. He looked down to find the moist-eyed youth, the son of the witch-doctor, standing only a few feet away from him, regarding him dolefully.

"Hello, boy," Connolly greeted him. He pointed at the vanishing satellite. "See the star?"

The youth made a barely perceptible nod. He hesitated for a moment, his running eyes glowing like drowned moons, then stepped forward and touched Connolly's wristwatch, tapping the dial with his horny fingernail.

Puzzled, Connolly held it up for him to inspect. The youth watched the second hand sweep around the dial, an expression of rapt and ecstatic concentration on his face. Nodding vigorously, he pointed to the sky.

Connolly grinned. "So you understand? You've rumbled old man Ryker, have you?" He nodded encouragingly to the youth, who was tapping the watch eagerly, apparently in an effort to conjure up a second satellite. Connolly began to laugh. "Sorry, boy." He slapped the manual. "What you really need is this pack of jokers."

Connolly began to walk back to the bungalow when the youth darted forward impulsively and blocked his way, thin legs spread in an aggressive stance. Then, with immense ceremony, he drew from behind his back a round painted object with a glass face that Connolly remembered he had seen him carrying before.

"That looks interesting." Connolly bent down to examine the object, caught a glimpse in the thin light of a luminous instrument before the youth snatched it away.

"Wait a minute, boy. Let's have another look at that."

After a pause the pantomime was repeated, but the youth was reluctant to allow Connolly more than the briefest inspection. Again Connolly saw a calibrated dial and a wavering indicator. Then the youth stepped forward and touched Connolly's wrist.

Quickly Connolly unstrapped the metal chain. He tossed the watch to the youth, who instantly dropped the instrument, his barter achieved, and after a delighted yodel turned and darted off among the trees.

Bending down, careful not to touch the instrument with his hands, Connolly examined the dial. The metal housing around it was badly torn and scratched, as if the instrument had been pried from some control panel with a crude implement. But the glass face and the dial beneath it were still intact. Across the centre was the legend:

L U N A R   A L T I M E T E R
Miles: 100
G O L I A T H   7
General Electric Corporation,
Schenectady

Picking up the instrument, Connolly cradled it in his hands. The pressure seals were broken, and the gyro bath floated freely on its air cushion. Like a graceful bird the indicator needle glided up and down the scale.

The pier creaked under approaching footsteps. Connolly looked up at the perspiring figure of Captain Pereira, cap in one hand, monitor dangling from the other.

"My dear Lieutenant!" he panted. "Wait till I tell you, what a farce, it's fantastic! Do you know what Ryker's doing?—it's so simple it seems unbelievable that no one's thought of it before. It's nothing short of the most magnificent practical *joke*!" Gasping, he sat down on the bale of skins leaning against the gangway. "I'll give you a clue: Narcissus."

"*Echo,*" Connolly replied flatly, still staring at the instrument in his hands.

"You spotted it? Clever boy!" Pereira wiped his cap-band. "How did you guess? It wasn't that obvious." He took the manual Connolly handed him. "What the—? Ah, I see, this makes it even more clear. Of course." He slapped his knee with the manual. "You found this in his room? I take my hat off to Ryker," he continued as Connolly set the altimeter down on the pier and steadied it carefully. "Let's face it, it's something of a pretty clever trick. Can you imagine it, he comes here, finds a tribe with a strong cargo cult, opens his little manual and says, 'Presto, the great white bird will be arriving: *NOW!*' "

Connolly nodded, then stood up, wiping his hands on a strip of rattan. When Pereira's laughter had subsided, he pointed down to the glowing face of the altimeter at their feet. "Captain, something else arrived," he said quietly. "Never mind Ryker and the satellite. This cargo actually landed."

As Pereira knelt down and inspected the altimeter, whistling sharply to himself, Connolly walked over to the edge of the pier and looked out across the great back of the silent river at the giant trees which hung over the water, like forlorn mutes at some cataclysmic funeral, their thin silver voices carried away on the dead tide.

Half an hour before they set off the next morning, Connolly waited on the deck for Captain Pereira to conclude his interrogation of Ryker. The empty campong, deserted again by the Indians, basked in the heat, a single plume of smoke curling into the sky. The old witch-doctor and his son had disappeared, perhaps to try their skill with a neighbouring tribe, but the loss of his watch was unregretted by Connolly. Down below, safely stowed away among his baggage, was the altimeter, carefully sterilised and sealed. On the table in front of him, no more than two feet from the pistol in his belt, lay Ryker's manual.

For some reason he did not want to see Ryker, despite his contempt for him, and when Pereira emerged from the bungalow he was relieved to observe that he was alone. Connolly had decided that he would not return with the search-parties when they came to find the capsule; Pereira would serve adequately as a guide.

"Well?"

The captain smiled wanly. "Oh, he admitted it, of course." He sat down on the rail, and pointed to the manual. "After all, he had no choice. Without that his existence here would be untenable."

"He admitted that Colonel Spender landed here?"

Pereira nodded. "Not in so many words, but effectively.

The capsule is buried somewhere here—under the tumulus, I would guess. The Indians got hold of Colonel Spender, Ryker claims he could do nothing to help him."

"That's a lie. He saved me in the bush when the Indians thought I had landed."

With a shrug Pereira said: "Your positions were slightly different. Besides, my impression is that Spender was dying anyway, Ryker says the parachute was badly burnt. He probably accepted a *fait accompli*, simply decided to do nothing and hush the whole thing up, incorporating the landing into the cargo cult. Very useful too. He'd been tricking the Indians with the *Echo* satellite, but sooner or later they would have become impatient. After the *Goliath* crashed, of course, they were prepared to go on watching the *Echo* and waiting for the next landing forever." A faint smile touched his lips. "It goes without saying that he regards the episode as something of a macabre joke. On you and the whole civilised world."

A door slammed on the veranda, and Ryker stepped out into the sunlight. Bare-chested and hatless, he strode towards the launch.

"Connolly," he called down, "you've got my box of tricks there!"

Connolly reached forward and fingered the manual, the butt of his pistol tapping the table edge. He looked up at Ryker, at his big golden frame bathed in the morning light. Despite his still belligerent tone, a subtle change had come over Ryker. The ironic gleam in his eye had gone, and the inner core of wariness and suspicion which had warped the man and exiled him from the world was now visible. Connolly realised that, curiously, their respective roles had been reversed. He remembered Pereira reminding him that the Indians were at equilibrium with their environment, accepting its constraints and never seeking to dominate the towering arbors of the forest, in a sense an externalisation of their own unconscious psyches. Ryker had upset that equilibrium, and by using the *Echo* satellite had brought the twentieth century and its psychopathic projections into the heart of the Amazonian deep, transforming the Indians into a community of superstitious and materialistic sightseers, their whole culture oriented around the mythical god of the puppet star. It was Connolly who now accepted the jungle for what it was, seeing himself and the abortive spaceflight in this fresh perspective.

Pereira gestured to the helmsman, and with a muffled roar the engine started. The launch pulled lightly against its lines.

"Connolly!" Ryker's voice was shriller now, his bellicose shout overlayed by a higher note. For a moment the two men looked at each other, and in the eyes above him Connolly glimpsed the helpless isolation of Ryker, his futile attempt to identify himself with the forest.

Picking up the manual, Connolly leaned forward and tossed it through the air onto the pier. Ryker tried to catch it, then knelt down and picked it up before it slipped through the springing poles. Still kneeling, he watched as the lines were cast off and the launch surged ahead.

They moved out into the channel and plunged through the bowers of spray into the heavier swells of the open current.

As they reached a sheltering bend and the figure of Ryker faded for the last time among the creepers and sunlight, Connolly turned to Pereira. "Captain—what actually happened to Colonel Spender? You said the Indians wouldn't eat a white man."

"They eat their gods," Pereira said.

THE

DEAD

ASTRONAUT

CAPE KENNEDY HAS GONE NOW, ITS GANTRIES RISING FROM THE deserted dunes. Sand has come in across the Banana River, filling the creeks and turning the old space complex into a wilderness of swamps and broken concrete. In the summer, hunters build their blinds in the wrecked staff-cars; but by early November, when Judith and I arrived, the entire area was abandoned. Beyond Cocoa Beach, where I stopped the car, the ruined motels were half hidden in the saw grass. The launching towers rose into the evening air like the rusting ciphers of some forgotten algebra of the sky.

"The perimeter fence is half a mile ahead," I said. "We'll wait here until it's dark. Do you feel better now?"

Judith was staring at an immense funnel of cerise cloud that seemed to draw the day with it below the horizon, taking the light from her faded blonde hair. The previous afternoon, in the hotel in Tampa, she had fallen ill briefly with some unspecified complaint.

"What about the money?" she asked. "They may want more, now that we're here."

"Five thousand dollars? Ample, Judith. These relic hunters are a dying breed—few people are interested in Cape Kennedy any longer. What's the matter?"

Her thin fingers were fretting at the collar of her suede jacket. "I . . . it's just that perhaps I should have worn black."

"Why? Judith, this isn't a funeral. For heaven's sake, Robert died twenty years ago. I know all he meant to us, but. . . ."

Judith was staring at the debris of tyres and abandoned

cars, her pale eyes becalmed in her drawn face. "Philip, don't you understand, he's coming back now. Someone's got to be here. The memorial service over the radio was a horrible travesty—my God, that priest would have had a shock if Robert had talked back to him. There ought to be a full-scale committee, not just you and I and these empty nightclubs."

In a firmer voice, I said: "Judith, there would be a committee—*if* we told the NASA Foundation what we know. The remains would be interred in the NASA vault at Arlington, there'd be a band—even the President might be there. There's still time."

I waited for her to reply, but she was watching the gantries fade into the night sky. Fifteen years ago, when the dead astronaut orbiting the Earth in his burned-out capsule had been forgotten, Judith had constituted herself a memorial committee of one. Perhaps, in a few days, when she finally held the last relics of Robert Hamilton's body in her own hands, she would come to terms with her obsession.

"Philip, over there! Is that—"

High in the western sky, between the constellations Cepheus and Cassiopeia, a point of white light moved towards us, like a lost star searching for its zodiac. Within a few minutes it passed overhead, its faint beacon setting behind the cirrus over the sea.

"It's all right, Judith." I showed her the trajectory timetables pencilled into my diary. "The relic hunters read these orbits off the sky better than any computer. They must have been watching the pathways for years."

"Who was it?"

"A Russian woman pilot—Valentina Prokrovna. She was sent up from a site near the Urals twenty-five years ago to work on a television relay system."

"Television? I hope they enjoyed the programme."

This callous remark, uttered by Judith as she stepped from the car, made me realise once again her special motives for coming to Cape Kennedy. I watched the capsule of the dead woman disappear over the dark Atlantic stream, as always moved by the tragic but serene spectacle of one of these ghostly voyagers coming back after so many years from the tideways of space. All I knew of this dead Russian was her code name: Seagull. Yet, for some reason, I was glad to be there as she came down. Judith, on the other hand, felt nothing of this. During all the years she had sat in the garden in the cold evenings, too tired to bring herself to bed, she had been sustained by her concern for one only of the twelve dead astronauts orbiting the night sky.

As she waited, her back to the sea, I drove the car into the garage of an abandoned nightclub fifty yards from the road. From the trunk I took out two suitcases. One, a light travel-case, contained clothes for Judith and myself. The other, fitted with a foil inlay, reinforcing straps, and a second handle, was empty.

We set off north towards the perimeter fence, like two late visitors arriving at a resort abandoned years earlier.

It was twenty years now since the last rockets had left their launching platforms at Cape Kennedy. At the time, NASA had already moved Judith and me—I was a senior flight-programmer—to the great new Planetary Space Complex in New Mexico. Shortly after our arrival, we had met one of the trainee astronauts, Robert Hamilton. After two decades, all I could remember of this overpolite but sharp-eyed young man was his albino skin, so like Judith's pale eyes and opal hair, the same cold gene that crossed them both with its arctic pallor. We had been close friends for barely six weeks. Judith's infatuation was one of those confused sexual impulses that well-brought-up young women express in their own naive way; and as I watched them swim and play tennis together, I felt not so much resentful as concerned to sustain the whole passing illusion for her.

A year later, Robert Hamilton was dead. He had returned to Cape Kennedy for the last military flights before the launching grounds were closed. Three hours after lift-off, a freak meteorite collision ruptured his oxygen support system. He had lived on in his suit for another five hours. Although calm at first, his last radio transmissions were an incoherent babble Judith and I had never been allowed to hear.

A dozen astronauts had died in orbital accidents, their capsules left to revolve through the night sky like the stars of a new constellation; and at first, Judith had shown little response. Later, after her miscarriage, the figure of this dead astronaut circling the sky above us re-emerged in her mind as an obsession with time. For hours, she would stare at the bedroom clock, as if waiting for something to happen.

Five years later, after I resigned from NASA, we made our first trip to Cape Kennedy. A few military units still guarded the derelict gantries, but already the former launching site was being used as a satellite graveyard. As the dead capsules lost orbital velocity, they homed onto the master radio beacon. As well as the American vehicles, Russian and French satellites in the joint Euro-American space projects were brought down here, the burned-out hulks of the capsules exploding across the cracked concrete.

Already, too, the relic hunters were at Cape Kennedy, scouring the burning saw grass for instrument panels and flying suits and—most valuable of all—the mummified corpses of the dead astronauts.

These blackened fragments of collarbone and shin, kneecap and rib, were the unique relics of the Space Age, as treasured as the saintly bones of mediaeval shrines. After the first fatal accident in space, public outcry demanded that these orbiting biers be brought down to Earth. Unfortunately, when a returning moon rocket crashed into the Kalahari Desert, aboriginal tribesmen broke into the vehicle. Believing the crew to be dead gods, they cut off the eight hands and vanished into the bush. It had taken two years to track them down. From then on, the capsules were left in orbit to burn out on re-entry.

Whatever remains survived the crash landings in the satellite graveyard were scavenged by the relic hunters of Cape Kennedy. This band of nomads had lived for years in the wrecked cars and motels, stealing their icons under the feet of the wardens who patrolled the concrete decks. In early October, when a former NASA colleague told me that Robert Hamilton's satellite was becoming unstable, I drove down to Tampa and began to inquire about the purchase price of Robert's mortal remains. Five thousand dollars was a small price to pay for laying his ghost to rest in Judith's mind.

Eight hundred yards from the road, we crossed the perimeter fence. Crushed by the dunes, long sections of the twenty-foot-high palisade had collapsed, the saw grass growing through the steel mesh. Below us, the boundary road passed a derelict guardhouse and divided into two paved tracks. As we waited at this rendezvous, the headlamps of the wardens' half-tracks flared across the gantries near the beach.

Five minutes later, a small dark-faced man climbed from the rear seat of a car buried in the sand fifty yards away. Head down, he scuttled over to us.

"Mr. and Mrs. Groves?" After a pause to peer into our faces, he introduced himself tersely: "Quinton. Sam Quinton."

As he shook hands, his clawlike fingers examined the bones of my wrist and forearm. His sharp nose made circles in the air. He had the eyes of a nervous bird, forever searching the dunes and the grass. An Army webbing belt hung around his patched black denims. He moved his hands restlessly in the air, as if conducting a chamber ensemble hidden behind the sand-hills, and I noticed his badly scarred palms. Huge weals formed pale stars in the darkness.

For a moment, he seemed disappointed by us, almost reluctant to move on. Then he set off at a brisk pace across the dunes, now and then leaving us to blunder about helplessly. Half an hour later, when we entered a shallow basin near a farm of alkali-settling beds, Judith and I were exhausted, dragging the suitcases over the broken tyres and barbed wire.

A group of cabins had been dismantled from their original sites along the beach and re-erected in the basin. Isolated rooms tilted on the sloping sand, mantelpieces and flowered paper decorating the outer walls.

The basin was full of salvaged space material: sections of capsules, heat shields, antennas, and parachute canisters. Near the dented hull of a weather satellite, two sallow-faced men in sheepskin jackets sat on a car seat. The older wore a frayed Air Force cap over his eyes. With his scarred hands, he was polishing the steel visor of a space helmet. The other, a young man with a faint beard hiding his mouth, watched us approach with the detached and neutral gaze of an undertaker.

We entered the largest of the cabins, two rooms taken off

the rear of a beach-house. Quinton lit a paraffin lamp. He pointed around the dingy interior. "You'll be . . . comfortable," he said without conviction. As Judith stared at him with unconcealed distaste, he added pointedly: "We don't get many visitors."

I put the suitcases on the metal bed. Judith walked into the kitchen, and Quinton began to open the empty case. "It's in here?"

I took the two packets of $100 bills from my jacket. When I had handed them to him, I said: "The suitcase is for the . . . remains. Is it big enough?"

Quinton peered at me through the ruby light, as if baffled by our presence there. "You could have spared yourself the trouble. They've been up there a long time, Mr. Groves. After the impact"—for some reason, he cast a lewd eye in Judith's direction—"there might be enough for a chess set."

When he had gone, I went into the kitchen. Judith stood by the stove, hands on a carton of canned food. She was staring through the window at the metal salvage, refuse of the sky that still carried Robert Hamilton in its rusty centrifuge. For a moment, I had the feeling that the entire landscape of the Earth was covered with rubbish and that here, at Cape Kennedy, we had found its source.

I held her shoulders. "Judith, is there any point in this? Why don't we go back to Tampa? I could drive here in ten days' time when it's all over—"

She turned from me, her hands rubbing the suede where I had marked it. "Philip, I want to be here—no matter how unpleasant. Can't you understand?"

At midnight, when I finished making a small meal for us, she was standing on the concrete wall of the settling tank. The three relic hunters sitting on their car seats watched her without moving, scarred hands like flames in the darkness.

At three o'clock that morning, as we lay awake on the narrow bed, Valentina Prokrovna came down from the sky. Enthroned on a bier of burning aluminium three hundred yards wide, she soared past on her final orbit. When I went out into the night air, the relic hunters had gone. From the rim of the settling tank, I watched them race away among the dunes, leaping like hares over the tyres and wire.

I went back to the cabin. "Judith, she's coming down. Do you want to watch?"

Her blonde hair tied within a white towel, Judith lay on the bed, staring at the cracked plasterboard ceiling. Shortly after four o'clock, as I sat beside her, a phosphorescent light filled the hollow. There was the distant sound of explosions, muffled by the high wall of the dunes. Lights flared, followed by the noise of engines and sirens.

At dawn the relic hunters returned, hands wrapped in makeshift bandages, dragging their booty with them.

After this melancholy rehearsal, Judith entered a period of sudden and unexpected activity. As if preparing the cabin for some visitor, she rehung the curtains and swept out the two rooms with meticulous care, even bringing herself to ask Quinton for a bottle of cleanser. For hours she sat at the dressing-table, brushing and shaping her hair, trying out first one style and then another. I watched her feel the hollows of her cheeks, searching for the contours of a face that had vanished twenty years ago. As she spoke about Robert Hamilton, she almost seemed worried that she would appear old to him. At other times she referred to Robert as if he were a child, the son she and I had never been able to conceive since her miscarriage. These different roles followed one another like scenes in some private psychodrama. However, without knowing it, for years Judith and I had used Robert Hamilton for our own reasons. Waiting for him to land, and well aware that after this Judith would have no one to turn to except myself, I said nothing.

Meanwhile, the relic hunters worked on the fragments of Valentina Prokrovna's capsule: the blistered heat shield, the chassis of the radiotelemetry unit, and several cans of film that recorded her collision and act of death (these, if still intact, would fetch the highest prices, films of horrific and dreamlike violence played in the underground cinemas of Los Angeles, London, and Moscow). Passing the next cabin, I saw a tattered silver spacesuit spread-eagled on two automobile seats. Quinton and the relic hunters knelt beside it, their arms deep inside the legs and sleeves, gazing at me with the rapt and sensitive eyes of jewellers.

An hour before dawn, I was awakened by the sound of engines along the beach. In the darkness, the three relic hunters crouched by the settling tank, their pinched faces lit by the headlamps. A long convoy of trucks and half-tracks was moving into the launching ground. Soldiers jumped down from the tailboards, unloading tents and supplies.

"What are they doing?" I asked Quinton. "Are they looking for us?"

The old man cupped a scarred hand over his eyes. "It's the Army," he said uncertainly. "Manoeuvres, maybe. They haven't been here before like this."

"What about Hamilton?" I gripped his bony arm. "Are you sure—"

He pushed me away with a show of nervous temper. "We'll get him first. Don't worry, he'll be coming sooner than they think."

Two nights later, as Quinton prophesied, Robert Hamilton began his final descent. From the dunes near the settling tanks, we watched him emerge from the stars on his last run. Reflected in the windows of the buried cars, a thousand images of the capsule flared in the saw grass around us. Behind the satellite, a wide fan of silver spray opened in a phantom wake.

In the Army encampment by the gantries there was a surge of activity. A blaze of headlamps crossed the concrete lanes. Since the arrival of these military units, it had become plain to me, if not to Quinton, that far from being on manoeuvres, they were preparing for the landing of Robert Hamilton's capsule. A dozen half-tracks had been churning around the dunes, setting fire to the abandoned cabins and crushing the old car bodies. Platoons of soldiers were repairing the perimeter fence and replacing the sections of metalled road that the relic hunters had dismantled.

Shortly after midnight, at an elevation of forty-two degrees in the northwest, between Lyra and Hercules, Robert Hamilton appeared for the last time. As Judith stood up and shouted into the night air, an immense blade of light cleft the sky. The expanding corona sped towards us like a gigantic signal flare, illuminating every fragment of the landscape.

"Mrs. Groves!" Quinton darted after Judith and pulled her down into the grass as she ran towards the approaching satellite. Three hundred yards away, the silhouette of a half-track stood out on an isolated dune, its feeble spotlights drowned by the glare.

With a low metallic sigh, the burning capsule of the dead astronaut soared over our heads, the vaporising metal pouring from its hull. A few seconds later, as I shielded my eyes, an explosion of detonating sand rose from the ground behind me. A curtain of dust lifted into the darkening air like a vast spectre of powdered bone. The sounds of the impact rolled across the dunes. Near the launching gantries, fires flickered where fragments of the capsule had landed. A pall of phosphorescing gas hung in the air, particles within it beading and winking.

Judith had gone, running after the relic hunters through the swerving spotlights. When I caught up with them, the last fires of the explosion were dying among the gantries. The capsule had landed near the old Atlas launching pads, forming a shallow crater fifty yards in diameter. The slopes were scattered with glowing particles, sparkling like fading eyes. Judith ran distraughtly up and down, searching the fragments of smouldering metal.

Someone struck my shoulder. Quinton and his men, hot ash on their scarred hands, ran past like a troop of madmen, eyes wild in the crazed night. As we darted away through the flaring spotlights, I looked back at the beach. The gantries were enveloped in a pale-silver sheen that hovered there, and then moved away like a dying wraith over the sea.

At dawn, as the engines growled among the dunes, we collected the last remains of Robert Hamilton. The old man came into our cabin. As Judith watched from the kitchen, drying her hands on a towel, he gave me a cardboard shoe-box.

I held the box in my hands. "Is this all you could get?"

"It's all there was. Look at them, if you want."

"That's all right. We'll be leaving in half an hour."

He shook his head. "Not now. They're all around. If you move, they'll find us."

He waited for me to open the shoe-box, then grimaced and went out into the pale light.

We stayed for another four days, as the Army patrols searched the surrounding dunes. Day and night, the half-tracks lumbered among the wrecked cars and cabins. Once, as I watched with Quinton from a fallen water tower, a half-track and two jeeps came within four hundred yards of the basin, held back only by the stench from the settling beds and the cracked concrete causeways.

During this time, Judith sat in the cabin, the shoe-box on her lap. She said nothing to me, as if she had lost all interest in me and the salvage-filled hollow at Cape Kennedy. Mechanically she combed her hair, making and remaking her face.

On the second day, I came in after helping Quinton bury the cabins to their windows in the sand. Judith was standing by the table.

The shoe-box was open. In the centre of the table lay a pile of charred sticks, as if she had tried to light a small fire. Then I realised what was there. As she stirred the ash with her fingers, grey flakes fell from the joints, revealing the bony points of a clutch of ribs, a right hand and shoulder blade.

She looked at me with puzzled eyes. "They're black," she said.

Holding her in my arms, I lay with her on the bed. A loud-speaker reverberated among the dunes, fragments of the amplified commands drumming at the panes.

When they moved away, Judith said: "We can go now."

"In a little while, when it's clear. What about these?"

"Bury them. Anywhere, it doesn't matter." She seemed calm at last, giving me a brief smile, as if to agree that this grim charade was at last over.

Yet, when I had packed the bones into the shoe-box, scraping up Robert Hamilton's ash with a dessertspoon, she kept it with her, carrying it into the kitchen while she prepared our meals.

It was on the third day that we fell ill.

After a long noise-filled night, I found Judith sitting in front of the mirror, combing thick clumps of hair from her scalp. Her mouth was open, as if her lips were stained with acid. As she dusted the loose hair from her lap, I was struck by the leprous whiteness of her face.

Standing up with an effort, I walked listlessly into the kitchen and stared at the saucepan of cold coffee. A sense of indefinable exhaustion had come over me, as if the bones in my body had softened and lost their rigidity. On the lapels of my jacket, loose hair lay like spinning waste.

"Philip . . ." Judith swayed towards me. "Do you feel— What is it?"

"The water." I poured the coffee into the sink and massaged my throat. "It must be fouled."

"Can we leave?" She put a hand up to her forehead. Her brittle nails brought down a handful of frayed ash hair. "Philip, for God's sake—I'm losing all my hair!"

Neither of us was able to eat. After forcing myself through a few slices of cold meat, I went out and vomited behind the cabin.

Quinton and his men were crouched by the wall of the settling tank. As I walked towards them, steadying myself against the hull of the weather satellite, Quinton came down. When I told him that the water supplies were contaminated, he stared at me with his hard bird's eyes.

Half an hour later, they were gone.

The next day, our last there, we were worse. Judith lay on the bed, shivering in her jacket, the shoe-box held in one hand. I spent hours searching for fresh water in the cabins. Exhausted, I could barely cross the sandy basin. The Army patrols were closer. By now, I could hear the hard gear-changes of the half-tracks. The sounds from the loudspeakers drummed like fists on my head.

Then, as I looked down at Judith from the cabin doorway, a few words stuck for a moment in my mind.

"*. . . contaminated area . . . evacuate . . . radioactive . . .*"

I walked forward and pulled the box from Judith's hands.

"Philip . . ." She looked up at me weakly. "Give it back to me."

Her face was a puffy mask. On her wrists, white flecks were forming. Her left hand reached towards me like the claw of a cadaver.

I shook the box with blunted anger. The bones rattled inside. "For God's sake, it's *this!* Don't you see—why we're ill?"

"Philip—where are the others? The old man. Get them to help you."

"They've gone. They went yesterday, I told you." I let the box fall onto the table. The lid broke off, spilling the ribs tied together like a bundle of firewood. "Quinton knew what was happening—why the Army is here. They're trying to warn us."

"What do you mean?" Judith sat up, the focus of her eyes sustained only by a continuous effort. "Don't let them take Robert. Bury him here somewhere. We'll come back later."

"Judith!" I bent over the bed and shouted hoarsely at her. "Don't you realise—there was a *bomb* on board! Robert Hamilton was carrying an atomic weapon!" I pulled back the curtains from the window. "My God, what a joke. For twenty years I put up with him because I couldn't ever be really sure. . . ."

"Philip . . ."

"Don't worry, I used him—thinking about him was the only thing that kept us going. And all the time he was waiting up there to pay us back!"

There was a rumble of exhaust outside. A half-track with red crosses on its doors and hood had reached the edge of the basin. Two men in vinyl suits jumped down, counters raised in front of them.

"Judith, before we go, tell me. . . . I never asked you—"

Judith was sitting up, touching the hair on her pillow. One half of her scalp was almost bald. She stared at her weak hands with their silvering skin. On her face was an expression I had never seen before, the dumb anger of betrayal.

As she looked at me, and at the bones scattered across the table, I knew my answer.

MY DREAM
OF FLYING
TO
WAKE ISLAND

MELVILLE'S DREAM OF FLYING TO WAKE ISLAND—A HOPELESS ambition, given all his handicaps—came alive again when he found the crashed aircraft buried in the dunes above the beach-house. Until then, during these first three months at the abandoned resort built among the sand-hills, his obsession with Wake Island had rested on little more than a collection of fraying photographs of this Pacific atoll, a few vague memories of its immense concrete runways, and an unfulfilled vision of himself at the controls of a light aircraft, flying steadily westwards across the open sea.

With the discovery of the crashed bomber in the dunes, everything had changed. Instead of spending his time wandering aimlessly along the beach, or gazing from the balcony at the endless sand-flats that stretched towards the sea at low tide, Melville now devoted all his time to digging the aircraft out of the dunes. He cancelled his evening games of chess with Dr. Laing, his only neighbour at the empty resort, went to bed before the television programmes began, and was up by five, dragging his spades and land-lines across the sand to the excavation site.

The activity suited Melville, distracting him from the sharp frontal migraines that had begun to affect him again. These returning memories of the prolonged ECT treatment unsettled him more than he had expected, with their unequivocal warning that in the margins of his mind the elements of a less pleasant world were waiting to reconstitute themselves. The dream of escaping to Wake Island was a compass bearing of sorts, but the discovery of the crashed aircraft gave him a chance to engage all his energies and, with luck, hold these migraine attacks at bay.

A number of wartime aircraft were buried near this empty resort. Walking across the sand-flats on what Dr. Laing believed were marine-biology specimen hunts, Melville often found pieces of Allied and enemy fighters shot down over the Channel. Rusting engine blocks and sections of cannon breeches emerged from the sand, somehow brought to the surface by the transits of the sea, and then subsided again without trace. During the summer weekends a few souvenir hunters and World War II enthusiasts picked over the sand, now and then finding a complete engine or wing spar. Too heavy to move, these relics were left where they lay. However, one of the weekend groups, led by a former advertising executive named Tennant, had found an intact Messerschmitt 109 a few feet below the sand half a mile along the coast. The members of the party parked their sports-cars at the bottom of the road below Melville's beach-house, and set off with elaborate pumps and lifting tackle in a reconditioned DUKW.

Melville noticed that Tennant was usually suspicious and standoffish with any visitors who approached the Messerschmitt, but the advertising man was clearly intrigued by this solitary resident of the deserted resort who spent his time ambling through the debris on the beach. He offered Melville a chance of looking at the aircraft. They drove out across the wet sand to where the fighter lay like a winged saurian inside its galvanised-iron retaining wall a few feet below the surface of the flat. Tennant helped to lower Melville into the blackened cockpit, an experience which promptly brought on his first fugue.

Later, when Tennant and his co-workers had returned him to the beach-house, Melville sat for hours massaging his arms and hands, uneasily aware of certain complex digital skills that he wanted to forget but were beginning to reassert themselves in unexpected ways. Laing's solarium, with its dials and shutters, its capsulelike interior, unsettled him even more than the cockpit of the 109.

Impressive though the find was, the rusting hulk of the World War II fighter was insignificant beside Melville's discovery. He had been aware of the bomber, or at least of a large engineered structure, for some time. Wandering among the dunes above the beach-house during the warm afternoons, he had been too preoccupied at first with the task of settling in at the abandoned resort, and above all with doing nothing. Despite the endless hours he had spent in the hospital gymnasium, during his long recuperation after the aviation accident, he found that the effort of walking through the deep sand soon exhausted him.

At this stage, too, he had other matters to think about. After arriving at the resort he had contacted Dr. Laing, as instructed by the after-care officers at the hospital, expecting the physician to follow him everywhere. But whether deliberately or not, Laing had not been particularly interested in Melville, this ex-pilot who had turned up here impulsively in his expensive car and was now prowling restlessly around the solarium as if hunting for a chromium rat. Laing worked at the Science Research Council laboratory five miles inland, and clearly valued the privacy of the prefabricated solarium he had erected on the sand-bar at the southern end of the resort. He greeted Melville without comment, handed him the keys to the beach-house, and left him to it.

This lack of interest was a relief to Melville, but at the same time threw him onto himself. He had arrived with two suitcases, one filled with newly purchased and unfamiliar clothes, the other holding the hospital X-ray plates of his head and the photographs of Wake Island. The X-ray plates he passed to Dr. Laing, who raised them to the light, scrutinising these negatives of Melville's skull as if about to point out some design error in its construction. The photographs of Wake Island he returned without comment.

These illustrations of the Pacific atoll, with its vast concrete runways, he had collected over the previous months. During his convalescence at the hospital he had joined a wildlife conservation society, ostensibly in support of its campaign to save the Wake Island albatross from extinction —tens of thousands of the goony birds nested at the ends of the runways, and would rise in huge flocks into the flight-paths of airliners at takeoff. Melville's real interest had been in the island itself, a World War II airbase and now refuelling point for trans-Pacific passenger jets. The combination of scuffed sand and concrete, metal shacks rusting by the runways, the total psychological reduction of this man-made landscape, seized his mind in a powerful but ambiguous way. For all its arid, oceanic isolation, the Wake Island in Melville's mind soon became a zone of intense possibility. He daydreamed of flying there in a light aircraft, island-hopping across the Pacific. Once he touched down he knew that the migraines would go away forever. He had been discharged from the Air Force in confused circumstances, and during his convalescence after the accident the military psychiatrists had been only too glad to play their parts in what soon turned out to be an underrehearsed conspiracy of silence. When he told them that he had rented a house from a doctor in this abandoned resort, and intended to live there for a year on his back pay, they had been relieved to see him go, carrying away the X-ray plates of his head and the photographs of Wake Island.

"But why Wake Island?" Dr. Laing asked him on their third chess evening. He pointed to the illustrations that Melville had pinned to the mantelpiece, and the technical abstracts lavishly documenting its geology, rainfall, seismology, flora, and fauna. "Why not Guam? Or Midway? Or the Hawaiian chain?"

"Midway would do, but it's a naval base now—I doubt if they'll give me landing clearance. Anyway, the atmosphere is wrong." Discussing the rival merits of various Pacific islands always animated Melville, feeding this potent re-mythologising of himself. "Guam is forty miles long, covered with mountains and dense jungle, New Guinea in miniature. The Hawaiian islands are an offshore suburb of the United States. Only Wake has real time."

"You were brought up in the Far East?"

"In Manila. My father ran a textile company there."

"So the Pacific area has a special appeal for you."

"To some extent. But Wake is a long way from the Philippines."

Laing never asked if Melville had actually been to Wake Island. Clearly Melville's vision of flying to this remote Pacific atoll was unlikely to take place outside his own head.

However, Melville then had the good luck to discover the aircraft buried in the dunes.

When the tide was in, covering the sand-flats, Melville was forced to walk among the dunes above his beach-house. Driven and shaped by the wind, the contours of the dunes varied from day to day, but one afternoon Melville noticed that a section below the ridge retained its rectilinear form, indicating that some man-made structure lay below the sand, possibly the detached room of a metal barn or boat-house.

Irritated by the familiar drone of a single-engined aircraft flying from the light airfield behind the resort, Melville clambered up to the ridge through the flowing sand and sat down on the horizontal ledge that ran among the clumps of wild grass. The aircraft, a privately owned Cessna, flew in from the sea directly towards him, banked steeply and circled overhead. Its pilot, a dentist and aviation enthusiast in her early thirties, had been curious about Melville for some time—the mushy drone of her flat six was forever dividing the sky over his head. Often, as he walked across the sand-flats four hundred yards from the shore, she would fly past him, wheels almost touching the streaming sand, throttling up her engine as if trying to din something into his head. She appeared to be testing various types of auxiliary fuel tank. Now and then he saw her driving her American sedan through the deserted streets of the resort towards the airfield. For some reason the noise of her light aircraft began to unsettle him, as if the furniture of his brain was being shifted around behind some dark curtain.

The Cessna circled above him like a dull, unwearying bird. Trying to look as though he was engaged in his study of beach ecology, Melville cleared away the sand between his feet. Without realising it, he had exposed a section of grey, riveted metal, the skin of an all-too-familiar aerodynamic structure. He stood up and worked away with both hands, soon revealing the unmistakable profile of an aerofoil curvature.

The Cessna had gone, taking the lady dentist back to the airstrip. Melville had forgotten about her as he pushed the heavy sand away, steering it down the saddle between the dunes. Although nearly exhausted, he continued to clear the starboard wing-tip now emerging from the dune. He took off his jacket and beat away the coarse white grains, at last revealing the combat insignia, star and bars of a USAAF roundel.

As he knew within a few minutes, he had discovered an intact wartime B-17. Two days later, by a sustained effort, he had dug away several tons of sand and exposed to view almost the entire starboard wing, the tail and rear turret. The bomber was virtually undamaged—Melville assumed that the pilot had run out of fuel while crossing the Channel and tried to land on the sand-flats at low tide, overshot the wet surface and ploughed straight through the dunes above the beach. A write-off, the Fortress had been abandoned where it lay, soon to be covered by the shifting sand-hills. The small resort had been built, flourished briefly, and declined without anyone's realising that this relic of World War II lay in the ridge a hundred yards behind the town.

Systematically, Melville organised himself in the task of digging out, and then renovating, this antique bomber. Working by himself, he estimated that it would take three months to expose the aircraft, and a further two years to strip it down and rebuild it from scratch. The precise details of how he would straighten the warped propeller blades and replace the Wright Cyclone engines remained hazy in his mind, but already he visualised the shingle-reinforced earth-and-sand ramp which he would construct with a rented bulldozer from the crest of the dunes down to the beach. When the sea was out, after a long late-summer day, the sand along the tide-line was smooth and hard. . . .

Few people came to watch him. Tennant, the former advertising man leading the group digging out the Messerschmitt, came across the sand-flats and gazed philosophically at the emerging wings and fuselage of the Fortress. Neither of the men spoke to each other—both, as Melville knew, had something more important on their minds.

In the evening, when Melville was still working on the aircraft, Dr. Laing walked along the beach from his solarium.

He climbed the shadow-filled dunes, watching Melville clear away the sand from the chin-turret.

"What about the bomb-load?" he asked. "I'd hate to see the whole town levelled."

"It's an officially abandoned wreck." Melville pointed to the stripped-down gun turret. "Everything has been removed, including the machine-guns and bomb-sight. I think you're safe from me, Doctor."

"A hundred years ago you'd have been digging a diplodocus out of a chalk cliff," Laing remarked. The Cessna was circling the sand-bar at the southern end of the resort, returning after a navigation exercise. "If you're keen to fly, perhaps Helen Winthrop will take you on as a copilot. She was asking me something about you the other day. She's planning to break the single-engine record to Cape Town."

This item of news intrigued Melville. The next day, as he worked at his excavation site, he listened for the sound of the Cessna's engine. The image of this determined woman preparing for her solo flight across Africa, testing her aircraft at this abandoned airfield beside the dunes, coincided powerfully with his own dream of flying to Wake Island. He knew full well now that the elderly Fortress he was laboriously digging from the sand-dunes would never leave its perch on the ridge, let alone take off from the beach. But the woman's aircraft offered a feasible alternative. Already he mapped out a route in his mind, calculating the capacity of her auxiliary tanks and the refuelling points in the Azores and Newfoundland.

Afraid that she might leave without him, Melville decided to approach her directly. He drove his car through the deserted streets of the resort, turned onto the unmade road that led to the airfield, and parked beside her American sedan. The Cessna, its engine cowlings removed, stood at the end of the runway.

She was working at an engineering bench in the hangar, welding together the sections of a fuel tank. As Melville approached she switched off the blowtorch and removed her mask, her intelligent face shielded by her hands.

"I see we're involved in a race to get away first," she called out reassuringly to him when he paused in the entrance to the hangar. "Dr. Laing told me that you'd know how to strengthen these fuel tanks."

For Melville, her nervous smile cloaked a complex sexual metaphor.

From the start Melville took it for granted that she would abandon her plan to fly to Cape Town, and instead embark on a round-the-world flight with himself as her copilot. He outlined his plans for their westward flight, calculating the reduced fuel load they would carry to compensate for his weight. He showed her his designs for the wing spars and braces that would support the auxiliary tanks.

"Melville, I'm flying to Cape Town," she told him wearily. "It's taken me years to arrange this—there's no question of setting out anywhere else. You're obsessed with this absurd island."

"You'll understand when we get there," Melville assured her. "Don't worry about the aircraft. After Wake you'll be on your own. I'll strip off the tanks and cut all these braces away."

"You intend to stay on Wake Island?" Helen Winthrop seemed unsure of Melville's seriousness, as if listening to an overenthusiastic patient in her surgery chair outlining the elaborate dental treatment he had set his heart on.

"Stay there? Of course . . ." Melville prowled along the mantelpiece of the beach-house, slapping the line of photographs. "Look at those runways, everything is there. A big airport like the Wake field is a zone of tremendous possibility —a place of beginnings, by the way, not ends."

Helen Winthrop made no comment on this, watching Melville quietly. She no longer slept in the hangar at the airstrip, and during her weekend visits moved into Melville's beach-house. Needing his help to increase the Cessna's range, and so reduce the number of refuelling stops with their built-in delays, she put up with his restlessness and childlike excitement, only concerned by his growing dependence on her. As he worked on the Cessna, she listened for hours to him describing the runways of the island. However, she was careful never to leave him alone with the ignition keys.

While she was away, working at her dental practice, Melville returned to the dunes, continuing to dig out the crashed bomber. The port and starboard wings were now free of the sand, soon followed by the upper section of the fuselage. The weekends he devoted to preparing the Cessna for its long westward flight. For all his excitability, the state of controlled euphoria which his soon-to-be-realised dream of flying to Wake Island had brought about, his navigation plans and structural modification to the Cessna's airframe were carefully and professionally carried through.

Even the intense migraines that began to disturb Melville's sleep did little to dent his good humour. He assumed that these fragments of the past had been brought to the surface of his mind by the strains of his involvement with this overserious aviatrix, but later he knew that these elements of an unforgotten nightmare had been cued in by the aircraft emerging around him on all sides—Helen Winthrop's Cessna, the Fortress he was exposing to light, the blackened Messerschmitt which the advertising man was lifting from the seabed.

After a storm had disturbed the sand-flats, he stood on the balcony of the beach-house inhaling the carbonated air, trying to free himself from the uneasy dreams that had filled the night, a system of demented metaphors. In front of him the surface of the sand-flats was covered with dozens of pieces of rusting metal, aircraft parts shaken loose by the storm. As Helen Winthrop watched from the bedroom window, he stepped onto the beach and walked across the ruffled sand, counting the fragments of carburettor and exhaust manifold, trim-tab and tail-wheel, that lay around him as if left here by the receding tide of his dreams.

Already other memories were massing around him, fragments that he was certain belonged to another man's life, details from the case-history of an imaginary patient whose role he had been tricked into playing. As he worked on the Fortress high among the dunes, brushing the sand away from the cylinder vanes of the radial engines, he remembered other aircraft he had been involved with, vehicles without wings.

The bomber was completely exposed now. Knowing that

his work was almost over, Melville opened the ventral crew hatch behind the chin turret. Ever since he had first revealed the cockpit of the plane he had been tempted to climb through the broken starboard windshield and take his seat at the controls, but the experience of the Messerschmitt cautioned him. With Helen Winthrop, however, he would be safe.

Throwing down his spade, he clambered across the sand to the beach-house.

"Helen! Come up here!" He pointed with pride to the exposed aircraft on the ridge, poised on its belly as if at the end of a takeoff ramp. While Helen Winthrop tried to calm him, he steered her up the shifting slopes, hand over hand along the rope-line.

As they climbed through the crew hatch, he looked back for the last time across the sand-flats, littered with their rusting aircraft parts. Inside the fuselage they searched their way around the barbette of the roof turret, stepping through the debris of old R/T gear, life-jackets, and ammunition boxes. After all his efforts, the interior of the fuselage seemed to Melville like a magical arbour, the grottolike cavern within some archaic machine.

Sitting beside Helen in the cockpit, happy that she was with him as she would be on their flight across the Pacific, he took her through the controls, moving the throttles and trim wheels.

"Right, now. Mixture rich, carb heat cold, pitch full fine, flaps down for takeoff. . . ."

As she held his shoulders, trying to pull him away from the controls, Melville could hear the engines of the Fortress starting up within his head. As if watching a film, he remembered his years as a military test-pilot, and his single abortive mission as an astronaut. By some grotesque turn of fate, he had become the first astronaut to suffer a mental breakdown in space. His nightmare ramblings had disturbed millions of television viewers around the world, as if the terrifying image of a man going mad in space had triggered off some long-buried innate releasing mechanism.

Later that evening, Melville lay by the window in his bedroom, watching the calm sea that covered the sand-flats. He remembered Helen Winthrop leaving him in the cockpit, and running away along the beach to find Dr. Laing. Careful though he was, the physician was no more successful at dealing with Melville than the doctors at the institute of aviation medicine, who had tried to free him from his obsession that he had seen a fourth figure on board the three-man craft. This mysterious figure, either man or bird, he was convinced he had killed. Had he, also, committed the first murder in space? After his release he resolved to make his worldwide journey, externally to Wake Island, and internally across the planets of his mind.

As the summer ended and the time of their departure drew nearer, Melville was forced to renew his efforts at digging out the crashed Fortress. In the cooler weather the night winds moved the sand across the ridge, once again covering the fuselage of the aircraft.

Dr. Laing visited him more frequently. Worried by Melville's deteriorating condition, he watched him struggle with the tons of sliding sand.

"Melville, you're exhausting yourself." Laing took the spade from him and began to shovel away. Melville sat down on the wing. He was careful now never to enter the cockpit. Across the sand-flats Tennant and his team were leaving for the winter, the broken-backed Me 109 carried away on two trucks. Conserving his strength, he waited for the day when he and Helen Winthrop would leave this abandoned resort and take off into the western sky.

"All the radio aids are ready," he told her on the weekend before they were due to leave. "All you need to do now is file your flight plan."

Helen Winthrop watched him sympathetically as he stood by the mantelpiece. Unable to stand his nervous vomiting, she had moved back to the hangar. Despite, or perhaps because of, their brief sexual involvement, their relationship now was almost matter-of-factly neutral, but she tried to reassure him.

"How much luggage have you got? You've packed nothing."

"I'm taking nothing—only the photographs."

"You won't need them once you get to Wake Island."

"Perhaps—they're more real for me now than the island could ever be."

When Helen Winthrop left without him, Melville was surprised, but not disappointed. He was working up on the dunes as the heavily laden Cessna, fitted with the wing tanks he had installed, took off from the airstrip. He knew immediately from the pitch of the engine that this was not a trial flight. Sitting on the roof turret of the Fortress, he watched her climb away across the sand-flats, make a steady right-hand turn towards the sea and set off downwind across the Channel.

Long before she was out of sight, Melville had forgotten her. He would make his own way to the Pacific. During the following weeks he spent much of his time sheltering under the aircraft, watching the wind blow the sand back across the fuselage. With the departure of Helen Winthrop and the advertising executive with his Messerschmitt he found that his dreams grew calmer, shutting away his memories of the spaceflights. At times he was certain that his entire memory of having trained as an astronaut was a fantasy, part of some complex delusional system, an extreme metaphor of his real ambition. This conviction brought about a marked improvement in his health and self-confidence.

Even when Dr. Laing climbed the dunes and told him that Helen Winthrop had died two weeks after crashing her Cessna at Nairobi airport, Melville had recovered sufficiently to feel several days of true grief. He drove to the airfield and wandered around the empty hangar. Traces of her overhurried departure, a suitcase of clothes and a spare set of rescue flares, lay among the empty oil-drums.

Returning to the dunes, he continued to dig the crashed bomber from the sand, careful not to expose too much of it to the air. Although often exhausted in the damp winter air, he felt increasingly calm, sustained by the huge bulk of the Fortress, whose cockpit he never entered, and by his dream of flying to Wake Island.

NEWS

FROM

THE

SUN

IN THE EVENINGS, AS FRANKLIN RESTED ON THE ROOF OF THE ABAN-
doned clinic, he would often remember Trippett, and the last
drive he had taken into the desert with the dying astronaut
and his daughter. On impulse he had given in to the girl's
request, when he found her waiting for him in the dismantled laboratory, her father's flight jacket and solar glasses
in her hands, shabby mementoes of the vanished age of
space. In many ways it had been a sentimental gesture, but
Trippett was the last man to walk on the moon, and the
untended landscape around the clinic more and more
resembled the lunar terrain. Under that cyanide-blue sky
perhaps something would stir, a lost memory engage, for
a few moments Trippett might even feel at home again.

Followed by the daughter, Franklin entered the darkened
ward. The other patients had been transferred, and Trippett
sat alone in the wheelchair at the foot of his bed. By now,
on the eve of the clinic's closure, the old astronaut had
entered his terminal phase and was conscious for only a few
seconds each day. Soon he would lapse into his last deep
fugue, an invisible dream of the great tideways of space.

Franklin lifted the old man from his chair, and carried his
childlike body through the corridors to the car-park at the
rear of the clinic. Already, however, as they moved into the
needle-sharp sunlight, Franklin regretted his decision,
aware that he had been manipulated by the young woman.
Ursula rarely spoke to Franklin and, like everyone at the
hippy commune, seemed to have all the time in the world
to stare at him. But her patient, homely features and un-

innocent gaze disturbed him in a curious way. Sometimes he suspected that he had kept Trippett at the clinic simply so that he could see the daughter. The younger doctors thought of her as dumpy and unsexed, but Franklin was sure that her matronly body concealed a sexual conundrum of a special kind.

These suspicions aside, her father's condition reminded Franklin of his own accelerating fugues. For a year these had lasted little more than a few minutes each day, manageable within the context of the hours he spent at his desk, and at times barely distinguishable from musing. But in the past few weeks, as if prompted by the decision to close the clinic, they had lengthened to more than thirty minutes at a stretch. In three months he would be housebound, in six be fully awake for only an hour each day.

The fugues came so swiftly, time poured in a torrent from the cracked glass of their lives. The previous summer, during their first excursions into the desert, Trippett's waking periods had lasted at least half an hour. He had taken a touching pleasure in the derelict landscape, in the abandoned motels and weed-choked swimming-pools of the small town near the air base, in the silent runways with their dusty jets sitting on flattened tyres, in the overbright hills waiting with the infinite guile of the geological kingdom for the organic world to end and a more vivid mineral realm to begin.

Now, sadly, the old astronaut was unaware of all this. He sat beside Franklin in the front seat, his blanched eyes open behind the glasses but his mind set to some private time. Even the motion of the speeding car failed to rouse him, and Ursula had to hold his shoulders as he tottered like a stuffed toy into the windshield.

"Go on, Doctor—he likes the speed. . . ." Sitting forward, she tapped Franklin's head, wide eyes fixed on the speedometer. Franklin forced himself to concentrate on the road, conscious of the girl's breath on his neck. This highway madonna, with her secret dream of speed, he found it difficult to keep his hands and mind off her. Was she planning to abduct her father from the clinic? She lived in the small commune that had taken over the old solar city up in the hills, Soleri II. Every morning she cycled in, bringing Trippett his ration of raisins and macrobiotic cheer. She sat calmly beside him like his young mother as he played with the food, making strange patterns on his paper plate.

"Faster, Dr. Franklin—I've watched you drive. You're always speeding."

"So you've seen me? I'm not sure. If I had a blackout now. . . ." Giving in again, Franklin steered the Mercedes into the centre of the road and eased the speedometer needle towards fifty. There was a flare of headlights as they overtook the weekly bus to Las Vegas, a medley of warning shouts from the passengers left behind in a tornado of dust. The Mercedes was already moving at more than twice the legal limit. At twenty miles an hour, theoretically, a driver entering a sudden fugue had time to pass the controls to the obligatory front-seat passenger. In fact, few people drove at all. The desert on either side of the road was littered with the wrecks of cars that had veered off the soft shoulder and ended up in a sand-hill a mile away, their drivers dying of exposure before they could wake from their fugues.

Yet, for all the danger, Franklin loved to drive, illicit high-speed runs at dusk when he seemed to be alone on a forgotten planet. In a locked hangar at the air base were a Porsche and an antique Jaguar. His colleagues at the clinic disapproved, but he pursued his own maverick way, as he did in the laboratory, shielding himself behind a front of calculated eccentricity that excused certain obsessions with speed, time, sex. . . . He needed the speed more than the sex now. But soon he would have to stop, already the fast driving had become a dangerous game spurred on by the infantile hope that speed in some way would keep the clock hands turning.

The concrete towers and domes of the solar city approached on their left, Paulo Soleri's charming fantasy of a self-sufficient community. Franklin slowed to avoid running down a young woman in a sari who stood like a mannequin in the centre of the highway. Her eyes stared at the dust, a palaeontology of hopes. In an hour she would snap out of it, and complete her walk to the bus stop without realising that time, and the bus, had passed her by.

Ursula sombrely embraced her father, beckoning Franklin to accelerate.

"We're dawdling, Doctor. What's the matter? You enjoyed the speed. And so did Dad."

"Ursula, he doesn't even know he's here."

Franklin looked out at the desert, trying to imagine it through Trippett's eyes. The landscape was not so much desolate as derelict—the untended irrigation canals, the rusting dish of a radio-telescope on a nearby peak, a poor man's begging bowl held up to the banquet of the universe. The hills were waiting for them to go away. A crime had been committed, a cosmic misdemeanour carried on the shoulders of this fine old astronaut sitting beside him. Every night Trippett wept in his sleep. Spectres strode through his unlit dreams, trying to find a way out of his head.

The best astronauts, Franklin had noticed during his work for NASA, never dreamed. Or, at least, not until ten years after their flights, when the nightmares began and they returned to the institutes of aviation medicine which had first helped to recruit them.

Light flickered at them from the desert, and raced like a momentary cathode trace across the black lenses of Trippett's glasses. Thousands of steel mirrors were laid out in a semicircular tract beside the road, one of the solar farms that would have provided electric current for the inhabitants of Soleri II, unlimited power donated in a perhaps too kindly gesture by the economy of the sun.

Watching the reflected light dance in Trippett's eyes, Franklin turned the car onto the service road that ran down to the farm.

"Ursula, we'll rest here—I think I'm more tired than your father."

Franklin stepped from the car, and strolled across the white calcinated soil towards the nearest of the mirrors. In his eye he followed the focal lines that converged onto the steel tower two hundred feet away. A section of the collector dish had fallen onto the ground, but Franklin could see images of himself flung up into the sky, the outstretched sleeves of his white jacket like the wings of a deformed bird.

"Ursula, bring your father. . . ." The old astronaut could once again see himself suspended in space, this time upside down in the inverted image, hung by his heels from the yardarm of the sky.

Surprised by the perverse pleasure he took in this notion, Franklin walked back to the car. But as they helped Trippett from his seat, trying to reassure the old man, there was a clatter of metallic noise across the desert. An angular shadow flashed over their faces, and a small aircraft soared past, little more than twenty feet above the ground. It scuttled along like a demented gnat, minute engine buzzing up a storm, its wired wings strung around an open fuselage.

A white-haired man sat astride the miniature controls, naked except for the aviator's goggles tied around his head. He handled the plane in an erratic but stylish way, exploiting the sky to display his showy physique.

Ursula tried to steady her father, but the old man broke away from her and tottered off among the mirrors, his clenched fists pummelling the air. Seeing him, the pilot banked steeply around the sun-tower, then dived straight towards him, pulling up at the last moment in a blare of noise and dust. As Franklin ran forward and pressed Trippett to the ground, the plane banked and came round again in a wide turn. The pilot steered the craft with his bare knees, arms trailing at his sides as if mimicking Franklin's image in the dish above the tower.

"Slade! Calm down, for once. . . ." Franklin wiped the stinging grit from his mouth. He had seen the man up to too many extravagant tricks ever to be sure what he would do next. This former Air Force pilot and would-be astronaut, whose application Franklin had rejected three years earlier when he was chairman of the medical appeals board, had now returned to plague him with these absurd antics—spraying flocks of swallows with gold paint, erecting a circle of towers out in the desert ("my private space programme," he termed it proudly), building a cargo cult airport with wooden control tower and planes in the air base car-park, a cruel parody intended to punish the few remaining servicemen.

And this incessant stunt flying. Had Slade recognised Franklin's distant reflection as he sped across the desert in the inverted aircraft, then decided to buzz the Mercedes for the fun of it, impress Trippett and Ursula, even himself, perhaps?

The plane was coming back at them, engine wound up

to a scream. Franklin saw Ursula shouting at him soundlessly. The old astronaut was shaking like an unstuffed scarecrow, one hand pointing to the mirrors. Reflected in the metal panes were the multiple images of the black aircraft, hundreds of vulturelike birds that hungrily circled the ground.

"Ursula, into the car!" Franklin took off his jacket and ran through the mirrors, hoping to draw the aircraft away from Trippett. But Slade had decided to land. Cutting the engine, he let the microlight die in the air, then stalled the flapping machine onto the service road. As it trundled towards the Mercedes with its still spinning propeller, Franklin held off the starboard wing, almost tearing the doped fabric.

"Doctor! You've already grounded me once too often. . . ." Slade inspected the dented fabric, then pointed to Franklin's trembling fingers. "Those hands . . . I hope you aren't allowed to operate on your patients."

Franklin looked down at the white-haired pilot. His own hands *were* shaking, an understandable reflex of alarm. For all Slade's ironic drawl, his naked body was as taut as a trap, every muscle tense with hostility. His eyes surveyed Franklin with the ever-alert but curiously dead gaze of a psychopath. His pallid skin was almost luminous, as if after ending his career as an astronaut he had made some private pact with the sun. A narrow lap belt held him to the seat, but his shoulders bore the scars of a strange harness—the restraining straps of a psychiatric unit, Franklin guessed, or some kind of sexual fetishism.

"My hands, yes. They're always the first to let me down. You'll be glad to hear that I retire this week." Quietly, Franklin added: "I didn't ground you."

Slade pondered this, shaking his head. "Doctor, you practically closed the entire space programme down single-handed. It must have provoked you in a special way. Don't worry, though, I've started my own space programme now, another one." He pointed to Trippett, who was being soothed by Ursula in the car. "Why are you still bothering the old man? He won't buy off any unease."

"He enjoys the drives—speed seems to do him good. And you too, I take it. Be careful of those fugues. If you want to, visit me at the clinic."

"Franklin . . ." Controlling his irritation, Slade carefully relaxed his jaw and mouth, as if dismantling an offensive weapon. "I don't have the fugues any longer. I found a way of . . . dealing with them."

"All this flying around? You frightened the old boy."

"I doubt it." He watched Trippett nodding to himself. "In fact, I'd like to take him with me—we'll fly out into space again, one day. Just for him I'll build a gentle spacecraft, made of rice paper and bamboo. . . ."

"That sounds your best idea yet."

"It is." Slade stared at Franklin with sudden concern and the almost boyish smile of a pupil before a favourite teacher. "There is a way out, Doctor, a way out of time."

"Show me, Slade. I haven't much time left."

"I know that, Doctor. That's what I wanted to tell you. Together, Marion and I are going to help you."

"Marion—?" But before Franklin could speak, the aircraft's engine racketed into life. Fanning the tailplane, Slade deftly turned the craft within its own length. He replaced the goggles over his eyes, and took off in a funnel of dust that blanched the paintwork of the Mercedes. Safely airborne, he made a final circuit, gave a curious underhand salute, and soared away.

Franklin walked to the car and leaned against the roof, catching his breath. The old man was quiet again, his brief fit forgotten.

"That was Slade. Do you know him, Ursula?"

"Everyone does. Sometimes he works on our computer at Soleri, or just starts a fight. He's a bit crazy, trying all the time not to fugue."

Franklin nodded, watching the plane disappear towards Las Vegas, lost among the hotel towers. "He was a trainee astronaut once. My wife thinks he's trying to kill me."

"Perhaps she's right. I remember now—he said that except for you he would have gone to the moon."

"We all went to the moon. That was the trouble. . . ."

Franklin reversed the Mercedes along the service road. As they set off along the highway he thought of Slade's puzzling reference to Marion. It was time to be wary. Slade's fugues should have been lengthening for months, yet somehow he kept them at bay. All that violent energy contained

in his skull would one day push apart the sutures, burst out
in some ugly act of revenge. . . .

"Dr. Franklin! Listen!"

Franklin felt Ursula's hands on his shoulder. In a panic
he slowed down and began to search the sky for the returning microlight.

"It's Dad, Doctor! Look!"

The old man had sat up, and was peering through the window in a surprisingly alert way. The slack musculature of
his face had drilled itself into the brisk profile of a sometime
naval officer. He seemed uninterested in his daughter or
Franklin, but stared sharply at a threadbare palm tree beside
a wayside motel, and at the tepid water in the partly drained
pool.

As the car swayed across the camber Trippett nodded to
himself, thoroughly approving of the whole arid landscape.
He took his daughter's hand, emphasising some conversa-
tional point that had been interrupted by a pothole.

". . . it's green here, more like Texas than Nevada. Peaceful, too. Plenty of cool trees and pasturage, all these fields
and sweet lakes. I'd like to stop and sleep for a while. We'll
come out and swim, dear, perhaps tomorrow. Would you
like that?"

He squeezed his daughter's hand with sudden affection.
But before he could speak again, a door closed within his
face and he had gone.

They reached the clinic and returned Trippett to his darkened ward. Later, while Ursula cycled away down the silent
runways, Franklin sat at his desk in the dismantled laboratory. His fingers sparred with each other as he thought of
Trippett's curious utterance. In some way Slade's appearance in the sky had set it off. The old astronaut's brief
emergence into the world of time, those few lucid seconds,
gave him hope. Was it possible that the fugues could be
reversed? He was tempted to go back to the ward, and bundle Trippett into the car for another drive.

Then he remembered Slade's aircraft speeding towards
him across the solar mirrors, the small, vicious propeller
that shredded the light and air, time and space. This failed
astronaut had first come to the clinic seven months earlier.

While Franklin was away at a conference, Slade arrived by Air Force ambulance, posing as a terminal patient. With his white hair and obsessive gaze, he had instantly charmed the clinic's director, Dr. Rachel Vaisey, into giving him the complete run of the place. Moving about the laboratories and corridors, Slade took over any disused cupboards and desk drawers, where he constructed a series of little tableaux, psychosexual shrines to the strange gods inside his head.

He built the first of the shrines in Rachel Vaisey's bidet, an ugly assemblage of hypodermic syringes, fractured sunglasses, and blood-stained tampons. Other shrines appeared in corridor alcoves and unoccupied beds, relics of a yet to be experienced future left here as some kind of psychic deposit against his treatment's probable failure. After an outraged Dr. Vaisey insisted on a thorough inspection, Slade discharged himself from the clinic and made a new home in the sky.

The shrines were cleared away, but one alone had been carefully preserved. Franklin opened the centre drawer of his desk and stared at the assemblage laid out like a corpse on its bier of surgical cotton. There was a labelled fragment of lunar rock stolen from the NASA museum in Houston; a photograph taken with a zoom lens of Marion in a hotel bathroom, her white body almost merging into the tiles of the shower stall; a faded reproduction of Dali's *Persistence of Memory,* with its soft watches and expiring embryo; a set of leucotomes whose points were masked by metal peas; and an emergency organ-donor card bequeathing to anyone in need his own brain. Together the items formed an accurate antiportrait of all Franklin's obsessions, a side-chapel of his head. But Slade had always been a keen observer, more interested in Franklin than in anyone else.

How did he elude the fugues? When Franklin had last seen him at the clinic, Slade was already suffering from fugues that lasted an hour or more. Yet somehow he had sprung a trapdoor in Trippett's mind, given him his vision of green fields.

When Rachel Vaisey called to complain about the unauthorised drive, Franklin brushed this aside. He tried to convey his excitement over Trippett's outburst.

"He was there, Rachel, completely himself, for something

like thirty seconds. And there was no effort involved, no need to remember who he was. It's frightening to think that I'd given him up for lost."

"It is strange—one of those inexplicable remissions. But try not to read too much into it." Dr. Vaisey stared with distaste at the perimeter camera mounted beside its large turntable. Like most members of her staff, she was only too glad that the clinic was closing, and that the few remaining patients would soon be transferred to some distant sanatorium or memorial home. Within a month she and her colleagues would return to the universities from which they had been seconded. None of them had yet been affected by the fugues, and that Franklin should be the only one to succumb seemed doubly cruel, confirming all their long-standing suspicions about this wayward physician. Franklin had been the first of the NASA psychiatrists to identify the time-sickness, to have seen the astronauts' original fugues for what they were.

Sobered by the prospect facing Franklin, she managed a conciliatory smile. "You say he spoke coherently. What did he talk about?"

"He babbled of green fields." Franklin stood behind his desk, staring at the open drawer hidden from Dr. Vaisey's suspicious gaze. "I'm sure he actually saw them."

"A childhood memory? Poor man, at least he seems happy, wherever he really is."

"Rachel . . . !" Franklin drove the drawer into the desk. "Trippett was staring at the desert along the road—nothing but rock, dust, and a few dying palms, yet he saw green fields, lakes, forests of trees. We've got to keep the clinic open a little longer, I feel I have a chance now. I want to go back to the beginning and think everything through again."

Before Dr. Vaisey could stop him, Franklin had started to pace the floor, talking to his desk. "Perhaps the fugues are a preparation for something, and we've been wrong to fear them. The symptoms are so widespread, there's virtually an invisible epidemic, one in a hundred of the population involved, probably another five unaware that they've been affected, certainly out here in Nevada."

"It's the desert—topography clearly plays a part in the fugues. It's been bad for you, Robert. For all of us."

"All the more reason to stay and face it. Rachel, listen: I'm willing to work with the others more than I have done, this time we'll be a true team."

"That is a concession." Dr. Vaisey spoke without irony. "But too late, Robert. You've tried everything."

"I've tried nothing. . . ." Franklin placed a hand on the huge lens of the perimeter camera, hiding the deformed figure who mimicked his gestures from the glass cell. Distorted reflections of himself had pursued him all day, as if he were being presented with brief clips from an obscene film in which he would shortly star. If only he had spent more time on Trippett, rather than on the volunteer panels of housewives and Air Force personnel. But the old astronaut intimidated him, touched all his feelings of guilt over his complicity in the space programme. As a member of the medical support team, he had helped to put the last astronauts into space, made possible the year-long flights that had set off the whole time-plague, cracked the cosmic hourglass. . . .

"And Trippett? Where are you going to hide him away?"

"We aren't. His daughter has volunteered to take him. She seems a reasonable girl."

Giving in to her concern, Dr. Vaisey stepped forward and took Franklin's hand from the camera lens. "Robert—are you going to be all right? Your wife will look after you, you say. I wish you'd let me meet her. I could insist. . . ."

Franklin was thinking about Trippett—the news that the old astronaut would still be there, presumably living up in Soleri II, had given him hope. The work could go on. . . .

He felt a sudden need to be alone in the empty clinic, to be rid of Dr. Vaisey, this well-meaning middle-aged neurologist with her closed mind and closed world. She was staring at him across the desk, clearly unsure what to do about Franklin, her eyes distracted by the gold and silver swallows that swooped across the runways. Dr. Vaisey had always regretted her brief infatuation with Slade. Franklin remembered their last meeting in her office, when Slade had taken out his penis and masturbated in front of her, then insisted on mounting his hot semen on a slide. Through the microscope eyepiece Rachel Vaisey had watched the thousand replicas of this young psychotic frantically swimming. After ten minutes they began to falter. Within an hour they were all dead.

"Don't worry, I'll be fine. Marion knows exactly what I need. And Slade will be around to help her."

"Slade? How on Earth . . .?"

Franklin eased the centre drawer from his desk. Carefully, as if handling an explosive device, he offered the shrine to Dr. Vaisey's appalled gaze.

"Take it, Rachel. It's the blueprint of our joint space programme. You might care to come along. . . ."

When Dr. Vaisey had gone, Franklin returned to his desk. First, he took off his wristwatch and massaged the raw skin of his forearm. Every fifteen minutes he returned the hand of the stopwatch to zero. This nervous tic, a time-twitch, had long been a joke around the clinic. But after the onset of a fugue the accumulating total gave him a reasonably exact record of its duration. A crude device, he was almost glad that he would soon escape from time altogether.

Though not yet. Calming himself, he looked at the last pages of his diary.

> June 19—fugues: 8:30 to 9:11 A.M.; 11:45 to 12:27 A.M.; 5:15 to 6:08 P.M.; 11:30 to 12:14 P.M. Total: 3 hours.

The totals were gaining on him. June 20—3 hours 14 min.; June 21—3 hours 30 min.; June 22—3 hours 46 min. This gave him little more than ten weeks, unless the fugues began to slow down, or he found that trapdoor through which Trippett had briefly poked his head.

Franklin closed the diary and stared back at the watching lens of the perimeter camera. Curiously, he had never allowed himself to be photographed by the machine, as if the contours of his body constituted a secret terrain whose codes had to be held in reserve for his last attempt to escape. Standing or reclining on the rotating platform, the volunteer patients had been photographed in a continuous scan that transformed them into a landscape of undulating hills and valleys, not unlike the desert outside. Could they take an aerial photograph of the Sahara and Gobi deserts, reverse the process, and reconstitute the vast figure of some sleeping goddess, an Aphrodite born from a sea of dunes? Franklin had become obsessed with the camera, photographing everything from cubes and spheres to cups and saucers and then the naked patients themselves, in the hope of finding the dimension of time locked in those undulating spaces.

The volunteers had long since retired to their terminal wards, but their photographs were still pinned to the walls— a retired dentist, a police sergeant on the Las Vegas force, a middle-aged hair stylist, an attractive mother of year-old twins, an air-traffic controller from the base. Their splayed features and distorted anatomies resembled the nightmarish jumble seen by all patients if they were deliberately roused from their fugues by powerful stimulants or electric shock— oozing forms in an elastic world, giddying and unpleasant. Without time, a moving face seemed to smear itself across the air, the human body became a surrealist monster.

For Franklin, and the tens of thousands of fellow sufferers, the fugues had begun in the same way, with the briefest moments of inattention. An overlong pause in the middle of a sentence, some mysteriously burnt-out scrambled egg, the Air Force sergeant who looked after the Mercedes annoyed by his offhand rudeness, together led on to longer stretches of missed time. Subjectively, the moment to moment flow of consciousness seemed to be uninterrupted. But time drained away, leaking slowly from his life. Only the previous day he had been standing at the window, looking at the line of cars in the late afternoon sunlight, and the next moment there was dusk outside and a deserted parking lot.

All victims told the same story—there were forgotten appointments, inexplicable car crashes, untended infants rescued by police and neighbours. The victims would "wake" at midnight in empty office blocks, find themselves in stagnant baths, be arrested for jay-walking, forget to feed themselves. Within six months they would be conscious for only half the day, afraid to drive or go out into the streets, desperately filling every room with clocks and timepieces. A week would flash past in a jumble of sunsets and dawns. By the end of the first year they would be alert for only a few minutes each day, no longer able to feed or care for themselves, and soon after would enter one of the dozens of state hospitals and sanatoria.

After his arrival at the clinic Franklin's first patient was a badly burned fighter pilot who had taxied his jet through the doors of a hangar. The second was one of the last of the astronauts, a former naval captain named Trippett. The pilot was soon beyond reach in a perpetual dusk, but Trippett had hung on, lucid for a few minutes each day. Franklin had learned a great deal from Trippett, the last man to have walked on the moon and the last to hold out against the fugues—all the early astronauts had long since retreated into a timeless world. The hundreds of fragmentary conversations, and the mysterious guilt that Trippett shared with his colleagues, like them weeping in his dreams, convinced Franklin that the sources of the malaise were to be found in the space programme itself.

By leaving his planet and setting off into outer space man had committed an evolutionary crime, a breach of the rules governing his tenancy of the universe, and of the laws of time and space. Perhaps the right to travel through space belonged to another order of beings, but his crime was being punished just as surely as would be any attempt to ignore the laws of gravity. Certainly the unhappy lives of the astronauts bore all the signs of a deepening sense of guilt. The relapse into alcoholism, silence, and pseudomysticism, and the mental breakdowns, suggested profound anxieties about the moral and biological rightness of space exploration.

Sadly, not only the astronauts were affected. Each space-launch left its trace in the minds of those watching the expeditions. Each flight to the moon and each journey around the sun was a trauma that warped their perception of time and space. The brute-force ejection of themselves from their planet had been an act of evolutionary piracy, for which they were now being expelled from the world of time.

Preoccupied with his memories of the astronauts, Franklin was the last to leave the clinic. He had expected his usual afternoon fugue, and sat at his desk in the silent laboratory, finger on his stopwatch. But the fugue had not occurred, perhaps deflected by his buoyant mood after the drive with Trippett. As he walked across the car-park he looked out over the deserted air base. Two hundred yards from the control tower, a young woman with an apron around her waist stood on the concrete runway, lost in her fugue. Half a mile away, two more women stood in the centre of the huge cargo runway. All of them came from the nearby town. At twilight these women of the runways left their homes and trailers and strayed across the air base, staring into the dusk like the wives of forgotten astronauts waiting for their husbands to return from the tideways of space.

The sight of these women always touched Franklin in a disturbing way, and he had to force himself to start the car. As he drove towards Las Vegas the desert seemed almost lunar in the evening light. No one came to Nevada now, and most of the local population had long since left, fearing the uneasy perspectives of the desert. When he reached home, the dusk filtered through a cerise haze that lay over the old casinos and hotels, a ghostly memory of the electric night.

Franklin liked the abandoned gambling resort. The other physicians lived within a short drive of the clinic, but Franklin had chosen one of the half-empty motels in the northern suburbs of the city. In the evenings, after visiting his few patients in their retirement homes, he would often drive down the silent Strip, below the sunset façades of the vast hotels, and wander for hours through the shadows among the drained swimming-pools. This city of spent dreams, which had once boasted that it contained no clocks, now seemed itself to be in fugue.

As he parked in the forecourt of the motel he noted that Marion's car was missing. The third-floor apartment was empty. The television set was drawn up by the bed, playing silently to a clutch of medical textbooks Marion had taken from his shelves and an overflowing ashtray like a vent of Vesuvius. Franklin hung the unracked dresses in the wardrobe. As he counted the fresh cigarette burns in the carpet he reflected on the remarkable disarray that Marion could achieve in a few hours, here as in everything else. Were her fugues real or simulated? Sometimes he suspected that she half-consciously mimicked the time-slips, in an effort to enter that one realm where Franklin was free of her, safe from all her frustration at having come back to him.

Franklin went onto the balcony and glanced down at the empty swimming-pool. Often Marion sunbathed nude on the floor at the deep end, and perhaps had been trapped there by her fugue. He listened to the drone of a light aircraft circling the distant hotels, and learned from the retired geologist in the next apartment that Marion had driven away only minutes before his arrival.

As he set off in the car he realised that his afternoon fugue had still not occurred. Had Marion seen his headlamps approaching across the desert, and then decided on impulse to disappear into the unlit evening of the Strip hotels? She had known Slade at Houston three years earlier, when he tried to persuade her to intercede with Franklin. Now he seemed to be courting her from the sky, for reasons that Marion probably failed to realise. Even their original affair had been part of his elaborate stalking of Franklin.

The aircraft had vanished, disappearing across the desert. Franklin drove along the Strip, turning in and out of the hotel forecourts. In an empty car-park he saw one of the ghosts of the twilight, a middle-aged man in a shabby tuxedo, some retired croupier or cardiologist returning to these dreaming hulks. Caught in midthought, he stared sightlessly at a dead neon sign. Not far away, a strong-hipped young woman stood among the dusty pool-furniture, her statuesque figure transformed by the fugue into that of a Delvaux muse.

Franklin stopped to help them, if possible rouse them before they froze in the cold desert night. But as he stepped from his car he saw that the headlamps were reflected in the stationary propeller blade of a small aircraft parked on the Strip.

Slade leaned from the cockpit of his microlight, his white skin an unhealthy ivory in the electric beams. He was still naked, gesturing in an intimate way at a handsome woman in a streetwalker's fur who was playfully inspecting his cockpit. He beckoned her towards the narrow seat, like some cruising driver of old trying to entice a passerby.

Admiring Slade for his nerve in using the sky to accost his wife, Franklin broke into a run. Slade had taken Marion's waist and was trying to pull her into the cockpit.

"Leave her, Slade!" Fifty feet from them, Franklin stumbled over a discarded tyre. He stopped to catch his breath as —an engine of noise hurtled towards him out of the darkness, the same metallic blare he had heard in the desert that morning. Slade's aircraft raced along the Strip, wheels bouncing on the road, its propeller lit by the car's head-lamps. As Franklin fell to his knees the plane banked to avoid him, climbed steeply, and soared away into the sky.

Hunting for Slade, the excited air surged around Frank-lin. He stood up, hands raised to shield his face from the stinging dust. The darkness was filled with rotating blades. Silver lassoes spiralled out of the night, images of the pro-peller that launched themselves one after another from the wake of the vanished aircraft.

Still stunned by the violent attack of the machine, Frank-lin listened to its last drone across the desert. He watched the retinal display that had transformed the shadowy streets. Silver coils spun away over his head and disap-peared among the hotels, a glistening flight-path that he could almost touch with his hands. Steadying himself against the hard pavement under his feet, he turned to follow his wife as she fled from him through the drained swimming-pools and deserted car-parks of the newly lit city.

"Poor man—couldn't you see him? He flew straight at you. Robert . . . ?"

"Of course I saw him. I don't think I'd be here otherwise."

"But you stood there, totally mesmerised. I know he's always fascinated you, but that was carrying it too far. If that propeller had. . . ."

"It was a small experiment," Franklin said. "I wanted to see what he was trying to do."

"He was trying to kill you!"

Franklin sat on the end of the bed, staring at the cigarette burns in the carpet. They had reached the apartment fifteen minutes earlier, but he was still trying to calm himself. He thought of the rotating blade that had devoured the dark-ness. Delayed all afternoon, his fugue had begun as he tripped over the tyre, and had lasted almost an hour. For her own reasons Marion was pretending that the fugue had not occurred, but when he woke his skin was frozen. What had she and Slade been doing during the lost time? Too eas-ily, Franklin imagined them together in Marion's car, or even in the cockpit of the aircraft, watched by the sightless husband. That would please Slade, put him in just the mood to scare the wits out of Franklin as he took off.

Through the open door Franklin stared at his wife's naked body in the white cube of the bathroom. A wet cigarette smouldered in the soap dish. There were clusters of small bruises on her thighs and hips, marks of some stylised grapple. One day soon, when the time drained out of her, the contours of her breasts and thighs would migrate to the polished walls, calm as the dunes and valleys of the perimeter photographs.

Sitting down at the dressing-table, Marion peered over her powdered shoulder with some concern. "Are you going to be all right? I'm finding it difficult enough to cope with myself. That wasn't an attack . . .?"

"Of course not." For months now they had kept up the pretence that neither of them was affected by the fugues. Marion needed the illusion, more in Franklin's case than in her own. "But I may not always be immune."

"Robert, if anyone's immune, you are. Think of yourself, what you've always wanted—alone in the world, just you and these empty hotels. But be careful of Slade."

"I am." Casually, Franklin added: "I want you to see more of him. Arrange a meeting."

"What?" Marion looked round at her husband again, her left contact lens trapped under her eyelid. "He was naked, you know."

"So I saw. That's part of his code. Slade's trying to tell me something. He needs me, in a special way."

"Needs you? He doesn't need you, believe me. But for you he would have gone to the moon. You took that away from him, Robert."

"And I can give it back to him."

"How? Are the two of you going to start your own space programme?"

"In a sense we already have. But we really need you to help us."

Franklin waited for her to reply, but Marion sat raptly in front of the mirror, lens case in one hand, fingers retracting her upper and lower eyelids around the trapped lens. Fused with her own reflection in the finger-stained glass, she seemed to be shooting the sun with a miniature sextant, finding her bearings in this city of empty mirrors. He remembered their last month together after the end at Cape Kennedy, the long drive down the dead Florida coast. The space programme had expressed all its failure in that terminal moraine of deserted hotels and apartment houses, a cryptic architecture like the forgotten codes of a discarded geometric language. He remembered Marion's blood flowing into the hand-basin from her slashed palms, and the constant arguments that warped themselves out of the air.

Yet curiously those had been happy days, filled with the quickening excitements of her illness. He had dreamed of her promiscuity, the deranged favours granted to waitresses and bellboys. He came back alone from Miami, resting beside the swimming-pools of the empty hotels, remembering the intoxications of abandoned parking lots. In a sense that drive had been his first conscious experiment with time and space, placing that body and its unhappy mind in a sequence of bathrooms and pools, watching her with her lovers in the diagrammed car-parks, emotions hung on these abstract webs of space.

Affectionately, Franklin placed his hands on Marion's shoulders, feeling the familiar clammy skin of the fugue. He lowered her hands to her lap, and then removed the contact lens from her eyeball, careful not to cut the cornea. Franklin smiled down at her blanched face, counting the small scars and blemishes that had appeared around her mouth. Like all women, Marion never really feared the fugues, accepting the popular myth that during these periods of lapsed time the body refused to age.

Sitting beside her on the stool, Franklin embraced her gently. He held her breasts in his palms, for a moment shoring up their slipping curvatures. For all his fondness for Marion, he would have to use her in his duel with Slade. The planes of her thighs and shoulders were segments of a secret runway along which he would one day fly to safety.

JULY 5.

Not one of my best days. Five long fugues, each lasting over an hour. The first started at 9:00 A.M. as I was walking around the pool towards the car. Suddenly I found myself

standing by the deep end in much steeper sunlight, the old
geologist poking me in a concerned way. Marion had told
him not to disturb me, I was deep in thought! I must remember to wear a hat in future, the sunlight brought out a viral
rash on my lips. An excuse for Marion not to kiss me, without realising it she's eager to get away from here, can't pre-
tend for much longer that the fugues don't exist. Does she
guess that in some way I plan to exploit that keening sex
of hers?

These long fugues are strange, for the first time since the
airplane attack I have a vague memory of the dead time. The
geometry of that drained pool acted like a mirror, the sky
seemed to be full of suns. Perhaps Marion knew what she
was doing when she sunbathed there. I ought to climb down
that rusty chromium ladder into a new kind of time? *Lost
time total:* 6 hours 50 min.

JULY 11.

A dangerous fugue today, and what may have been another attempt on my life by Slade. I nearly killed myself driving to the clinic, must think hard about going there again.
The first fugue came at 8:15 A.M., synchronised with
Marion's—our sole connubial activity now. I must have
spent an hour opening the bathroom door, staring at her as
she stood motionless in the shower stall. Curious after-
images, sections of her anatomy seemed to be splayed across
the walls and ceiling, even over the car-park outside. For
the first time I felt that it might be possible to stay awake
during the fugues. A weird world, spatial change perceived
independently of time.

Fired by all this, I set off for the clinic, eager to try something out on the perimeter camera. But only a mile down
the highway I must have gone straight off the road, found
myself in the parking lot of some abandoned hypermarket,
surrounded by a crowd of staring faces. In fact, they were
department-store mannequins. Suddenly there was a volley
of gunshots, fibreglass arms and heads were flying everywhere. Slade at his games again, this time with a pump-gun
on the roof of the hypermarket. He must have seen me
stranded there and placed the mannequins around me. The

timeless people, the only mementoes of *Homo sapiens* when we've all gone, waiting here with their idiotic smiles for the first stellar visitor.

How does Slade repress the fugues? Perhaps violence, like pornography, is some kind of evolutionary standby system, a last-resort device for throwing a wild joker into the game? A widespread taste for pornography means that nature is alerting us to some threat of extinction. I keep thinking about Ursula, incidentally. . . . *Total time lost:* 8 hours 17 min.

July 15.

Must get out of this motel more often. A curious by-product of the fugues is that I'm losing all sense of urgency. Sat here for the last three days, calmly watching time run through my fingers. Almost convinces me that the fugues are a good thing, a sign that some great biological step forward is about to take place, set off by the spaceflights. Alternatively, my mind is simply numbing itself through sheer fear. . . .

This morning I forced myself into the sunlight. I drove slowly around Las Vegas, looking out for Marion and thinking about the links between gambling and time. One could devise a random world, where the length of each time interval depended on chance. Perhaps the high-rollers who came to Vegas were nearer the truth than they realised. "Clock time" is a neurophysiological construct, a measuring rod confined to *Homo sapiens.* The old labrador owned by the geologist next door obviously has a different sense of time, likewise the cicadas beside the pool. Even the materials of my body and the lower levels of my brain have a very different sense of time from my cerebrum—that uninvited guest within my skull.

Simultaneity? It's possible to imagine that everything is happening at once, all the events "past" and "future" which constitute the universe are taking place together. Perhaps our sense of time is a primitive mental structure that we inherited from our less intelligent forebears. For prehistoric man the invention of time (a brilliant conceptual leap) was a way of classifying and storing the huge flood of events which his dawning mind had opened for him. Like a dog burying a large bone, the invention of time allowed him to postpone the recognition of an event-system too large for him to grasp at one bite.

If time *is* a primitive mental structure we have inherited, then we ought to welcome its atrophy, embrace the fugues —*Total time lost:* 9 hours 15 min.

JULY 25.

Everything is slowing down, I have to force myself to remember to eat and shower. It's all rather pleasant, no fear even though I'm left with only six or seven hours of conscious time each day. Marion comes and goes, we literally have no time to talk to each other. A day passes as quickly as an afternoon. At lunch I was looking at some album photographs of my mother and father, and a formal wedding portrait of Marion and myself, and suddenly it was evening. I feel a strange nostalgia for my childhood friends, as if I'm about to meet them for the first time, an awakening premonition of the past. I can see the past coming alive in the dust on the balcony, in the dried leaves at the bottom of the pool, part of an immense granary of past time whose doors we can open with the right key. Nothing is older than the very new—a newborn baby with its head emerging from its mother has the smooth, time-worn features of Pharaoh. The whole process of life is the discovery of the immanent past contained in the present.

At the same time, I feel a growing nostalgia for the future, a memory of the future I have already experienced but somehow forgotten. In our lives we try to repeat those significant events which have already taken place in the future. As we grow older we feel an increasing nostalgia for our own deaths, through which we have already passed. Equally, we have a growing premonition of our births, which are about to take place. At any moment we may be born for the first time. *Total time lost:* 10 hours 5 min.

JULY 29.

Slade has been here. I suspect that he's been entering the apartment while I fugue. I had an uncanny memory of some-

one in the bedroom this morning, when I came out of the
11:00 A.M. fugue there was a curious afterimage, almost a
Pentecostal presence, a vaguely biomorphic blur that hung
in the air like a photograph taken with the perimeter
camera. My pistol had been removed from the dressing-table
drawer and placed on my pillow. There's a small diagram
of white paint on the back of my left hand. Some kind of
cryptic pattern, a geometric key.

Has Slade been reading my diary? This afternoon someone painted the same pattern across the canted floor of the
swimming-pool and over the gravel in the car-park. Presumably all part of Slade's serious games with time and
space. He's trying to rally me, force me out of the apartment,
but the fugues leave me with no more than two hours at a
stretch of conscious time. I'm not the only one affected. Las
Vegas is almost deserted, everyone has retreated indoors.
The old geologist and his wife sit all day in their bedroom,
each in a straight-backed chair on either side of the bed.
I gave them a vitamin shot, but they're so emaciated they
won't last much longer. No reply from the police or ambulance services. Marion is away again, hunting the empty
hotels of the Strip for any sign of Slade. No doubt she thinks
that he alone can save her. *Total time lost:* 12 hours 35 min.

AUGUST 12.

Rachel Vaisey called today, concerned about me and disappointed not to find Marion here. The clinic has closed, and
she's about to go east. A strange pantomime, we talked
stiffly for ten minutes. She was clearly baffled by my calm
appearance, despite my beard and coffee-stained trousers,
and kept staring at the white pattern on my hand and at the
similar shapes on the bedroom ceiling, the car-park outside,
and even a section of a small apartment house half a mile
away. I'm now at the focus of a huge geometric puzzle radiating from my left hand through the open window and out
across Las Vegas and the desert.

I was relieved when she had gone. Ordinary time—so-
called "real time"—now seems totally unreal. With her dis-
crete existence, her prissy point-to-point consciousness,
Rachel reminded me of a figure in an animated tableau of

Time Man in an anthropological museum of the future. All the same, it's difficult to be too optimistic. I wish Marion were here. *Total time lost:* 15 hours 7 min.

AUGUST 21.

Down now to a few stretches of consciousness that last barely an hour at the most. Time seems continuous, but the days go by in a blur of dawns and sunsets. Almost continuously eating, or I'll die of starvation. I only hope that Marion can look after herself, she doesn't seem to have been here for weeks—

—the pen snapped in Franklin's hand. As he woke, he found himself slumped across his diary. Torn pages lay on the carpet around his feet. During the two-hour fugue a violent struggle had taken place, his books were scattered around an overturned lamp, there were heel marks in the cigarette ash on the floor. Franklin touched his bruised shoulders. Someone had seized him as he sat there in his fugue, trying to shake him into life, and had torn the watch from his wrist.

A familiar noise sounded from the sky. The clacking engine of a light aircraft crossed the nearby rooftops. Franklin stood up, shielding his eyes from the vivid air on the balcony. He watched the aircraft circle the surrounding streets and then speed towards him. A molten light dripped from the propeller, spraying the motel with liquid platinum, a retinal tincture that briefly turned the street dust to silver.

The plane flew past, heading north from Las Vegas, and he saw that Slade had recruited a passenger. A blonde woman in a ragged fur sat behind the naked pilot, hands clasped around his waist. Like a startled dreamer, she stared down at Franklin.

As the microlight soared away, Franklin went into the bathroom. Rallying himself, he gazed at the sallow, bearded figure in the mirror, a ghost of himself. Already sections of his mind were migrating towards the peaceful geometry of the bathroom walls. But at least Marion was still alive. Had she tried to intercede as Slade attacked him? There was a faint image on the air of a wounded woman. . . .

Las Vegas was deserted. Here and there, as he set off in the car, he saw a grey face at a window, or a blanket draped across two pairs of knees on a balcony. All the clocks had stopped, and without his watch he could no longer tell how long the fugues had lasted, or when the next was about to begin.

Driving at a cautious ten miles an hour, Franklin slowed to a halt every five miles, then waited until he found himself sitting in the car with a cold engine. The temperature dial became his clock. It was almost noon when he reached the air base. The clinic was silent, its car-park empty. Weeds grew through the fading marker lines, an empty report sheet left behind by those unhappy psychiatrists and their now vanished patients.

Franklin let himself into the building and walked through the deserted wards and laboratories. His colleagues' equipment had been shipped away, but when he unlocked the doors to his own laboratory he found the packing cases where he had left them.

In front of the perimeter camera a rubber mattress lay on the turntable. Next to it an ashtray overflowed with cigarette ends that had burned the wooden planks.

So Slade had turned his talents to a special kind of photography—a pornography in the round. Pinned to the walls behind the camera was a gallery of huge prints. These strange landscapes resembled aerial photographs of a desert convulsed by a series of titanic earthquakes, as if one geological era were giving birth to another. Elongated clefts and gullies stretched across the prints, their contours so like those that had lingered in the apartment after Marion's showers.

But a second geometry overlaid the first, a scarred and aggressive musculature he had seen borne on the wind. The aircraft was parked outside the window, its cockpit and passenger seat empty in the sunlight. A naked man sat behind the desk in Franklin's office, goggles around his forehead. Looking at him, Franklin realised why Slade had always appeared naked.

"Come in, Doctor. God knows it's taken you long enough to get here." He weighed Franklin's wristwatch in his hand, clearly disappointed by the shabby figure in front of him. He had removed the centre drawer from the desk, and was playing with Franklin's shrine. To the original objects Slade had added a small chromium pistol. Deciding against the wristwatch, he tossed it into the wastebasket.

"I don't think that's really part of you any longer. You're a man without time. I've moved into your office, Franklin. Think of it as my mission-control centre."

"Slade . . ." Franklin felt a sudden queasiness, a warning of the onset of the next fugue. The air seemed to warp itself around him. Holding the door-frame, he restrained himself from rushing to the wastebasket. "Marion's here with you. I need to see her."

"See her, then. . . ." Slade pointed to the perimeter photographs. "I'm sure you recognise her, Franklin. You've been using her for the last ten years. That's why you joined NASA. You've been pilfering from your wife and the agency in the same way, stealing the parts for your space machine. I've even helped you myself."

"Helped . . .? Marion told me that—"

"Franklin!" Slade stood up angrily, knocking the chromium pistol onto the floor. His hands worked clumsily at his scarred ribs, as if he were forcing himself to breathe. Watching him, Franklin could almost believe that Slade had held back the fugues by a sheer effort of will, by a sustained anger against the very dimensions of time and space.

"This time, Doctor, you can't ground me. But for you, I would have walked on the moon!"

Franklin was watching the pistol at his feet, uncertain how to pacify this manic figure. "Slade, but for me you'd be with the others. If you'd flown with the space-crews, you'd be like Trippett."

"I am like Trippett." Calm again, Slade stepped to the window and stared at the empty runways. "I'm taking the old boy, Franklin. He's coming with me to the sun. It's a pity you're not coming. But don't worry, you'll find a way out of the fugues. In fact, I'm relying on it."

He stepped around the desk and picked the pistol from the floor. As Franklin swayed, he touched the physician's cooling forehead with the weapon. "I'm going to kill you,

Franklin. Not now, but right at the end, as we go out into that last fugue. Trippett and I will be flying to the sun, and you . . . you'll die forever."

There were fifteen minutes, at the most, before the next fugue. Slade had vanished, taking the aircraft into the sky. Franklin gazed round the silent laboratory, listening to the empty air. He retrieved his wristwatch from the wastebasket and left. As he reached the parking lot, searching for his car among the maze of diagonal lines, the desert landscape around the air base resembled the perimeter photographs of Marion and Slade together. The hills wavered and shimmered, excited echoes of that single sexual act, mimicking every caress.

Already the moisture in his body was being leached away by the sun. His skin prickled with an attack of hives. He left the clinic and drove through the town, slowing to avoid the filling-station proprietor, his wife, and child who stood in the centre of the road. They stared sightlessly into the haze as if waiting for the last car in the world.

He set off towards Las Vegas, trying not to look at the surrounding hills. Ravines fondled each other, rock-towers undulated as if the Earth itself were on its marriage bed. Irritated by his own sweat and the oozing hills, Franklin urged on the accelerator, pushing the car's speed to forty miles an hour. The whole mineral world seemed intent on taking its revenge on him. Light stabbed at his retinas from the exposed quartz veins, from the rusting bowls of the radar dishes on the hill crests. Franklin fixed his eyes on the speeding marker line between the car's wheels, dreaming of Las Vegas, that dusty Samarkand.

Then time sidestepped in front of him again.

He woke to find himself lying under the torn ceiling liner of the overturned car, his legs stretched through the broken windshield. Burst from their locks, the open doors hung above him in a haze of idle dust. Franklin pushed aside the loose seats that had fallen across him and climbed from the car. A faint steam rose from the fractured radiator, and the last of the coolant trickled into the culvert of the old irrigation system into which the car had slewed. The blue liquid formed a small pool, then, as he watched it, sank into the sand.

A single kite circled the sky over his head, but the landscape was empty. Half a mile away was the tarry strip of the highway. As he fugued the car had veered off the road, then sped in a wide circle across the scrub, upending itself as it jumped the first of the irrigation ditches. Franklin brushed the sand from his face and beard. He had been unconscious for almost two hours, part-concussion and part-fugue, and the harsh noon light had driven all shadows from the sandy soil. The northern suburbs of Las Vegas were ten miles away, too far for him to walk, but the white domes of Soleri II rose from the foothills to the west of the highway, little more than two miles across the desert. He could see the metallic flicker of the solar mirrors as one of the canted dishes caught the sun.

Still jarred by the crash, Franklin turned his back to the road and set off along the causeway between the irrigation ditches. After only a hundred yards he sank to his knees. The sand liquefied at his feet, sucking at his shoes as if eager to strip the clothes from his back and expose him to the sun.

Playing its private game with Franklin, the sun changed places in the sky. The fugues were coming at fifteen-minute intervals. He found himself leaning against a rusting pump-head. Huge pipes emerged thirstlessly from the forgotten ground. His shadow hid behind him, scuttling under his heels. Franklin waved away the circling kite. All too easily he could imagine the bird perching on his shoulder as he fugued, and lunching off his eyes. He was still more than a mile from the solar mirrors, but their sharp light cut at his retinas. If he could reach the tower, climb a few of its steps, and signal with a fragment of broken glass, someone might . . .

. . . the sun was trying to trick him again. More confident now, his shadow had emerged from beneath his heels and slid silkily along the stony ground, unafraid of this tottering scarecrow who made an ordeal of each step. Franklin sat down in the dust. Lying on his side, he felt the blisters on his eyelids, lymph-filled sacs that had almost closed his orbits. Any more fugues and he would die here; blood, life, and time would run out of him at the same moment.

He stood up and steadied himself against the air. The hills undulated around him, the copulating bodies of all the women he had known, together conceiving this mineral world for him to die within.

Three hundred yards away, between himself and the solar mirrors, a single palm tree dipped its green parasol. Franklin stepped gingerly through the strange light, nervous of this mirage. As he moved forward a second palm appeared, then a third and fourth. There was a glimmer of blue water, the calm surface of an oasis pool.

His body had given up, the heavy arms and legs that emerged from his trunk had slipped into the next fugue. But his mind had scrambled free inside his skull. Franklin knew that even if this oasis was a mirage, it was a mirage that he could see, and that for the first time he was conscious during a fugue. Like the driver of a slow-witted automaton, he propelled himself across the sandy ground, a half-roused sleepwalker clinging to the blue pool before his eyes. More trees had appeared, groves of palms lowered their fronds to the glassy surface of a serpentine lake.

Franklin hobbled forward, ignoring the two kites in the sky above his head. The air was engorged with light, a flood of photons crowded around him. A third kite appeared, joined almost at once by half a dozen more.

But Franklin was looking at the green valley spread out in front of him, at the forest of palms that shaded an archipelago of lakes and pools, together fed by cool streams that ran down from the surrounding hills. Everything seemed calm and yet vivid, the young earth seen for the first time, where all Franklin's ills would be soothed and assuaged in its sweet waters. Within this fertile valley everything multiplied itself without effort. From his outstretched arms fell a dozen shadows, each cast by one of the twelve suns above his head.

Towards the end, while he made his last attempt to reach the lake, he saw a young woman walking towards him. She moved through the palm trees with concerned eyes, hands clasped at her waist, as if searching for a child or elderly parent who had strayed into the wilderness. As Franklin waved to her she was joined by her twin, another grave-faced young woman who walked with the same cautious step. Behind them came other sisters, moving through the palms like schoolgirls from their class, concubines from a pavilion cooled by the lake. Kneeling before them, Franklin waited for the women to find him, to take him away from the desert to the meadows of the valley.

Time, in a brief act of kindness, flowed back into Franklin. He lay in a domed room, behind a veranda shaded by a glass awning. Through the railings he could see the towers and apartment terraces of Soleri II, its concrete architecture a reassuring shoulder against the light. An old man sat on a terrace across the square. Although deeply asleep, he remained inwardly alert and gestured with his hands in a rhythmic way, happily conducting an orchestra of stones and creosote bushes.

Franklin was glad to see the old astronaut. All day Trippett sat in his chair, conducting the desert through its repertory of invisible music. Now and then he sipped a little water that Ursula brought him, and then returned to his colloquy with the sun and the dust.

The three of them lived alone in Soleri II, in this empty city of a future without time. Only Franklin's wristwatch and its restless second hand linked them to the past world.

"Dr. Franklin, why don't you throw it away?" Ursula asked him, as she fed Franklin the soup she prepared each morning on the solar fireplace in the piazza. "You don't need it anymore. There's no time to tell."

"Ursula, I know. It's some kind of link, I suppose, a telephone line left open to a world we're leaving behind. Just in case . . ."

Ursula raised his head and dusted the sand from his pillow. With only an hour left to her each day, housework played little part in her life. Yet her broad face and handsome body expressed all the myths of the maternal child. She had seen Franklin wandering across the desert as she sat on her veranda during an early afternoon fugue.

"I'm sorry I couldn't find you, Doctor. There were hundreds of you, the desert was covered with dying men, like some kind of lost army. I didn't know which one to pick."

"I'm glad you came, Ursula. I saw you as a crowd of dreamy schoolgirls. There's so much to learn. . . ."

"You've made a start, Doctor. I knew it months ago when we drove Dad out here. There's enough time."

They both laughed at this, as the old man across the piazza conducted the orchestral sands. Enough time, when time was what they were most eager to escape. Franklin held the young woman's wrist and listened to her calm pulse, impatient for the next fugue to begin. He looked out over the arid valley below, at the cloud-filled mirrors of the solar farm and the rusting tower with its cracked collector dish. Where were those groves of palms and magic lakes, the sweet streams and pastures, from which the grave and beautiful young women had emerged to carry him away to safety? During the fugues that followed his recovery they had begun to return, but not as vividly as he had seen them from the desert floor in the hours after his crash. Each fugue, though, gave him a glimpse of that real world, streams flowed to fill the lakes again.

Ursula and her father, of course, could see the valley bloom, a dense and vivid forest as rich as the Amazon's.

"You see the trees, Ursula, the same ones your father saw?"

"All of them, and millions of flowers, too. Nevada's a wonderful garden now. Our eyes are filling the whole state with blossom. One flower makes the desert bloom."

"And one tree becomes a forest, one drop of water a whole lake. Time took that away from us, Ursula, though for a brief while the first men and women probably saw the world as a paradise. When did you learn to see?"

"When I brought Dad out here, after they shut the clinic. But it started during our drive. Later we went back to the mirrors. They helped me open my eyes. Dad's already were open."

"The solar mirrors—I should have gone back myself."

"Slade waited for you, Doctor. He waited for months. He's almost out of time now—I think he only has enough time for one more flight." Ursula dusted the sand from the sheet. For all the Amazon blaze during their fugues, clouds of dust blew into the apartment, a gritty reminder of a different world. She listened to the silent wind. "Never mind, Doctor, there are so many doors. For us it was the mirrors, for you it was that strange camera and your wife's body in sex."

She fell silent, staring at the veranda with eyes from which time had suddenly drained. Her hand was open, letting the sand run away, fingers outstretched like a child's to catch the brilliant air. Smiling at everything around her, she tried to talk to Franklin, but the sounds came out like a baby's burble.

Franklin held her cold hands, happy to be with her during the fugue. He liked to listen to her murmuring talk. So-called articulate speech was an artefact of time. But the babbling infant, and this young woman, spoke with the lucidity of the timeless, that same lucidity that others tried to achieve in delirium and brain-damage. The babbling newborn were telling their mothers of that realm of wonder from which they had just been expelled. He urged Ursula on, eager to understand her. Soon they would go into the light together, into that last fugue which would free them from the world of appearances.

He waited for the hands to multiply on his watch-dial, the sure sign of the next fugue. In the real world beyond the clock, serial time gave way to simultaneity. Like a camera with its shutter left open indefinitely, the eye perceived a moving object as a series of separate images. Ursula's walking figure as she searched for Franklin had left a hundred replicas of herself behind her, seeded the air with a host of identical twins. Seen from the speeding car, the few frayed palm trees along the road had multiplied themselves across the screen of Trippett's mind, the same forest of palms that Franklin had perceived as he moved across the desert. The lakes had been the multiplied images of the water in that tepid motel pool, and the blue streams were the engine coolant running from the radiator of his overturned car.

During the following days, when he left his bed and began to move around the apartment, Franklin happily embraced the fugues. Each day he shed another two or three minutes. Within only a few weeks, time would cease to exist. Now, however, he was awake during the fugues, able to explore this empty suburb of the radiant city. He had been freed by the ambiguous dream that had sustained him for so long, the vision of his wife with Slade, then copulating with the surrounding hills, in this ultimate infidelity with the mineral kingdom and with time and space themselves.

In the mornings he watched Ursula bathe in the piazza below his veranda. As she strolled around the fountain, drying herself under a dozen suns, Soleri II seemed filled with beautiful naked women bathing themselves in a city of waterfalls, a seraglio beyond all the fantasies of Franklin's childhood.

At noon, during a few last minutes of time, Franklin stared at himself in the wardrobe mirror. He felt embarrassed by the continued presence of his body, by the sticklike arms and legs, a collection of bones discarded at the foot of the clock. As the fugue began he raised his arms and filled the room with replicas of himself, a procession of winged men each dressed in his coronation armour. Free from time, the light had become richer, gilding his skin with layer upon layer of golden leaf. Confident now, he knew that death was merely a failure of time, and that if he died this would be in a small and unimportant way. Long before they died, he and Ursula would become the people of the sun.

It was the last day of past time, and the first of the day of forever.

Franklin woke in the white room to feel Ursula slapping his shoulders. The exhausted girl lay across his chest, sobbing into her fists. She held his wristwatch in her hand, and pressed it against his forehead.

". . . wake, Doctor. Come back just once. . . ."

"Ursula, you're cutting—"

"Doctor!" Relieved to see him awake, she rubbed her tears into his forehead. "It's Dad, Doctor."

"The old man? What is it? Has he died?"

"No, he won't die." She shook her head, and then pointed to the empty terrace across the piazza. "Slade's been here. He's taken Dad!"

She swayed against the mirror as Franklin dressed. He searched unsteadily for a hat to shield himself from the sun, listening to the rackety engine of Slade's microlight. It was parked on the service road near the solar farm, and the reflected light from its propeller filled the air with knives. Since his arrival at Soleri he had seen nothing of Slade, and hoped that he had flown away, taking Marion with him. Now the noise and violence of the engine were tearing apart the new world he had constructed so carefully. Within only a few more hours he and Ursula would escape from time forever.

Franklin leaned against the rim of the washbasin, no longer recognising the monklike figure who stared at him from the shaving mirror. Already he felt exhausted by the effort of coping with this small segment of conscious time, an adult forced to play a child's frantic game. During the past three weeks time had been running out at an ever faster rate. All that was left was a single brief period of a few minutes each day, useful only for the task of feeding himself and the girl. Ursula had lost interest in cooking for them, and devoted herself to drifting through the arcades and sundecks of the city, deep in her fugues.

Aware that they would both perish unless he mastered the fugues, Franklin steered himself into the kitchen. In the warm afternoons the steam from the soup tureen soon turned the solar city into an island of clouds. Gradually, though, he was teaching Ursula to eat, to talk and respond to him, even during the fugues. There was a new language to learn, sentences whose nouns and verbs were separated by days, syllables whose vowels were marked by the phases of the sun and moon. This was a language outside time, whose grammar was shaped by the contours of Ursula's breasts in his hands, by the geometry of the apartment. The angle between two walls became a Homeric myth. He and Ursula lisped at each other, lovers talking between the transits of the moon, in the language of birds, wolves, and whales. From the start, their sex together had taken away all Franklin's fears. Ursula's ample figure at last proved itself in the fugues. Nature had prepared her for a world without time, and he lay between her breasts like Trippett sleeping in his meadows.

Now he was back in a realm of harsh light and rigid perspectives, wristwatch in hand, its mark on his forehead.

"Ursula, try not to follow me." At the city gates he steadied her against the portico, trying to rub a few more seconds of time into her cooling hands. If they both went out into the desert, they would soon perish in the heat of that angry and lonely sun. Like all things, the sun needed its companions, needed time leached away from it. . . .

As Franklin set off across the desert the microlight's engine began to race at full bore, choked itself, and stuttered

to a stop. Slade stepped from the cockpit, uninterested in
Franklin's approach. He was still naked, except for his goggles, and his white skin was covered with weals and sun-
sores, as if time itself were an infective plague from which
he now intended to escape. He swung the propeller, shouting
at the flooded engine. Strapped into the passenger seat of
the aircraft was a grey-haired old man, a scarecrow stuffed
inside an oversize flying jacket. Clearly missing the vivid
flash of the propeller, Trippett moved his hands up and
down, a juggler palming pieces of light in the air.

"Slade! Leave the old man!"

Franklin ran forward into the sun. His next fugue would
begin in a few minutes, leaving him exposed to the dreamlike violence of Slade's propeller. He fell to his knees against
the nearest of the mirrors as the engine clattered into life.

Satisfied, Slade stepped back from the propeller, smiling
at the old astronaut. Trippett swayed in his seat, eager for
the flight to begin. Slade patted his head, and then surveyed
the surrounding landscape. His gaunt face seemed calm for
the first time, as if he now accepted the logic of the air and
the light, the vibrating propeller and the happy old man in
his passenger seat. Watching him, Franklin knew that Slade
was delaying his flight until the last moment, so that he
would take off into his own fugue. As they soared towards
the sun, he and the old astronaut would make their way into
space again, on their forever journey to the stars.

"Slade, we want the old man here! You don't need him
now!"

Slade frowned at Franklin's shout, this hoarse voice from
the empty mirrors. Turning from the cockpit, he brushed
his sunburnt shoulder against the starboard wing. He
winced, and dropped the chromium pistol onto the sand.

Before he could retrieve it, Franklin stood up and ran
through the lines of mirrors. High above, he could see the
reflection of himself in the collector dish, a stumbling crip-
ple who had pirated the sky. Even Trippett had noticed him,
and rollicked in his seat, urging on this lunatic aerialist. He
reached the last of the mirrors, straddled the metal plate,
and walked towards Slade, brushing the dust from his
trousers.

"Doctor, you're too late." Slade shook his head, impatient with Franklin's derelict appearance. "A whole life too late. We're taking off now."

"Leave Trippett. . . ." Franklin tried to speak, but the words slurred on his tongue. "I'll take his place. . . ."

"I don't think so, Doctor. Besides, Marion is out there somewhere." He gestured to the desert. "I left her on the runways for you."

Franklin swayed against the brightening air. Trippett was still conducting the propeller, impatient to join the sky. Shadows doubled themselves from Slade's heels. Franklin pressed the wound on his forehead, forcing himself to remain in time long enough to reach the aircraft. But the fugue was already beginning, the light glazed everything around him. Slade was a naked angel pinioned against the stained glass of the air.

"Doctor? I could save. . . ." Slade beckoned to him, his arm forming a winged replica of itself. As he moved towards Franklin his body began to disassemble. Isolated eyes watched Franklin, mouths grimaced in the vivid light. The silver pistols multiplied.

Like dragonflies, they hovered in the air around Franklin long after the aircraft had taken off into the sky.

The sky was filled with winged men. Franklin stood among the mirrors, as the aircraft multiplied in the air and crowded the sky with endless armadas. Ursula was coming for him, she and her sisters walking across the desert from the gates of the solar city. Franklin waited for her to fetch him, glad that she had learned to feed herself. He knew that he would soon have to leave her and Soleri II, and set off in search of his wife. Happy now to be free of time, he embraced the great fugue. All the light in the universe had come here to greet him, an immense congregation of particles.

Franklin revelled in the light, as he would do when he returned to the clinic. After the long journey on foot across the desert, he at last reached the empty air base. In the evenings he sat on the roof above the runways, and remembered his drive with the old astronaut. There he rested, learning the language of the birds, waiting for his wife to emerge from the runways and bring him news from the sun.

MEMORIES OF THE SPACE AGE

I

ALL DAY THIS STRANGE PILOT HAD FLOWN HIS ANTIQUE AERO-
plane over the abandoned Space Centre, a frantic machine
lost in the silence of Florida. The flapping engine of the old
Curtiss biplane woke Dr. Mallory soon after dawn, as he lay
asleep beside his exhausted wife on the fifth floor of the
empty hotel in Titusville. Dreams of the Space Age had filled
the night, memories of white runways as calm as glaciers,
now broken by this eccentric aircraft veering around like
the fragment of a disturbed mind.

From his balcony Mallory watched the ancient biplane circle the rusty gantries of Cape Kennedy. The sunlight flared
against the pilot's helmet, illuminating the cat's cradle of
silver wires that pinioned the open fuselage between the
wings, a puzzle from which the pilot was trying to escape
by a series of loops and rolls. Ignoring him, the plane flew
back and forth above the forest canopy, its engine calling
across the immense deserted decks, as if this ghost of the
pioneer days of aviation could summon the sleeping titans
of the Apollo programme from their graves beneath the
cracked concrete.

Giving up for the moment, the Curtiss turned from the
gantries and set course inland for Titusville. As it clattered
over the hotel Mallory recognised the familiar hard stare
behind the pilot's goggles. Each morning the same pilot appeared, flying a succession of antique craft—relics, Mallory
assumed, from some forgotten museum at a private airfield
nearby. There were a Spad and a Sopwith Camel, a replica
of the Wright Flyer, and a Fokker triplane that had buzzed

the NASA causeway the previous day, driving inland thousands of frantic gulls and swallows, denying them any share of the sky.

Standing naked on the balcony, Mallory let the amber air warm his skin. He counted the ribs below his shoulder blades, aware that for the first time he could feel his kidneys. Despite the hours spent foraging each day, and the canned food looted from the abandoned supermarkets, it was difficult to keep up his body weight. In the two months since they set out from Vancouver on the slow, nervous drive back to Florida, he and Anne had each lost more than thirty pounds, as if their bodies were carrying out a re-inventory of themselves for the coming world without time. But the bones endured. His skeleton seemed to grow stronger and heavier, preparing itself for the unnourished sleep of the grave.

Already sweating in the humid air, Mallory returned to the bedroom. Anne had woken, but lay motionless in the centre of the bed, strands of blonde hair caught like a child's in her mouth. With its fixed and empty expression, her face resembled a clock that had just stopped. Mallory sat down and placed his hands on her diaphragm, gently respiring her. Every morning he feared that time would run out for Anne while she slept, leaving her forever in the middle of a nightmare.

She stared at Mallory, as if surprised to wake in this shabby resort hotel with a man she had possibly known for years but for some reason failed to recognise.

"Hinton?"

"Not yet." Mallory steered the hair from her mouth. "Do I look like him now?"

"God, I'm going blind." Anne wiped her nose on the pillow. She raised her wrists, and stared at the two watches that formed a pair of time-cuffs. The stores in Florida were filled with clocks and watches that had been left behind in case they might be contaminated, and each day Anne selected a new set of timepieces. She touched Mallory reassuringly. "All men look the same, Edward. That's streetwalker's wisdom for you. But I meant the plane."

"I'm not sure. It wasn't a spotter aircraft. Clearly the police don't bother to come to Cape Kennedy anymore."

"I don't blame them. It's an evil place. Edward, we ought to leave, let's get out this morning."

Mallory held her shoulders, trying to calm this frayed but still handsome woman. He needed her to look her best for Hinton. "Anne, we've only been here a week—let's give it a little more time."

"Time? Edward . . ." She took Mallory's hands in a sudden show of affection. "Dear, that's one thing we've run out of. I'm getting those headaches again, just like the ones I had fifteen years ago. It's uncanny, I can feel the same nerves. . . ."

"I'll give you something, you can sleep this afternoon."

"No . . . They're a warning. I want to feel every twinge." She pressed the wristwatches to her temples, as if trying to tune her brain to their signal. "We were mad to come here, and even more mad to stay for a second longer than we need."

"I know. It's a long shot but worth a try. I've learned one thing in all these years—if there's a way out, we'll find it at Cape Kennedy."

"We won't! Everything's poisoned here. We should go to Australia, like all the other NASA people." Anne rooted in her handbag on the floor, heaving aside an illustrated encyclopaedia of birds she had found in a Titusville bookstore. "I looked it up—western Australia is as far from Florida as you can go. It's almost the exact antipodes. Edward, my sister lives in *Perth*. I knew there was a reason why she invited us there."

Mallory stared at the distant gantries of Cape Kennedy. It was difficult to believe that he had once worked there. "I don't think even Perth, Australia, is far enough. We need to set out into space again. . . ."

Anne shuddered. "Edward, don't say that—a *crime* was committed here, everyone knows that's how it all began." As they listened to the distant drone of the aircraft she gazed at her broad hips and soft thighs. Equal to the challenge, her chin lifted. "Noisy, isn't it? Do you think Hinton is here? He may not remember me."

"He'll remember you. You were the only one who liked him."

"Well, in a sort of way. How long was he in prison before he escaped? Twenty years?"

"A long time. Perhaps he'll take you flying again. You enjoyed that."

"Yes . . . He was strange. But even if he is here, can he help? He was the one who started it all."

"No, not Hinton." Mallory listened to his voice in the empty hotel. It seemed deeper and more resonant, as the slowing time stretched out the frequencies. "In point of fact, I started it all."

Anne had turned from him and lay on her side, a watch pressed to each ear. Mallory reminded himself to go out and begin his morning search for food. Food, a vitamin shot, and a clean pair of sheets. Sex with Anne, which he had hoped would keep them bickering and awake, had generated affection instead. Suppose they conceived a child, here at Cape Kennedy, within the shadow of the gantries . . . ?

He remembered the mongol and autistic children he had left behind at the clinic in Vancouver, and his firm belief—strongly contested by his fellow physicians and the worn-out parents—that these were diseases of time, malfunctions of the temporal sense that marooned these children on small islands of awareness, a few minutes in the case of the mongols, a span of microseconds for the autistics. A child conceived and born here at Cape Kennedy would be born into a world without time, an indefinite and unending present, that primeval paradise that the old brain remembered so vividly, seen both by those living for the first time and by those dying for the first time. It was curious that images of heaven or paradise always presented a static world, not the kinetic eternity one would expect, the roller-coaster of a hyperactive funfair, the screaming Luna Parks of LSD and psilocybin. It was a strange paradox that given eternity, an infinity of time, they chose to eliminate the very element offered in such abundance.

Still, if they stayed much longer at Cape Kennedy he and Anne would soon return to the world of the old brain, like those first tragic astronauts he had helped to put into space.

During the previous year in Vancouver there had been too many attacks, those periods of largo when time seemed to slow, an afternoon at his desk stretched into days. His own lapses in concentration both he and his colleagues put down to eccentricity, but Anne's growing vagueness had been impossible to ignore, the first clear signs of the space sickness that began to slow the clock, as it had done first for the astronauts and then for all the other NASA personnel based in Florida. Within the last months the attacks had come five or six times a day, periods when everything began to slow down, he would apparently spend all day shaving or signing a cheque.

Time, like a film reel running through a faulty projector, was moving at an erratic pace, at moments backing up and almost coming to a halt, then speeding on again. One day soon it would stop, freeze forever on one frame. Had it really taken them two months to drive from Vancouver, weeks alone from Jacksonville to Cape Kennedy?

He thought of the long journey down the Florida coast, a world of immense empty hotels and glutinous time, of strange meetings with Anne in deserted corridors, of sex-acts that seemed to last for days. Now and then, in forgotten bedrooms, they came across other couples who had strayed into Florida, into the eternal present of this timeless zone, Paolo and Francesca forever embracing in the Fontainebleau Hotel. In some of those eyes there had been horror. . . .

As for Anne and himself, time had run out of their marriage fifteen years ago, driven away by the spectres of the space complex, and by memories of Hinton. They had come back here like Adam and Eve returning to the Edenic paradise with an unfortunate dose of VD. Thankfully, as time evaporated, so did memory. He looked at his few possessions, now almost meaningless—the tape machine on which he recorded his steady decline; an album of nude Polaroid poses of a woman doctor he had known in Vancouver; his Gray's *Anatomy* from his student days, a unique work of fiction, pages still stained with formalin from the dissecting-room cadavers; a paperback selection of Muybridge's stop-frame photographs; and a psychoanalytic study of Simon Magus.

"Anne . . .?" The light in the bedroom had become brighter, there was a curious glare, like the white runways of his dreams. Nothing moved, for a moment Mallory felt that they were waxworks in a museum tableau, or in a painting by Edward Hopper of a tired couple in a provincial hotel. The dream-time was creeping up on him, about to enfold him. As always he felt no fear, his pulse was calmer. . . .

There was a blare of noise outside, a shadow flashed across the balcony. The Curtiss biplane roared overhead, then sped low across the rooftops of Titusville. Roused by the sudden movement, Mallory stood up and shook himself, slapping his thighs to spur on his heart. The plane had caught him just in time.

"Anne, I think that was Hinton. . . ."

She lay on her side, the watches to her ears. Mallory stroked her cheeks, but her eyes rolled away from him. She breathed peacefully with her upper lungs, her pulse as slow as a hibernating mammal's. He drew the sheet across her shoulders. She would wake in an hour's time, with a vivid memory of a single image, a rehearsal for those last seconds before time finally froze. . . .

II

Medical case in hand, Mallory stepped into the street through the broken plate-glass window of the supermarket. The abandoned store had become his chief source of supplies. Tall palms split the sidewalks in front of the boarded-up shops and bars, providing a shaded promenade through the empty town. Several times he had been caught out in the open during an attack, but the palms had shielded his skin from the Florida sun. For a reason he had yet to understand, he liked to walk naked through the silent streets, watched by the orioles and parakeets. The naked doctor, physician to the birds . . . perhaps they would pay him in feathers, the midnight-blue tail-plumes of the macaws, the golden wings of the orioles, sufficient fees for him to build a flying machine of his own?

The medical case was heavy, loaded with packet rice, sugar, cartons of pasta. He would light a small fire on another balcony and cook up a starchy meal, carefully boiling the brackish water in the roof tank. Mallory paused in the hotel car-park, gathering his strength for the climb to the fifth floor, above the rat and cockroach line. He rested in the front seat of the police patrol car they had commandeered in a deserted suburb of Jacksonville. Anne had regretted leaving behind her classy Toyota, but the exchange had been sensible. Not only would the unexpected sight of this squad car confuse any military spotter planes, but the hotted-up Dodge could outrun most light aircraft.

Mallory was relying on the car's power to trap the mysterious pilot who appeared each morning in his antique aeroplanes. He had noticed that as every day passed these veteran machines tended to be of increasingly older vintage. Sooner or later the pilot would find himself well within Mallory's reach, unable to shake off the pursuing Dodge before being forced to land at his secret airfield.

Mallory listened to the police radio, the tuneless static that reflected the huge void that lay over Florida. By contrast the air-traffic frequencies were a babel of intercom chatter, both from the big jets landing at Mobile, Atlanta, and Savannah, and from military craft overflying the Bahamas. All gave Florida a wide berth. To the north of the thirty-first parallel life in the United States went on as before, but south of that unfenced and rarely patrolled frontier was an immense silence of deserted marinas and shopping malls, abandoned citrus farms and retirement estates, silent ghettoes and airports.

Losing interest in Mallory, the birds were rising into the air. A dappled shadow crossed the car-park, and Mallory looked up as a graceful slender-winged aircraft drifted lazily past the roof of the hotel. Its twin-bladed propeller struck the air like a child's paddle, driven at a leisurely pace by the pilot sitting astride the bicycle pedals within the transparent fuselage. A man-powered glider of advanced design, it soared silently above the rooftops, buoyed by the thermals rising from the empty town.

"Hinton!" Certain now that he could catch the former astronaut, Mallory abandoned his groceries and pulled himself behind the wheel of the police car. By the time he started the flooded engine he had lost sight of the glider. Its delicate wings, almost as long as an airliner's, had drifted across the forest canopy, kept company by the flocks of swallows and martins that rose to inspect this timorous intruder of their airspace. Mallory reversed out of the car-park and set off after the glider, veering in and out of the palms that lifted from the centre of the street.

Calming himself, he scanned the side roads, and caught sight of the machine circling the jai alai stadium on the southern outskirts of the town. A cloud of gulls surrounded the glider, some mobbing its lazy propeller, others taking up their station above its wing-tips. The pilot seemed to be urging them to follow him, enticing them with gentle rolls and yaws, drawing them back towards the sea and to the forest causeways of the space complex.

Reducing his speed, Mallory followed three hundred yards behind the glider. They crossed the bridge over the Banana River, heading towards the NASA causeway and the derelict bars and motels of Cocoa Beach. The nearest of the gantries was still over a mile away to the north, but Mallory was aware that he had entered the outer zone of the space grounds. A threatening aura emanated from these ancient towers, as old in their way as the great temple columns of Karnak, bearers of a different cosmic order, symbols of a view of the universe that had been abandoned along with the state of Florida that had given them birth.

Looking down at the now clear waters of the Banana River, Mallory found himself avoiding the sombre forests that packed the causeways and concrete decks of the space complex, smothering the signs and fences, the camera towers and observation bunkers. Time was different here, as it had been at Alamogordo and Eniwetok, a psychic fissure had riven both time and space, then run deep into the minds of the people who worked here. Through that new suture in his skull, time leaked into the slack water below the car. The forest oaks were waiting for him to feed their roots, these motionless trees were as insane as anything in the visions of Max Ernst. There were the same insatiable birds, feeding on the vegetation that sprang from the corpses of trapped aircraft. . . .

Above the causeway the gulls were wheeling in alarm, screaming against the sky. The powered glider side-slipped

out of the air, circled and soared along the bridge, its miniature undercarriage only ten feet above the police car. The
pilot pedalled rapidly, propeller flashing at the alarmed sun,
and Mallory caught a glimpse of blonde hair and a woman's
face in the transparent cockpit. A red silk scarf flew from
her throat.

"Hinton!" As Mallory shouted into the noisy air the pilot
leaned from the cockpit and pointed to a slip road running
through the forest towards Cocoa Beach, then banked behind the trees and vanished.

Hinton? For some bizarre reason the former astronaut was
now masquerading as a woman in a blonde wig, luring him
back to the space complex. The birds had been in league
with him. . . .

The sky was empty, the gulls had vanished across the
river into the forest. Mallory stopped the car. He was about
to step onto the road when he heard the drone of an aero-
engine. The Fokker triplane had emerged from the Space
Centre. It made a tight circuit of the gantries and came in
over the sea. Fifty feet above the beach, it swept across the
palmettos and saw grass, its twin machine-guns pointing
straight towards the police car.

Mallory began to restart the engine when the machine-
guns above the pilot's windshield opened fire at him. He
assumed that the pilot was shooting blank ammunition left
over from some air display. Then the first bullets struck the
metalled road a hundred feet ahead. The second burst threw
the car onto its flattened front tyres, severed the door pillar
by the passenger seat, and filled the cabin with exploding
glass. As the plane climbed steeply, about to make its second pass at him, Mallory brushed the blood-flecked glass
from his chest and thighs. He leapt from the car and vaulted
over the metal railing into the shallow culvert beside the
bridge, as his blood ran away through the water towards the
waiting forest of the space grounds.

III

From the shelter of the culvert, Mallory watched the police
car burning on the bridge. The column of oily smoke rose
a thousand feet into the empty sky, a beacon visible for ten

miles around the Cape. The flocks of gulls had vanished. The powered glider and its woman pilot—he remembered her warning him of the Fokker's approach—had slipped away to its lair somewhere south along the coast.

Too stunned to rest, Mallory stared at the mile-long causeway. It would take him half an hour to walk back to the mainland, an easy target for Hinton as he waited in the Fokker above the clouds. Had the former astronaut recognised Mallory and immediately guessed why the sometime NASA physician had come to search for him?

Too exhausted to swim the Banana River, Mallory waded ashore and set off through the trees. He decided to spend the afternoon in one of the abandoned motels in Cocoa Beach, then make his way back to Titusville after dark.

The forest floor was cool against his bare feet, but a soft light fell through the forest canopy and warmed his skin. Already the blood had dried on his chest and shoulders, a vivid tracery like an aboriginal tattoo that seemed more suitable wear for this violent and uncertain realm than the clothes he had left behind at the hotel. He passed the rusting hulk of an Airstream trailer, its steel capsule overgrown with lianas and ground ivy, as if the trees had reached up to seize a passing spacecraft and dragged it down into the undergrowth. There were abandoned cars and the remains of camping equipment, moss-covered chairs and tables around old barbecue spits left here twenty years earlier when the sightseers had hurriedly vacated the state.

Mallory stepped through this terminal moraine, the elements of a forgotten theme-park arranged by a demolition squad. Already he felt that he belonged to an older world within the forest, a realm of darkness, patience, and unseen life. The beach was a hundred yards away, the Atlantic breakers washing the empty sand. A school of dolphins leapt cleanly through the water, on their way south to the Gulf. The birds had gone, but the fish were ready to take their place in the air.

Mallory welcomed them. He knew that he had been walking down this sand-bar for little more than half an hour, but at the same time he felt that he had been there for days, even possibly weeks and months. In part of his mind he had always been there. The minutes were beginning to stretch, urged on by this eventless universe free of birds and aircraft. His memory faltered, he was forgetting his past, the clinic at Vancouver and its wounded children, his wife asleep in the hotel at Titusville, even his own identity. A single moment was a small instalment of forever—he plucked a fern leaf and watched it for minutes as it fell slowly to the ground, deferring to gravity in the most elegant way.

Aware now that he was entering the dream-time, Mallory ran on through the trees. He was moving in slow-motion, his weak legs carrying him across the leafy ground with the grace of an Olympic athlete. He raised his hand to touch a butterfly apparently asleep on the wing, embarking his outstretched fingers on an endless journey.

The forest that covered the sand-bar began to thin out, giving way to the beach-houses and motels of Cocoa Beach. A derelict hotel sat among the trees, its gates collapsed across the drive, Spanish moss hanging from a sign that advertised a zoo and theme-park devoted to the Space Age. Through the waist-high palmettos the chromium and neon rockets rose from their stands like figures on amusement-park carousels.

Laughing to himself, Mallory vaulted the gates and ran on past the rusting spaceships. Behind the theme-park were overgrown tennis courts, a swimming-pool, and the remains of the small zoo, with an alligator pit, mammal cages, and aviary. Happily, Mallory saw that the tenants had returned to their homes. An overweight zebra dozed in his concrete enclosure, a bored tiger stared in a cross-eyed way at his own nose, and an elderly caiman sunbathed on the grass beside the alligator pit.

Time was slowing now, coming almost to a halt. Mallory hung in midstep, his bare feet in the air above the ground. Parked on the tiled path beside the swimming-pool was a huge transparent dragonfly, the powered glider he had chased that morning.

Two wizened cheetahs sat in the shade under its wing, watching Mallory with their prim eyes. One of them rose from the ground and slowly launched itself towards him, but it was twenty feet away and Mallory knew that it would never reach him. Its threadbare coat, refashioned from some old carpetbag, stretched itself into a lazy arch that seemed to freeze forever in midframe.

Mallory waited for time to stop. The waves were no longer running towards the beach, and were frozen ruffs of icing sugar. Fish hung in the sky, the wise dolphins happy to be in their new realm, faces smiling in the sun. The water spraying from the fountain at the shallow end of the pool now formed a glass parasol.

Only the cheetah was moving, still able to outrun time. It was now ten feet from him, its head tilted to one side as it aimed itself at Mallory's throat, its yellow claws more pointed than Hinton's bullets. But Mallory felt no fear for this violent cat. Without time it could never reach him, without time the lion could at last lie down with the lamb, the eagle with the vole.

He looked up at the vivid light, noticing the figure of a young woman who hung in the air with outstretched arms above the diving board. Suspended over the water in a swallow dive, her naked body flew as serenely as the dolphins above the sea. Her calm face gazed at the glass floor ten feet below her small extended palms. She seemed unaware of Mallory, her eyes fixed on the mystery of her own flight, and he could see clearly the red marks left on her shoulders by the harness straps of the glider, and the silver arrow of her appendix scar pointing to her childlike pubis.

The cheetah was closer now, its claws picking at the threads of dried blood that laced Mallory's shoulders, its grey muzzle retracted to show its ulcerated gums and stained teeth. If he reached out he could embrace it, comfort all the memories of Africa, soothe the violence from its old pelt. . . .

IV

Time had flowed out of Florida, as it had from the Space Age. After a brief pause, like a trapped film reel running free, it sped on again, rekindling a kinetic world.

Mallory sat in a deck chair beside the pool, watching the cheetahs as they rested in the shade under the glider. They crossed and uncrossed their paws like card-dealers palming an ace, now and then lifting their noses at the scent of this strange man and his blood.

Despite their sharp teeth, Mallory felt calm and rested, a sleeper waking from a complex but satisfying dream. He was glad to be surrounded by this little zoo with its backdrop of playful rockets, as innocent as an illustration from a children's book.

The young woman stood next to Mallory, keeping a concerned watch on him. She had dressed while Mallory recovered from his collision with the cheetah. After dragging away the boisterous beast she settled Mallory in the deck chair, then pulled on a patched leather flying suit. Was this the only clothing she had ever worn? A true child of the air, born and sleeping on the wing. With her overbright mascara and blonde hair brushed into a vivid peruke, she resembled a leather-garbed parakeet, a punk madonna of the airways. Worn NASA flashes on her shoulder gave her a biker's swagger. On the nameplate above her right breast was printed: *Nightingale.*

"Poor man—are you back? You're far, far away." Behind the childlike features, the soft mouth and boneless nose, a pair of adult eyes watched him warily. "Hey, you—what happened to your uniform? Are you in the police?"

Mallory took her hand, touching the heavy Apollo signet ring she wore on her wedding finger. From somewhere came the absurd notion that she was married to Hinton. Then he noticed her enlarged pupils, a hint of fever.

"Don't worry—I'm a doctor, Edward Mallory. I'm on holiday here with my wife."

"Holiday?" The girl shook her head, relieved but baffled. "That patrol car—I thought someone had stolen your uniform while you were . . . out. Dear Doctor, no one comes on holiday to Florida anymore. If you don't leave soon, this is one vacation that may last forever."

"I know. . . ." Mallory looked round at the zoo with its dozing tiger, the gay fountain and cheerful rockets. This was the amiable world of the Douanier Rousseau's *Merry Jesters.* He accepted the jeans and shirt which the girl gave him. He had liked being naked, not from any exhibitionist urge, but because it suited the vanished realm he had just visited. The impassive tiger with his skin of fire belonged to that world of light. "Perhaps I've come to the right place, though —I'd like to spend forever here. To tell the truth, I've just had a small taste of what forever is going to be like."

"No, thanks." Intrigued by Mallory, the girl squatted on the grass beside him. "Tell me, how often are you getting the attacks?"

"Every day. Probably more than I realise. And you . . . ?" When she shook her head a little too quickly, Mallory added: "They're not that frightening, you know. In a way you want to go back."

"I can see. Doctor, you ought to be worried by that. Take your wife and leave—any moment now all the clocks are going to stop."

"That's why we're here—it's our one chance. My wife has even less time left than I have. We want to come to terms with everything—whatever that means. Not much any-more."

"Doctor . . . The real Cape Kennedy is inside your head, not out here." Clearly unsettled by the presence of this marooned physician, the girl pulled on her flying helmet. She scanned the sky, where the gulls and swallows were again gathering, drawn into the air by the distant drone of an aero-engine. "Listen—an hour ago you were nearly killed. I tried to warn you. Our local stunt pilot doesn't like the police."

"So I found out. I'm glad he didn't hit you. I thought he was flying your glider."

"Hinton? He wouldn't be seen dead in that. He needs speed. Hinton's trying to join the birds."

"Hinton . . ." Repeating the name, Mallory felt a surge of fear and relief, realising that he was committed now to the course of action he had planned months ago when he left the clinic in Vancouver. "So Hinton is here."

"He's here." The girl nodded at Mallory, still unsure that he was not a policeman. "Not many people remember Hinton."

"I remember Hinton." As she fingered the Apollo signet ring he asked: "You're not married to him?"

"To Hinton? Doctor, you have some strange ideas. What are your patients like?"

"I often wonder. But you know Hinton?"

"Who does? He has other things in his mind. He fixed the pool here, and brought me the glider from the museum at Orlando." She added, archly: "Disneyland East—that's what they called Cape Kennedy in the early days."

"I remember—twenty years ago I worked for NASA."

"So did my father." She spoke sharply, angered by the mention of the space agency. "He was the last astronaut— Alan Shepley—the only one who didn't come back. And the only one they didn't wait for."

"Shepley was your father?" Startled, Mallory turned to look at the distant gantries of the launching grounds. "He died in the shuttle. Then you know that Hinton. . . ."

"Doctor, I don't think it was Hinton who really killed my father." Before Mallory could speak, she lowered her goggles over her eyes. "Anyway, it doesn't matter now. The important thing is that someone will be here when he comes down."

"You're waiting for him?"

"Shouldn't I, Doctor?"

"Yes . . . but it was a long time ago. Besides, it's a million to one against him coming down here."

"That's not true. According to Hinton, Dad may actually come down somewhere along this coast. Hinton says the orbits are starting to decay. I search the beaches every day."

Mallory smiled at her encouragingly, admiring this spunky but sad child. He remembered the news photographs of the astronaut's daughter, Gale Shepley, a babe in arms fiercely cradled by the widow outside the courtroom after the verdict. "I hope he comes. And your little zoo, Gale?"

"Nightingale," she corrected. "The zoo is for Dad. I want the world to be a special place for us when we go."

"You're leaving together?"

"In a sense—like you, Doctor, and everyone else here."

"So you do get the attacks."

"Not often—that's why I keep moving. The birds are teaching me how to fly. Did you know that, Doctor? The birds are trying to get out of time."

Already she was distracted by the unswept sky and the massing birds. After tying up the cheetahs she made her way quickly to the glider. "I have to leave, Doctor. Can you ride a motorcycle? There's a Yamaha in the hotel lobby you can borrow."

But before taking off she confided to Mallory: "It's all wishful thinking, Doctor, for Hinton too. When Dad comes it won't matter anymore."

Mallory tried to help her launch the glider, but the filmy craft took off within its own length. Pedalling swiftly, she propelled it into the air, climbing over the chromium rockets of the theme-park. The glider circled the hotel, then levelled its long tapering wings and set off for the empty beaches of the north.

Restless without her, the tiger began to wrestle with the truck tyre suspended from the ceiling of its cage. For a moment Mallory was tempted to unlock the door and join it. Avoiding the cheetahs chained to the diving board, he entered the empty hotel and took the staircase to the roof. From the ladder of the elevator house he watched the glider moving towards the Space Centre.

Alan Shepley—the first man to be murdered in space. All too well Mallory remembered the young pilot of the shuttle, one of the last astronauts to be launched from Cape Kennedy before the curtain came down on the Space Age. A former Apollo pilot, Shepley had been a dedicated but likeable young man, as ambitious as the other astronauts and yet curiously naive.

Mallory, like everyone else, had much preferred him to the shuttle's copilot, a research physicist who was then the token civilian among the astronauts. Mallory remembered how he had instinctively disliked Hinton on their first meeting at the medical centre. But from the start he had been fascinated by the man's awkwardness and irritability. In its closing days, the space programme had begun to attract people who were slightly unbalanced, and he recognised that Hinton belonged to this second generation of astronauts, mavericks with complex motives of their own, quite unlike the disciplined service pilots who had furnished the Mercury and Apollo flight-crews. Hinton had the intense and obsessive temperament of a Cortez, Pizarro, or Drake, the hot blood and cold heart. It was Hinton who had exposed for the first time so many of the latent conundrums at the

heart of the space programme, those psychological dimensions that had been ignored from its start and subsequently
revealed, too late, in the crack-ups of the early astronauts,
their slides into mysticism and melancholia.

"The best astronauts never dream," Russell Schweickart
had once remarked. Not only did Hinton dream, he had torn
the whole fabric of time and space, cracked the hourglass
from which time was running. Mallory was aware of his own
complicity, he had been chiefly responsible for putting
Shepley and Hinton together, guessing that the repressed
and earnest Shepley might provide the trigger for a metaphysical experiment of a special sort.

At all events, Shepley's death had been the first murder
in space, a crisis that Mallory had both stage-managed and
unconsciously welcomed. The murder of the astronaut and
the public unease that followed had marked the end of the
Space Age, an awareness that man had committed an evolutionary crime by travelling into space, that he was tamper-
ing with the elements of his own consciousness. The fracture of that fragile continuum erected by the human psyche
through millions of years had soon shown itself, in the confused sense of time displayed by the astronauts and NASA
personnel, and then by the inhabitants of the towns near
the Space Centre. Cape Kennedy and the whole of Florida
itself became a poisoned land to be forever avoided like the
nuclear testing grounds of Nevada and Utah.

Yet, perhaps, instead of going mad in space, Hinton had
been the first man to "go sane." During his trial he pleaded
his innocence and then refused to defend himself, viewing
the international media circus with a stoicism that at times
seemed bizarre. That silence had unnerved everyone—how
could Hinton believe himself innocent of a murder (he had
locked Shepley into the docking module, vented his air supply, and then cast him loose in his coffin, keeping up a
matter-of-fact commentary the whole while) committed in
full view of a thousand million television witnesses?

Alcatraz had been recommissioned for Hinton, for this
solitary prisoner isolated on the frigid island, to prevent his
contaminating the rest of the human race. After twenty
years he was safely forgotten, and even the report of his
escape was only briefly mentioned. He was presumed to

have died, after crashing into the icy waters of the bay in a small aircraft he had secretly constructed. Mallory had travelled down to San Francisco to see the waterlogged craft, a curious ornithopter built from the yew trees that Hinton had been allowed to grow in the prison island's stony soil, boosted by a homemade rocket engine powered by a fertiliser-based explosive. He had waited twenty years for the slow-growing evergreens to be strong enough to form the wings that would carry him to freedom.

Then, only six months after Hinton's death, Mallory had been told by an old NASA colleague of the strange stunt pilot who had been seen flying his antique aircraft at Cape Kennedy, some native of the air who had so far eluded the half-hearted attempts to ground him. The descriptions of the bird-cage aeroplanes reminded Mallory of the drowned ornithopter dragged up onto the winter beach. . . .

So Hinton had returned to Cape Kennedy. As Mallory set off on the Yamaha along the coast road, past the deserted motels and cocktail bars of Cocoa Beach, he looked out at the bright Atlantic sand, so unlike the rocky shingle of the prison island. But was the ornithopter a decoy, like all the antique aircraft that Hinton flew above the Space Centre, machines that concealed some other aim?

Some other escape?

V

Fifteen minutes later, as Mallory sped along the NASA causeway towards Titusville, he was overtaken by an old Wright biplane. Crossing the Banana River, he noticed that the noise of a second engine had drowned the Yamaha's. The venerable flying machine appeared above the trees, the familiar gaunt-faced pilot sitting in the open cockpit. Barely managing to pull ahead of the Yamaha, the pilot flew down to within ten feet of the road, gesturing to Mallory to stop, then cut back his engine and settled the craft onto the weed-grown concrete.

"Mallory, I've been looking for you! Come on, Doctor!"

Mallory hesitated, the gritty backwash of the Wright's props stinging the open wounds under his shirt. As he peered among the struts Hinton seized his arm and lifted him onto the passenger seat.

"Mallory, yes . . . it's you still!" Hinton pushed his goggles back onto his bony forehead, revealing a pair of blood-flecked eyes. He gazed at Mallory with open amazement, as if surprised that Mallory had aged at all in the past twenty years, but delighted that he had somehow survived. "Nightingale just told me you were here. Doctor Mysterium . . . I nearly killed you!"

"You're trying again . . . !" Mallory clung to the frayed seat straps as Hinton opened the throttle. The biplane gazelled into the air. In a gust of wind across the exposed causeway it flew backwards for a few seconds, then climbed vertically and banked across the trees towards the distant gantries. Thousands of swallows and martins overtook them on all sides, ignoring Hinton as if well accustomed to this erratic aviator and his absurd machines.

As Hinton worked the rudder tiller, Mallory glanced at this feverish and undernourished man. The years in prison and the rushing air above Cape Kennedy had leached all trace of iron salts from his pallid skin. His raw eyelids, the nail-picked septum of his strong nose, and his scarred lips were blanched almost silver in the wind. He had gone beyond exhaustion and malnutrition into a nervous realm where the rival elements of his warring mind were locked together like the cogs of an overwound clock. As he pummelled Mallory's arm it was clear that he had already forgotten the years since their last meeting. He pointed to the forest below them, to the viaducts, concrete decks, and blockhouses, eager to show off his domain.

They had reached the heart of the space complex, where the gantries rose like gallows put out to rent. In the centre was the giant crawler, the last of the shuttles mounted vertically on its launching platform. Its rusting tracks lay around it, the chains of an unshackled colossus.

Here at Cape Kennedy time had not stood still but moved into reverse. The huge fuel tank and auxiliary motors of the shuttle resembled the domes and minarets of a replica Taj Mahal. Lines of antique aircraft were drawn up on the runway below the crawler—a Lilienthal glider lying on its side

like an ornate fan window; a Mignet Flying Flea; the Fokker, Spad, and Sopwith Camel; and a Wright Flyer that went
back to the earliest days of aviation. As they circled the
launch platform Mallory almost expected to see a crowd of
Edwardian aviators thronging this display of ancient craft,
pilots in gaiters and overcoats, women passengers in hats
fitted with leather straps.

Other ghosts haunted the daylight at Cape Kennedy. When
they landed Mallory stepped into the shadow of the launch
platform, an iron cathedral shunned by the sky. An unsettling silence came in from the dense forest that filled the
once open decks of the Space Centre, from the eyeless
bunkers and rusting camera towers.

"Mallory, I'm glad you came!" Hinton pulled off his flying helmet, exposing a lumpy scalp under his close-cropped
hair—Mallory remembered that he had once been attacked
by a berserk warder. "I couldn't believe it was you! And
Anne? Is she all right?"

"She's here, at the hotel in Titusville."

"I know, I've just seen her on the roof. She looked. . . ."
Hinton's voice dropped, in his concern he had forgotten
what he was doing. He began to walk in a circle, and then
rallied himself. "Still, it's good to see you. It's more than
I hoped for—you were the one person who knew what was
going on here."

"Did I?" Mallory searched for the sun, hidden behind the
cold bulk of the launch platform. Cape Kennedy was even
more sinister than he had expected, like some ancient death
camp. "I don't think I—"

"Of course you knew! In a way we were collaborators
—believe me, Mallory, we will be again. I've a lot to tell
you. . . ." Happy to see Mallory, but concerned for the shivering physician, Hinton embraced him with his restless hands.
When Mallory flinched, trying to protect his shoulders, Hinton whistled and peered solicitously inside his shirt.

"Mallory, I'm sorry—that police car confused me. They'll
be coming for me soon, we have to move fast. But you don't
look too well, Doctor. Time's running out, I suppose, it's difficult to understand at first. . . ."

"I'm starting to. What about you, Hinton? I need to talk to you about everything. You look—"

Hinton grimaced. He slapped his hip, impatient with his undernourished body, an atrophied organ that he would soon discard. "I had to starve myself, the wing-loading of that machine was so low. It took years, or they might have noticed. Those endless medical checks, they were terrified that I was brewing up an even more advanced psychosis— they couldn't grasp that I was opening the door to a new world." He gazed round at the Space Centre, at the empty wind. "We had to get out of time—that's what the space pro- gramme was all about. . . ."

He beckoned Mallory towards a steel staircase that led up to the assembly deck six storeys above them. "We'll go top- side. I'm living in the shuttle—there's a crew module of the Mars platform still inside the hold, a damn sight more com- fortable than most of the hotels in Florida." He added, with an ironic gleam: "I imagine it's the last place they'll come to look for me."

Mallory began to climb the staircase. He tried not to touch the greasy rivets and sweating rails, lowering his eyes from the tiled skin of the shuttle as it emerged above the assembly deck. After all the years of thinking about Cape Kennedy he was still unprepared for the strangeness of this vast reductive machine, a juggernaut that could be pushed by its worshippers across the planet, devouring the years and hours and seconds.

Even Hinton seemed subdued, scanning the sky as if wait- ing for Shepley to appear. He was careful not to turn his back on Mallory, clearly suspecting that the former NASA physi- cian had been sent to trap him.

"Flight and time, Mallory, they're bound together. The birds have always known that. To get out of time we first need to learn to fly. That's why I'm here. I'm teaching myself to fly, going back through all these old planes to the begin- ning. I want to fly without wings. . . ."

As the shuttle's delta wing fanned out above them, Mallory swayed against the rail. Exhausted by the climb, he tried to pump his lungs. The silence was too great, this stillness

at the centre of the stopped clock of the world. He searched
the breathless forest and runways for any sign of movement.
He needed one of Hinton's machines to take off and go
racketing across the sky.

"Mallory, you're going . . . ? Don't worry, I'll help you
through it." Hinton had taken his elbow and steadied him
on his feet. Mallory felt the light suddenly steepen, the intense white glare he had last seen as the cheetah sprang
towards him. Time left the air, wavered briefly as he struggled to retain his hold on the passing seconds.

A flock of martins swept across the assembly deck, swirled
like exploding soot around the shuttle. Were they trying to
warn him? Roused by the brief flurry, Mallory felt his eyes
clear. He had been able to shake off the attack, but it would
come again.

"Doctor—? You'll be all right." Hinton was plainly disappointed as he watched Mallory steady himself at the rail.
"Try not to fight it, Doctor, everyone makes that mistake."

"It's going. . . ." Mallory pushed him away. Hinton was
too close to the rail, the man's manic gestures could jostle
him over the edge. "The birds—"

"Of course, we'll join the birds! Mallory, we can all fly,
every one of us. Think of it, Doctor, true flight. We'll live
forever in the air!"

"Hinton . . ." Mallory backed along the deck as Hinton
seized the greasy rail, about to catapult himself onto the
wind. He needed to get away from this madman and his
lunatic schemes.

Hinton waved to the aircraft below, saluting the ghosts
in their cockpits. "Lilienthal and the Wrights, Curtiss and
Blériot, even old Mignet—they're here, Doctor. That's why
I came to Cape Kennedy. I needed to go back to the beginning, long before aviation sent us all off on the wrong track.
When time stops, Mallory, we'll step from this deck and fly
towards the sun. You and I, Doctor, and Anne. . . ."

Hinton's voice was deepening, a cavernous boom. The
white flank of the shuttle's hull was a lantern of translucent
bone, casting a spectral light over the sombre forest. Mallory
swayed forward, on some half-formed impulse he wanted
Hinton to vault the rail, step out onto the air, and challenge
the birds. If he pressed his shoulders. . . .

"Doctor—?"

Mallory raised his hands, but he was unable to draw any nearer to Hinton. Like the cheetah, he was forever a few inches away.

Hinton had taken his arm in a comforting gesture, urging him towards the rail.

"Fly, Doctor. . . ."

Mallory stood at the edge. His skin had become part of the air, invaded by the light. He needed to shrug aside the huge encumbrance of time and space, this rusting deck and the clumsy tracked vehicle. He could hang free, suspended forever above the forest, master of time and light. He would fly. . . .

A flurry of charged air struck his face. Fracture lines appeared in the wind around him. The transparent wings of a powered glider soared past, its propeller chopping at the sunlight.

Hinton's hands gripped his shoulders, bundling him impatiently over the rail. The glider slewed sideways, wheeled and flew towards them again. The sunlight lanced from its propeller, a stream of photons that drove time back into Mallory's eyes. Pulling himself free from Hinton, he fell to his knees as the young woman swept past in her glider. He saw her anxious face behind the goggles, and heard her voice shout warningly at Hinton.

But Hinton had already gone. His feet rang against the metal staircase. As he took off in the Fokker he called out angrily to Mallory, disappointed with him. Mallory knelt by the edge of the steel deck, waiting for time to flow back into his mind, hands gripping the oily rail with the strength of the newborn.

VI

TAPE 24: AUGUST 17.

Again, no sign of Hinton today.

Anne is asleep. An hour ago, when I returned from the drugstore, she looked at me with focused eyes for the first time in a week. By an effort I managed to feed her in the few minutes she was fully awake. Time has virtually stopped for her, there are long periods when she is clearly in an almost stationary world, a series of occasionally varying static tableaux. Then she wakes briefly and starts talking about Hinton and a flight to Miami she is going to make with him in his Cessna. Yet she seems refreshed by these journeys into the light, as if her mind is drawing nourishment from the very fact that no time is passing.

I feel the same, despite the infected wound on my shoulder —Hinton's dirty fingernails. The attacks come a dozen times a day, everything slows to a barely perceptible flux. The intensity of light is growing, photons backing up all the way to the sun. As I left the drugstore I watched a parakeet cross the road over my head, it seemed to take two hours to fly fifty feet.

Perhaps Anne has another week before time stops for her. As for myself, three weeks? It's curious to think that at, say, precisely 3:47 P.M., September 8, time will stop forever. A single microsecond will flash past unnoticed for everyone else, but for me will last an eternity. I'd better decide how I want to spend it!

TAPE 25: AUGUST 19.

A hectic two days, Anne had a relapse at noon yesterday, vasovagal shock brought on by waking just as Hinton strafed the hotel in his Wright Flyer. I could barely detect her heartbeat, spent hours massaging her calves and thighs (I'd happily go out into eternity caressing my wife). I managed to stand her up, walked her up and down the balcony in the hope that the noise of Hinton's aircraft might jolt her back onto the rails. In fact, this morning she spoke to me in a completely lucid way, obviously appalled by my derelict appearance. For her it's one of those quiet afternoons three weeks ago.

We could still leave, start up one of the abandoned cars, and reach the border at Jacksonville before the last minutes run out. I have to keep reminding myself why we came here in the first place. Running north will solve nothing. If there is a solution it's here, somewhere between Hinton's obsessions and Shepley's orbiting coffin, between the Space Centre and those bright, eerie transits that are all too visible at night. I hope I don't go out just as it arrives, spend the rest of eternity looking at the vaporising corpse of the man I helped to die in space. I keep thinking of that tiger. Somehow I can calm it.

TAPE 26: AUGUST 25.

3:30 P.M. The first uninterrupted hour of conscious time I've had in days. When I woke fifteen minutes ago Hinton had just finished strafing the hotel—the palms were shaking dust and insects all over the balcony. Clearly Hinton is trying to keep us awake, postponing the end until he's ready to play his last card, or perhaps until I'm out of the way and he's free to be with Anne.

I'm still thinking about his motives. He seems to have embraced the destruction of time, as if this whole malaise were an opportunity that we ought to seize, the next evolutionary step forward. He was steering me to the edge of the assembly deck, urging me to fly, if Gale Shepley hadn't appeared in her glider I would have dived over the rail. In a strange way he was helping me, guiding me into that new world without time. When he turned Shepley loose from the shuttle he didn't think he was killing him, but setting him free.

The ever-more primitive aircraft—Hinton's quest for a pure form of flight, which he will embark upon at the last moment. A Santos-Dumont flew over yesterday, an ungainly box-kite, he's given up his World War I machines. He's deliberately flying badly designed aircraft, all part of his attempt to escape from winged aviation into absolute flight, poetical rather than aeronautical structures.

The roots of shamanism and levitation, and the erotic cathexis of flight—can one see them as an attempt to escape from time? The shaman's supposed ability to leave his physical form and fly with his spiritual body, the psychopomp guiding the souls of the deceased and able to achieve a mastery of fire, together seem to be linked with those defects of the vestibular apparatus brought on by prolonged exposure to zero gravity during the spaceflights. We should have welcomed them.

That tiger—I'm becoming obsessed with the notion that it's on fire.

TAPE 27: AUGUST 28.

An immense silence today, not a murmur over the soft green deck of Florida. Hinton may have killed himself. Perhaps all this flying is some kind of expiatory ritual, when he dies the shaman's curse will be lifted. But do I want to go back into time? By contrast, that static world of brilliant light pulls at the heart like a vision of Eden. If time *is* a primitive mental structure, we're right to reject it. There's a sense in which not only the shaman's but all mystical and religious beliefs are an attempt to devise a world without time. Why did primitive man, who needed a brain only slightly larger than the tiger in Gale's zoo, in fact have a mind almost equal to those of Freud and Leonardo? Perhaps all that surplus neural capacity was there to release him from time, and it has taken the Space Age, and the sacrifice of the first astronaut, to achieve that single goal.

Kill Hinton. . . . How, though?

TAPE 28: SEPTEMBER 3.

Missing days. I'm barely aware of the flux of time any longer. Anne lies on the bed, wakes for a few minutes, and makes a futile attempt to reach the roof, as if the sky offers some kind of escape. I've just brought her down from the staircase. It's too much of an effort to forage for food, on my way to the supermarket this morning the light was so bright that I had to close my eyes, hand-holding my way around the streets like a blind beggar. I seemed to be standing on the floor of an immense furnace.

Anne is increasingly restless, murmuring to herself in some novel language, as if preparing for a journey. I recorded one of her drawn-out monologues, like some Gaelic love-poem, then speeded it up to normal time. An agonised "Hinton . . . Hinton . . ."

It's taken her twenty years to learn.

TAPE 29: SEPTEMBER 6.

There can't be more than a few days left. The dream-time comes on a dozen stretches each day, everything slows to a halt. From the balcony I've just watched a flock of orioles cross the street. They seemed to take hours, their unmoving wings supporting them as they hung above the trees.

At last the birds have learned to fly.

Anne is awake. . . .

(Anne): Who's learned to fly?

(EM): It's all right—the birds.

(Anne): Did you teach them? What am I talking about? How long have I been away?

(EM): Since dawn. Tell me what you were dreaming.

(Anne): Is this a dream? Help me up. God, it's dark in the street. There's no time left here. Edward, find Hinton. Do whatever he says.

VII

Kill Hinton. . . .

As the engine of the Yamaha clacked into life, Mallory straddled the seat and looked back at the hotel. At any moment, as if seizing the last few minutes left to her, Anne would leave the bedroom and try to make her way to the roof. The stationary clocks in Titusville were about to tell the real time for her, eternity for this lost woman would be a flight of steps around an empty elevator shaft.

Kill Hinton . . . he had no idea how. He set off through the streets to the east of Titusville, shakily weaving in and out of the abandoned cars. With its stiff gearbox and unsteady throttle the Yamaha was exhausting to control. He was driving through an unfamiliar suburb of the town, a terrain of tract houses, shopping malls, and car-parks laid out for the NASA employees in the building boom of the 1960s. He passed an overturned truck that had spilled its cargo of television sets across the road, and a laundry van that had careened through the window of a liquor store.

Three miles to the east were the gantries of the Space Centre. An aircraft hung in the air above them, a primitive helicopter with an overhead propeller. The tapering blades were stationary, as if Hinton had at last managed to dispense with wings.

Mallory pressed on towards the Cape, the engine of the motorcycle at full throttle. The tracts of suburban housing unravelled before him, endlessly repeating themselves, the same shopping malls, bars, and motels, the same stores and used-car lots that he and Anne had seen in their journey across the continent. He could almost believe that he was driving through Florida again, through the hundreds of small towns that merged together, a suburban universe in which these identical liquor stores, car-parks, and shopping malls formed the building blocks of a strand of urban DNA generated by the nucleus of the Space Centre. He had driven down this road, across these silent intersections, not for

minutes or hours but for years and decades. The unravel-
ling strand covered the entire surface of the globe, and then
swept out into space to pave the walls of the universe before
it curved back on itself to land here at its departure point
at the Space Centre. Again he passed the overturned truck
beside its scattered television sets, again the laundry van
in the liquor store window. He would forever pass them,
forever cross the same intersection, see the same rusty sign
above the same motel cabin. . . .

"Doctor . . . !"
The smell of burning flesh quickened in Mallory's nose.
His right calf was pressed against the exhaust manifold of
the idling Yamaha. Charred fragments of his cotton trouser
clung to the raw wound. As the young woman in the black
flying suit ran across the street Mallory pushed himself away
from the clumsy machine, stumbled over its spinning
wheels, and knelt in the road.
He had stopped at an intersection half a mile from the centre of Titusville. The vast planetary plain of parking lots had
withdrawn, swirled down some cosmic funnel, and then con-
tracted to this small suburban enclave of a single derelict
motel, two tract houses, and a bar. Twenty feet away the
blank screens of the television sets stared at him from the
road beside the overturned truck. A few steps further along
the sidewalk the laundry van lay in its liquor store window,
dusty bottles of vodka and bourbon shaded by the wing-tip
of the glider which Gale Shepley had landed in the street.
"Dr. Mallory! Can you hear me? Dear man . . ." She
pushed back Mallory's head and peered into his eyes, then
switched off the still clacking engine of the Yamaha. "I saw
you sitting here, there was something— My God, your leg!
Did Hinton . . . ?"
"No . . . I set fire to myself." Mallory climbed to his feet,
an arm around the girl's shoulder. He was still trying to clear
his head, there was something curiously beguiling about
that vast suburban world. .⁻. . "I was a fool trying to ride
it. I must see Hinton."
"Doctor, listen to me. . . ." The girl shook his hands, her
eyes wide with fever. Her mascara and hair were even more
bizarre than he remembered. "You're dying! A day or two

more, an hour maybe, you'll be gone. We'll find a car and I'll drive you north." With an effort she took her eyes from the sky. "I don't like to leave Dad, but you've got to get away from here, it's inside your head now."

Mallory tried to lift the heavy Yamaha. "Hinton—it's all that's left now. For Anne, too. Somehow I have to . . . kill him."

"He knows that, Doctor—" She broke off at the sound of an approaching aero-engine. An aircraft was hovering over the nearby streets, its shadowy bulk visible through the palm leaves, the flicker of a rotor blade across the sun. As they crouched among the television sets it passed above their heads. An antique autogyro, it lumbered through the air like an aerial harvester, its free-spinning rotor apparently powered by the sunlight. Sitting in the open cockpit, the pilot was too busy with his controls to search the streets below.

Besides, as Mallory knew, Hinton had already found his quarry. Standing on the roof of the hotel, a dressing gown around her shoulders, was Anne Mallory. At last she had managed to climb the stairs, driven on by her dream of the sky. She stared sightlessly at the autogyro, stepping back a single pace only when it circled the hotel and came in to land through a storm of leaves and dust. When it touched down on the roof the draught from its propeller stripped the gown from her shoulders. Naked, she turned to face the auto-gyro, lover of this strange machine come to save her from a time-reft world.

VIII

As they reached the NASA causeway huge columns of smoke were rising from the Space Centre. From the pillion seat of the motorcycle Mallory looked up at the billows boil-ing into the stained air. The forest was flushed with heat, the foliage glowing like furnace coals.

Had Hinton refuelled the shuttle's engines and prepared the craft for lift-off? He would take Anne with him, and cast them both loose into space as he had done with Shepley, joining the dead astronaut in his orbital bier.

Smoke moved through the trees ahead of them, driven by

the explosions coming from the launch site of the shuttle. Gale throttled back the Yamaha and pointed to a break in the clouds. The shuttle still sat on its platform, motors silent, the white hull reflecting the flash of explosions from the concrete runways.

Hinton had set fire to his antique planes. Thick with oily smoke, the flames lifted from the glowing shells slumped on their undercarts. The Curtiss biplane was burning briskly. A frantic blaze devoured the engine compartment of the Fokker, detonated the fuel tank, and set off the machine-gun ammunition. The exploding cartridges kicked through the wings as they folded like a house of cards.

Gale steadied the Yamaha with her feet, and skirted the glowing trees two hundred yards from the line of incandescent machines. The explosions flashed in her goggles, blanching her vivid makeup and giving her blonde hair an ashlike whiteness. The heat flared against Mallory's sallow face as he searched the aircraft for any sign of Hinton. Fanned by the flames that roared from its fuselage, the autogyro's propeller rotated swiftly, caught fire, and spun in a last blazing carnival. Beside it, flames raced along the wings of the Wright Flyer, in a shower of sparks the burning craft lifted into the air and fell onto its back upon the red-hot hulk of the Sopwith Camel. Ignited by the intense heat, the primed engine of the Flying Flea roared into life, propelled the tiny aircraft in a scurrying arc among the burning wrecks, setting off the Spad and Blériot before it overturned in a furnace of rolling flame.

"Doctor—on the assembly deck!"

Mallory followed the girl's raised hand. A hundred feet above them, Anne and Hinton stood side by side on the metal landing of the stairway. The flames from the burning aircraft wavered against their faces, as if they were already moving through the air together. Although Hinton's arm was around Anne's waist, they seemed unaware of each other when they stepped forward into the light.

IX

As always during his last afternoons at Cocoa Beach, Mallory rested by the swimming-pool of the abandoned hotel, watching the pale glider float patiently across the undisturbed skies of Cape Kennedy. In this peaceful arbour, surrounded by the drowsing inmates of the zoo, he listened to the fountain cast its crystal gems onto the grass beside his chair. The spray of water was now almost stationary, like the glider and the wind and the watching cheetahs, elements of an emblematic and glowing world.

As time slipped away from him, Mallory stood under the fountain, happy to see it transform itself into a glass tree that shed an opalescent fruit onto his shoulders and hands. Dolphins flew through the air over the nearby sea. Once he immersed himself in the pool, delighted to be embedded in this huge block of condensed time.

Fortunately, Gale Shepley had rescued him before he drowned. Mallory knew that she was becoming bored with him. She was intent now only on the search for her father, confident that he would soon be returning from the tideways of space. At night the trajectories were ever lower, tracks of charged particles that soared across the forest. She had almost ceased to eat, and Mallory was glad that once her father arrived she would at last give up her flying. Then the two of them would leave together.

Mallory had made his own preparations for departure. The key to the tiger cage he held always in his hand. There was little time left to him now, the light-filled world had transformed itself into a series of tableaux from a pageant that celebrated the founding days of creation. In the finale every element in the universe, however humble, would take its place on the stage in front of him.

He watched the tiger waiting for him at the bars of its cage. The great cats, like the reptiles before them, had always stood partly out of time. The flames that marked its pelt reminded him of the fire that had consumed the aircraft at the Space Centre, the fire through which Anne and Hinton still flew forever.

He left the pool and walked towards the tiger cage. He would unlock the door soon, embrace these flames, lie down with this beast in a world beyond time.

MYTHS OF THE NEAR FUTURE

AT DUSK SHEPPARD WAS STILL SITTING IN THE COCKPIT OF THE stranded aircraft, unconcerned by the evening tide that advanced towards him across the beach. Already the first waves had reached the wheels of the Cessna, kicking spurs of spray against the fuselage. Tirelessly, the dark night-water sluiced its luminous foam at the Florida shoreline, as if trying to rouse the spectral tenants of the abandoned bars and motels.

But Sheppard sat calmly at the controls, thinking of his dead wife and all the drained swimming-pools of Cocoa Beach, and of the strange nightclub he had glimpsed that afternoon through the forest canopy now covering the old Space Centre. Part Las Vegas casino with its flamboyant neon façade, and part Petit Trianon—a graceful classical pediment carried the chromium roof—it had suddenly materialised among the palms and tropical oaks, more unreal than any film set. As Sheppard soared past, only fifty feet above its mirrored roof, he had almost expected to see Marie Antoinette herself, in a Golden Nugget getup, playing the milkmaid to an audience of uneasy alligators.

Before their divorce, oddly enough, Elaine had always enjoyed their weekend expeditions from Toronto to Algonquin Park, proudly roughing the wilderness in the high-chrome luxury of their Airstream trailer, as incongruous among the pine cones and silver birch as this latter-day fragment of a neon Versailles. All the same, the sight of the bizarre nightclub hidden deep in the Cape Kennedy forests, and the curious behaviour of its tenants, convinced Sheppard that Elaine was still alive, and very probably held prisoner by

Philip Martinsen. The chromium nightclub, presumably built thirty years earlier by some classically minded Disneyland executive, would appeal to the young neurosurgeon's sense of the absurd, a suitably garish climax to the unhappy events that had brought them together in the sombre forests of the Florida peninsula.

However, Martinsen was devious enough to have picked the nightclub deliberately, part of his elaborate attempt to lure Sheppard into the open air. For weeks now he had been hanging around the deserted motels in Cocoa Beach, flying his kites and gliders, eager to talk to Sheppard but nervous of approaching the older man. From the safety of his darkened bedroom at the Starlight Motel—a huddle of dusty cabins on the coast road—Sheppard watched him through a crack in the double blinds. Every day Martinsen waited for Sheppard to appear, but was always careful to keep a drained swimming-pool between them.

At first the young doctor's obsession with birds had irritated Sheppard—everything from the papier-mâché condor-kites hanging like corpses above the motel to endless Picasso doves chalked on the cabin doors while Sheppard slept. Even now, as he sat on the beach in the wave-washed Cessna, he could see the snake-headed profile cut in the wet sand, part of an enormous Aztec bird across which he had landed an hour earlier.

The birds . . . Elaine had referred to them in the last of her Florida letters, but those were creatures who soared inside her own head, far more exotic than anything a neurosurgeon could devise, feathered and jewelled chimeras from the paradises of Gustave Moreau. Nonetheless, Sheppard had finally taken the bait, accepting that Martinsen wanted to talk to him, and on his own terms. He forced himself from the motel, hiding behind the largest sunglasses he could find among the hundreds that littered the floor of the swimming-pool, and drove to the light airfield at Titusville. For an hour he flew the rented Cessna across the forest canopy, searching the whole of Cape Kennedy for any sign of Martinsen and his kites.

Tempted to turn back, he soared to and fro above the abandoned space grounds, unsettling though they were, with their immense runways leading to no conceivable sky, and the rusting gantries like so many deaths propped up in their tattered coffins. Here at Cape Kennedy a small part of space had died. A rich emerald light glowed through the forest, as if from a huge lantern lit at the heart of the Space Centre. This resonant halo, perhaps the phosphorescence of some unusual fungi on the leaves and branches, was spreading outwards and already had reached the northern streets of Cocoa Beach and crossed the Indian River to Titusville. Even the ramshackle stores and houses vibrated in the same overlit way.

Around him the bright winds were like the open jaws of a crystal bird, the light flashing between its teeth. Sheppard clung to the safety of the jungle canopy, banking the Cessna among the huge flocks of flamingos and orioles that scattered out of his way. In Titusville a government patrol car moved down one of the few stretches of clear road, but no one else was tempted out of doors, the few inhabitants resting in their bedrooms as the forest climbed the Florida peninsula and closed around them.

Then, almost in the shadow of the *Apollo 12* gantry, Sheppard had seen the nightclub. Startled by its neon façade, he stalled the Cessna. The wheels rattled the palm fronds as he throttled up a saving burst of speed and began a second circuit. The nightclub sat in a forest clearing beside a shallow inlet of the Banana River, near a crumbling camera blockhouse at the end of a concrete runway. The jungle pressed towards the nightclub on three sides, a gaudy aviary of parakeets and macaws, some long-vanished tycoon's weekend paradise.

As the birds hurtled past the windshield, Sheppard saw two figures running towards the forest, a bald-headed woman in the grey shroud of a hospital gown followed by a familiar dark-faced man with the firm step of a warder at a private prison. Despite her age, the woman fled lightly along the ground and seemed almost to be trying to fly. Confused by the noise of the Cessna, her white hands waved a distraught semaphore at the startled macaws, as if hoping to borrow their lurid plumage to cover her bare scalp.

Trying to recognise his wife in this deranged figure, Sheppard turned away for another circuit, and lost his bearings among the maze of inlets and concrete causeways that lay beneath the forest canopy. When he again picked out the nightclub he throttled back and soared in above the trees, only to find his glide-path blocked by a man-powered aircraft that had lifted into the air from the forest clearing.

Twice the size of the Cessna, this creaking cat's cradle of plastic film and piano wire wavered to left and right in front of Sheppard, doing its best to distract him. Dazzled by his own propeller, Sheppard banked and overflew the glider, and caught a last glimpse of the dark-bearded Martinsen pedalling intently inside his transparent envelope, a desperate fish hung from the sky. Then the waiting bough of a forest oak clipped the Cessna as it overran its own slipstream. The sharp antlers stripped the fabric from the starboard wing and tore off the passenger door. Stunned by the roaring air, Sheppard limped the craft back to Cocoa Beach, and brought it down to a heavy landing on the wet sand within the diagram of the immense beaked raptor which Martinsen had carved for him that morning.

Waves washed into the open cabin of the Cessna, flicking a cold foam at Sheppard's ankles. Headlamps approached along the beach, and a government jeep raced down to the water's edge a hundred yards from the aircraft. The young driver stood against the windshield, shouting at Sheppard over her headlamps.

Sheppard released the harness, still reluctant to leave the Cessna. The night had come in from the sea, and now covered the shabby coastal town, but everything was still lit by that same luminescence he had glimpsed from the air, a flood of photons released from the pavilion in the forest where his wife was held prisoner. The waves that washed the propeller of the Cessna, the empty bars and motels along the beach, and the silent gantries of the Space Centre were decorated with millions of miniature lights, lode-points that marked the profiles of a new realm waiting to reconstitute itself around him. Thinking of the nightclub, Sheppard stared into the firefly darkness that enveloped Cape Kennedy. Already he suspected that this was a first glimpse of a small corner of the magnetic city, a suburb of the world beyond time that lay around and within him.

Holding its image to his mind, he forced the door against

the flood and jumped down into the waist-deep water as the last of the night came in on the waves. In the glare of the jeep's headlamps he felt Anne Godwin's angry hands on his shoulders, and fell headlong into the water. Skirt floating around her hips, she pulled him like a drowned pilot onto the beach and held him to the warm sand as the sea rushed into the silver gullies of the great bird whose wings embraced them.

Yet, for all the confusions of the flight, at least he had been able to go outside. Three months earlier, when Sheppard arrived at Cocoa Beach, he had broken into the first motel he could find and locked himself forever into the safety of a darkened bedroom. The journey from Toronto had been a succession of nightmare way-stations, long delays in semi-derelict bus depots and car-rental offices, queasy taxi-rides slumped in the rear seat behind two pairs of dark glasses, coat pulled over his head like a Victorian photographer nervous of his own lens. As he moved south into the steeper sunlight the landscapes of New Jersey, Virginia, and the Carolinas seemed both lurid and opaque, the half-empty towns and uncrowded highways perceived on a pair of raw retinas inflamed by LSD. At times he seemed to be looking at the interior of the sun from a precarious gondola suspended at its core, through an air like fire-glass that might melt the dusty windows of his taxi.

Even Toronto, and his rapid decline after the divorce from Elaine, had not warned him of the real extent of his retreat behind his own nerve-endings. Surrounded by the deserted city, Sheppard was surprised that he was one of the last to be affected, this outwardly cool architect who concealed what was in fact a powerful empathy for other people's psychological ills. A secretary's headache would send him on a restless tour of the design offices. Often he felt that he himself had invented the dying world around him.

It was now twenty years since the earliest symptoms of this strange malaise—the so-called "space sickness"—had made their appearance. At first touching only a small minority of the population, it took root like a lingering disease in the interstices of its victims' lives, in the slightest changes of habit and behaviour. Invariably there was the same reluctance to go out of doors, the abandonment of job, family, and friends, a dislike of daylight, a gradual loss of weight and retreat into a hibernating self. As the illness became more widespread, affecting one in a hundred of the population, blame seemed to lie with the depletion of the ozone layer that had continued apace during the 1980s and 1990s. Perhaps the symptoms of world-shyness and withdrawal were no more than a self-protective response to the hazards of ultraviolet radiation, the psychological equivalent of the sunglasses worn by the blind.

But always there was the exaggerated response to sunlight, the erratic migraines and smarting corneas that hinted at the nervous origins of the malaise. There was the taste for wayward and compulsive hobbies, like the marking of obsessional words in a novel, the construction of pointless arithmetical puzzles on a pocket calculator, the collecting of fragments of TV programmes on a video recorder, and the hours spent playing back particular facial grimaces or shots of staircases.

It was another symptom of the "space sickness," appearing in its terminal stages, that gave both its popular name and the first real clue to the disease. Almost without exception, the victims became convinced that they had once been astronauts. Thousands of the sufferers lay in their darkened hospital wards, or in the seedy bedrooms of back-street hotels, unaware of the world around them but certain that they had once travelled through space to Mars and Venus, walked beside Armstrong on the moon. All of them, in their last seconds of consciousness, became calm and serene, and murmured like drowsy passengers at the start of a new voyage, their journey home to the sun.

Sheppard could remember Elaine's final retreat, and his last visit to the white-walled clinic beside the St. Lawrence River. They had met only once in the two years since the divorce, and he had not been prepared for the transformation of this attractive and self-possessed dentist into a dreaming adolescent being dressed for her first dance. Elaine smiled brightly at him from her anonymous cot, a white hand trying to draw him onto her pillow.

"Roger, we're going soon. We're leaving together. . . ."

As he walked away through the shadowy wards, listening to the babble of voices, the fragments of half-forgotten space jargon picked up from a hundred television serials, he had felt that the entire human race was beginning its embarkation, preparing to repatriate itself to the sun.

Sheppard recalled his last conversation with the young director of the clinic, and the weary physician's gesture of irritation, less with Sheppard than with himself and his profession.

"A *radical* approach? I assume you're thinking of something like resurrection?" Seeing the suspicious tic that jumped across Sheppard's cheek, Martinsen had taken him by the arm in a show of sympathy. "I'm sorry—she was a remarkable woman. We talked for many hours, about you, much of the time. . . ." His small face, as intense as an undernourished child's, was broken by a bleak smile.

Before Sheppard left the clinic the young physician showed him the photographs he had taken of Elaine sitting in a deck-chair on the staff lawn earlier that summer. The first hint of radiant good humour was already on her vivid lips, as if this saucy dentist had been quietly tasting her own laughing gas. Martinsen had clearly been most impressed by her.

But was he on the wrong track, like the whole of the medical profession? The ECT treatments and sensory deprivation, the partial lobotomies and hallucinatory drugs, all seemed to miss the point. It was always best to take the mad on their own terms. What Elaine and the other victims were trying to do was to explore space, using their illness as an extreme metaphor with which to construct a space vehicle. The astronaut obsession was the key. It was curious how close the whole malaise was to the withdrawal symptoms shown by the original astronauts in the decades after the Apollo programme, the retreat into mysticism and silence. Could it be that travelling into outer space, even thinking about and watching it on television, was a forced evolutionary step with unforeseen consequences, the eating of a very special kind of forbidden fruit? Perhaps, for the central nervous system, space was not a linear structure at all, but a model for an advanced condition of time, a metaphor for eternity which they were wrong to try to grasp. . . .

Looking back, Sheppard realised that for years he had

174   MEMORIES OF THE SPACE AGE

been waiting for the first symptoms of the malaise to affect him, that he was all too eager to be inducted into the great voyage towards the sun. During the months before the divorce he had carefully observed the characteristic signs— the loss of weight and appetite, his cavalier neglect of both staff and clients at his architect's practice, his growing reluctance to go out of doors, the allergic skin rashes that sprang up if he stood for even a few seconds in the open sunlight. He tagged along on Elaine's expeditions to Algonquin Park, and spent the entire weekends sealed inside the chromium womb of the Airstream, itself so like an astronaut's capsule.

Was Elaine trying to provoke him? She hated his forced absentmindedness, his endless playing with bizarre clocks and architectural follies, and above all his interest in pornography. This sinister hobby had sprung out of his peculiar obsession with the surrealists, a school of painters which his entire education and cast of mind had previously closed to him. For some reason he found himself gazing for hours at reproductions of de Chirico's Turin, with its empty colonnades and reversed perspectives, its omens of departure. Then there were Magritte's dislocations of time and space, his skies transformed into a series of rectilinear blocks, and Dali's biomorphic anatomies.

These last had led him to his obsession with pornography. Sitting in the darkened bedroom, blinds drawn against the festering sunlight that clung to the balconies of the condominium, he gazed all day at the video-recordings of Elaine at her dressing-table and in the bathroom. Endlessly he played back the zooms and close-ups of her squatting on the bidet, drying herself on the edge of the bath, examining with a hopeful frown the geometry of her right breast. The magnified images of this huge hemisphere, its curvatures splayed between Sheppard's fingers, glowed against the walls and ceiling of the bedroom.

Eventually, even the tolerant Elaine had rebelled. "Roger, what are you doing to yourself—and to me? You've turned this bedroom into a porno-cinema, with me as your star." She held his face, compressing twenty years of affection into her desperate hands. "For God's sake, see someone!"

But Sheppard already had. In the event, three months later, it was Elaine who had gone. At about the time that he closed his office and summarily sacked his exhausted staff, she packed her bags and stepped away into the doubtful safety of the bright sunlight.

Soon after, the space trauma recruited another passenger.

Sheppard had last seen her at Martinsen's clinic, but within only six months he received news of her remarkable recovery, no doubt one of those temporary remissions that sometimes freed the terminal cases from their hospital beds. Martinsen had abandoned his post at the clinic, against the open criticism of his colleagues and allegations of misconduct. He and Elaine had left Canada and moved south to the warm Florida winter, and were now living near the old Space Centre at Cape Kennedy. She was up and about, having miraculously shaken off the deep fugues.

At first Sheppard was sceptical, and guessed that the young neurosurgeon had become obsessed with Elaine and was trying some dangerous and radical treatment in a misguided attempt to save her. He imagined Martinsen abducting Elaine, lifting the drowsy but still beautiful woman from her hospital bed and carrying her out to his car, setting off for the harsh Florida light.

However, Elaine seemed well enough. During this period of apparent recovery she wrote several letters to Sheppard, describing the dark, jewelled beauty of the overgrown forest that surrounded their empty hotel, with its view over the Banana River and the rusting gantries of the abandoned Space Centre. Reading her final letter in the flinty light of the Toronto spring, it seemed to Sheppard that the whole of Florida was transforming itself for Elaine into a vast replica of the cavernous grottoes of Gustave Moreau, a realm of opalised palaces and heraldic animals.

> "... I wish you could be here, Roger, this forest is filled with a deep marine light, almost as if the dark lagoons that once covered the Florida peninsula have come in from the past and submerged us again. There are strange creatures here that seem to have stepped off the surface of the sun. Looking out over the river this morning, I actually saw a unicorn walking on the water, its hooves shod in gold. Philip has moved my bed to the window, and I sit propped here all day, courting the birds, species I've never seen before that seem to have

come from some extraordinary future. I feel sure now that I shall never leave here. Crossing the garden yesterday, I found that I was dressed in light, a sheath of golden scales that fell from my skin onto the glowing grass. The intense sunlight plays strange tricks with time and space. I'm really certain that there's a new kind of time here, flowing in some way from the old Space Centre. Every leaf and flower, even the pen in my hand and these lines I'm writing to you, are surrounded by haloes of themselves.

"Everything moves very slowly now, it seems to take all day for a bird to cross the sky, it begins as a shabby little sparrow and transforms itself into an extravagant creature as plumed and ribboned as a lyre-bird. I'm glad we came, even though Philip was attacked at the time. Coming here was my last chance, he claims, I remember him saying we should seize the light, not fear it. All the same, I think he's got more than he bargained for, he's very tired, poor boy. He's frightened of my falling asleep, he says that when I dream I try to turn into a bird. I woke up by the window this afternoon and he was holding me down, as if I were about to fly off forever into the forest.

"I wish you were here, dear, it's a world the surrealists might have invented. I keep thinking that I will meet you somewhere. . . ."

Attached to the letter was a note from Martinsen, telling him that Elaine had died the following day, and that at her request she had been buried in the forest near the Space Centre. The death certificate was countersigned by the Canadian consul in Miami.

A week later Sheppard closed the Toronto apartment and set off for Cape Kennedy. During the past year he had waited impatiently for the malaise to affect him, ready to make his challenge. Like everyone else he rarely went out during the day, but through the window blinds the sight of this empty sunlit city which came alive only at dusk drove Sheppard into all kinds of restless activity. He would go out into the noon glare and wander among the deserted office blocks, striking stylised poses in the silent curtain-walling. A few heavily cowled policemen and taxi-drivers watched him like spectres on a furnace floor. But Sheppard liked to play with his own obsessions. On impulse he would run around the apartment and release the blinds, turning the rooms into a series of white cubes, so many machines for creating a new kind of time and space.

Thinking of all that Elaine had said in her last letter, and determined as yet not to grieve for her, he set off eagerly on his journey south. Too excited to drive himself, and wary of the steeper sunlight, he moved by bus, rented limousine, and taxi. Elaine had always been an accurate observer, and he was convinced that once he reached Florida he would soon rescue her from Martinsen and find respite for them both in the eternal quiet of the emerald forest.

In fact, he found only a shabby, derelict world of dust, drained swimming-pools, and silence. With the end of the Space Age thirty years earlier, the coastal towns near Cape Kennedy had been abandoned to the encroaching forest. Titusville, Cocoa Beach, and the old launching-grounds now constituted a psychic disaster area, a zone of ill omen. Lines of deserted bars and motels sat in the heat, their signs like rusty toys. Beside the handsome houses once owned by flight controllers and astrophysicists, the empty swimming-pools were a resting-place for dead insects and cracked sunglasses.

Shielded by the coat over his head, Sheppard paid off the uneasy cab driver. As he fumbled with his wallet the un-latched suitcase burst at his feet, exposing its contents to the driver's quizzical gaze: a framed reproduction of Magritte's *March of Summer*, a portable videocassette pro-jector, two tins of soup, a well-thumbed set of six *Kamera Klassic* magazines, a clutch of cassettes labelled *Elaine/Shower Stall I–XXV*, and a paperback selection of Marey's *Chronograms.*

The driver nodded pensively. "Samples? Exactly what is all that—a survival kit?"

"Of a special kind." Unaware of any irony in the man's voice, Sheppard explained: "They're the fusing device for a time-machine. I'll make one up for you. . . ."

"Too late. My son . . ." With a half-smile, the driver wound up his tinted windows and set off for Tampa in a cloud of glassy dust.

Picking the Starlight Motel at random, Sheppard let himself into an intact cabin overlooking the drained pool, the only guest apart from the elderly retriever that dozed on the office steps. He sealed the blinds and spent the next two days resting in the darkness on the musty bed, the suitcase beside him, this "survival kit" that would help him to find Elaine.

At dusk on the second day he left the bed and went to the window for his first careful look at Cocoa Beach. Through the plastic blinds he watched the shadows bisecting the empty pool, drawing a broken diagonal across the canted floor. He remembered his few words to the cab driver. The complex geometry of this three-dimensional sundial seemed to contain the operating codes of a primitive time-machine, repeated a hundred times in all the drained swimming-pools of Cape Kennedy.

Surrounding the motel was the shabby coastal town, its derelict bars and stores shielded from the subtropical dusk by the flamingo-tinted parasols of the palm trees that sprang through the cracked roads and sidewalks. Beyond Cocoa Beach was the Space Centre, its rusting gantries like old wounds in the sky. Staring at them through the sandy glass, Sheppard was aware for the first time of the curious delusion that he had once been an astronaut, lying on his contour couch atop the huge booster, dressed in a suit of silver foil. . . . An absurd idea, but the memory had come from somewhere. For all its fearfulness, the Space Centre was a magnetic zone.

But where was the visionary world which Elaine had described, filled with jewelled birds? The old golden retriever sleeping under the diving board would never walk the Banana River on golden hooves.

Although he rarely left the cabin during the day—the Florida sunlight was still far too strong for him to attempt a head-on confrontation—Sheppard forced himself to put together the elements of an organised life. First, he began to take more care of his own body. His weight had been falling for years, part of a long decline that he had never tried to reverse. Standing in front of the bathroom mirror, he stared at his unsavoury reflection—his wasted shoulders, sallow arms, and inert hands, but a fanatic's face, unshaven skin stretched across the bony points of his jaw and cheeks, orbits like the entrances to forgotten tunnels from which gleamed two penetrating lights. Everyone carried an image of himself that was ten years out of date, but Sheppard felt that he was growing older and younger at the same time— his past and future selves had arranged a mysterious rendez-vous in this motel bedroom.

Still, he forced down the cold soup. He needed to be strong enough to drive a car, map the forests and runways of Cape Kennedy, perhaps hire a light aircraft and carry out an aerial survey of the Space Centre.

At dusk, when the sky seemed to tilt and, thankfully, tipped its freight of cyclamen clouds into the Gulf of Mexico, Sheppard left the motel and foraged for food in the abandoned stores and supermarkets of Cocoa Beach. A few of the older townspeople lived on in the overgrown side-streets, and one bar was still open to the infrequent visitors. Derelicts slept in the rusting cars, and the occasional tramp wandered like a schizophrenic Crusoe among the wild palms and tamarinds. Long-retired engineers from the Space Centre, they hovered in their shabby whites by the deserted stores, forever hesitating to cross the shadowy streets.

As he carried a battery charger from an untended appliance store, Sheppard almost bumped into a former mission controller who had frequently appeared on television during the campaign to prevent the disbandment of NASA. With his dulled face, eyes crossed by the memories of forgotten trajectories, he resembled one of de Chirico's mannequins, heads marked with mathematical formulae.

"No . . ." He wavered away, and grimaced at Sheppard, the wild fracture lines in his face forming the algebra of an unrealisable future. "Another time . . . seventeen seconds . . ." He tottered off into the dusk, tapping the palm trees with one hand, preoccupied with this private countdown.

For the most part they kept to themselves, twilight guests of the abandoned motels where no rent would ever be charged and no memories ever be repaid. All of them avoided the government-aid centre by the bus depot. This unit, staffed by a psychologist from Miami University and two graduate students, distributed food parcels and medicines to the aged townspeople asleep on their rotting porches. It was also their task to round up the itinerant derelicts and persuade them to enter the state-run hospice in Tampa.

On his third evening, as he looted the local supermarket, Sheppard became aware of this alert young psychologist watching him over the dusty windshield of her jeep.

"Do you need any help breaking the law?" She came over and peered into Sheppard's carton. "I'm Anne Godwin, hello. Avocado purée, rice pudding, anchovies, you're all set for a midnight feast. But what about a filet steak, you really look as if you could use one?"

Sheppard tried to sidestep out of her way. "Nothing to worry about. I'm here on a working vacation . . . a scientific project."

She eyed him shrewdly. "Just another summer visitor—though you all have Ph.D.s, the remittance men of the Space Age. Where are you staying? We'll drive you back."

As Sheppard struggled with the heavy carton she signalled to the graduate students, who strolled across the shadowy pavement. At that moment a rusty Chevrolet turned into the street, a bearded man in a soft hat at the wheel. Blocked by the jeep, he stopped to reverse the heavy sedan, and Sheppard recognised the young physician he had last seen on the steps of the clinic overlooking the St. Lawrence.

"Dr. Martinsen!" Anne Godwin shouted as she released Sheppard's arm. "I've been wanting to talk to you, Doctor. Wait . . . ! That prescription you gave me, I take it you've reached the menopause—"

Punching the locked gear shift, Martinsen seemed only interested in avoiding Anne Godwin and her questions. Then he saw Sheppard's alert eyes staring at him above the carton. He paused, and gazed back at Sheppard, with the frank and almost impatient expression of an old friend who had long since come to terms with some act of treachery. He had grown his beard, as if to hide some disease of the mouth or jaw, but his face seemed almost adolescent and at the same time aged by some strange fever.

"Doctor . . . I've reported—" Anne Godwin reached Martinsen's car. He made a halfhearted attempt to hide a loosely tied bundle of brass curtain-rods on the seat beside him. Was he planning to hang the forest with priceless fabrics? Before Sheppard could ask, Martinsen engaged his gear lever and sped off, clipping Anne Godwin's outstretched hand with his wing-mirror.

But at least he knew now that Martinsen was here, and their brief meeting allowed Sheppard to slip away unobserved from Anne Godwin. Followed by the doddery retriever, Sheppard carried his stores back to the motel, and the two of them enjoyed a tasty snack in the darkness beside the drained swimming-pool.

Already he felt stronger, confident that he would soon have tracked down Martinsen and rescued Elaine. For the next week he slept during the mornings and spent the afternoons repairing the old Plymouth he had commandeered from a local garage.

As he guessed, Martinsen soon put in another appearance. A small bird-shaped kite began a series of regular flights in the sky above Cocoa Beach. Its silver line disappeared into the forest somewhere to the north of the town. Two others followed it into the air, and the trio swayed across the placid sky, flown by some enthusiast in the forest.

In the days that followed, other bird-emblems began to appear in the streets of Cocoa Beach, crude Picasso doves chalked on the boarded storefronts, on the dusty roofs of the cars, in the leafy slime on the drained floor of the Starlight pool, all of them presumably cryptic messages from Martinsen.

So the neurosurgeon was trying to lure him into the forest? Finally giving in to his curiosity, Sheppard drove late one afternoon to the light airfield at Titusville. Little traffic visited the shabby airstrip, and a retired commercial pilot dozed in his dusty office below a sign advertising pleasure trips around the Cape.

After a brief haggle, Sheppard rented a single-engined Cessna and took off into the softening dusk. He carried out a careful reconnaissance of the old Space Centre, and at last saw the strange nightclub in the forest, and caught a painful glimpse of the weird, bald-headed spectre racing through the trees. Then Martinsen sprang his surprise with the man-powered glider, clearly intending to ambush Sheppard and force him to crash-land the Cessna into the jungle. However,

Sheppard escaped, and limped back to Cocoa Beach and the incoming tide. Anne Godwin virtually dragged him from the swamped plane, but he managed to pacify her and slip away to the motel.

That evening he rested in his chair beside the empty pool, watching the videocassettes of his wife projected onto the wall at the deep end. Somewhere in these intimate conjunctions of flesh and geometry, of memory, tenderness, and desire, was a key to the vivid air, to that new time and space which the first astronauts had unwittingly revealed here at Cape Kennedy, and which he himself had glimpsed that evening from the cockpit of the drowned aircraft.

At dawn Sheppard fell asleep, only to be woken two hours later by a sudden shift of light in the darkened bedroom. A miniature eclipse of the sun was taking place. The light flickered, trembling against the window. Lying on the bed, Sheppard saw the profile of a woman's face and plumed hair projected onto the plastic blinds.

Bracing himself against the eager morning sunlight, and any unpleasant phobic rush, Sheppard eased the blinds apart. Two hundred feet away, suspended above the chairs on the far side of the swimming-pool, a large man-carrying kite hung in the air. The painted figure of a winged woman was silhouetted against the sun's disc, arms outstretched across the canvas panels. Her shadow tapped the plastic blinds, only inches from Sheppard's fingers, as if asking to be let into the safety of the darkened bedroom.

Was Martinsen offering him a lift in this giant kite? Eyes shielded behind his heaviest sunglasses, Sheppard left the cabin and made his way around the drained pool. It was time now to make a modest challenge to the sun. The kite hung above him, flapping faintly, its silver wire disappearing behind a boat-house half a mile along the beach.

Confident of himself, Sheppard set off along the beach road. During the night the Cessna had vanished, swept away by the sea. Behind the boat-house the kite-flier was winding in his huge craft, and the woman's shadow kept Sheppard company, the feathered train of her hair at his feet. Already he was sure that he would find Martinsen among the derelict speedboats, ravelling in whatever ambiguous message he had sent up into the fierce air.

Almost tripping over the woman's shadow, Sheppard paused to gaze around him. After so many weeks and months of avoiding the daylight, he felt uncertain of the overlit perspectives, of the sea lapping at the edges of his mind, its tongues flicking across the beach like some treacherous animal's. Ignoring it, he ran along the road. The kite-flier had vanished, slipping away into the palm-filled streets.

Sheppard threw away his sunglasses and looked up into the air. He was surprised that the sky was far closer to him than he remembered. It seemed almost vertical, constructed of cubicular blocks a mile in width, the wall of an immense inverted pyramid.

The waves pressed themselves into the wet sand at his feet, flattering courtiers in this palace of light. The beach seemed to tilt, the road reversed its camber. He stopped to steady himself against the roof of an abandoned car. His retinas smarted, stung by thousands of needles. A feverish glitter rose from the roofs of the bars and motels, from the rusty neon signs and the flinty dust at his feet, as if the whole landscape was at the point of ignition.

The boat-house swayed towards him, its roof tilting from side to side. Its cavernous doors opened abruptly, like the walls of an empty mountain. Sheppard stepped back, for a moment blinded by the darkness, as the figure of a winged man burst from the shadows and raced past him across the sand towards the safety of the nearby forest. Sheppard saw a bearded face under the feathered headdress, canvas wings on a wooden frame attached to the man's arms. Waving them up and down like an eccentric aviator, he sprinted between the trees, hindered more than helped by his clumsy wings, one of which sheared from his shoulder when he trapped himself among the palms. He vanished into the forest, still leaping up and down in an attempt to gain the air with his one wing.

Too surprised to laugh at Martinsen, Sheppard ran after him. He followed the line of metal thread that unravelled behind the neurosurgeon. The man-carrying kite had collapsed across the roof of a nearby drugstore, but Sheppard ignored it and ran on through the narrow streets. The line came to an end under the rear wheel of an abandoned truck, but he had already lost Martinsen.

On all sides were the bird-signs, chalked upon the fences and tree-trunks, hundreds of them forming a threatening aviary, as if Martinsen was trying to intimidate the original tenants of the forest and drive them away from the Cape. Sheppard sat on the running-board of the truck, holding the broken end of the kite-line between his fingers.

Why was Martinsen wearing his ludicrous wings, trying to turn himself into a bird? At the end of the road he had even constructed a crude bird-trap, large enough to take a condor, or a small winged man, a cage the size of a garden shed tilted back on a trip-balance of bamboo sticks.

Shielding his eyes from the glare, Sheppard climbed onto the bonnet of the truck and took his bearings. He had entered an unfamiliar part of Cocoa Beach, a maze of roads invaded by the forest. He was well within that zone of vibrant light he had seen from the Cessna, the dim lantern that seemed to extend outwards from the Space Centre, illuminating everything it touched. The light was deeper but more resonant, as if every leaf and flower were a window into a furnace.

Facing him, along the line of shabby bars and stores, was a curious laundromat. Sandwiched between a boarded-up appliance store and a derelict cafeteria, it resembled a miniature temple, with a roof of gilded tiles, chromium doors, and windows of finely etched glass. The whole structure was suffused with a deep interior light, like some lamp-lit grotto in a street of shrines.

The same bizarre architecture was repeated in the nearby roads that lost themselves in the forest. A dry-goods store, a filling station, and a car-wash glittered in the sunlight, apparently designed for some group of visiting space enthusiasts from Bangkok or Las Vegas. Overgrown by the tamarinds and Spanish moss, the gilded turrets and metalled windows formed a jewelled suburb in the forest.

Giving up his search for Martinsen, who by now could be hiding atop one of the Apollo gantries, Sheppard decided to return to his motel. He felt exhausted, as if his body were swathed in a heavy armour. He entered the pavilion beside the cafeteria, smiling at the extravagant interior of this modest laundromat. The washing-machines sat within bowers of ironwork and gilded glass, a series of side-chapels set aside for the worship of the space engineers' overalls and denims.

A ruby light glimmered around Sheppard, as if the pavilion were vibrating above a mild ground-quake. Sheppard touched the glassy wall with one hand, surprised to find that his palm seemed to merge with the surface, as if both were images being projected onto a screen. His fingers trembled, a hundred outlines superimposed upon one another. His feet drummed against the floor, sending the same rapid eddies through his legs and hips, as if he were being transformed into a holographic image, an infinity of replicas of himself. In the mirror above the cashier's metal desk, now a Byzantine throne, he glowed like an archangel. He picked up a glass paperweight from the desk, a tremulous jewel of vibrating coral that suddenly flushed within its own red sea. The ruby light that radiated from every surface within the laundromat was charged by his own bloodstream as it merged into the flicker of multiplying images.

Staring at his translucent hands, Sheppard left the pavilion and set off along the street through the intense sunlight. Beyond the tilting fences he could see the drained swimming-pools of Cocoa Beach, each a complex geometry of light and shadow, canted decks encoding the secret entrances to another dimension. He had entered a city of yantras, cosmic dials sunk into the earth outside each house and motel for the benefit of devout time-travellers.

The streets were deserted, but behind him he heard a familiar laboured pad. The old retriever plodded along the sidewalk, its coat shedding a tremulous golden fur. Sheppard stared at it, for a moment certain that he was seeing the unicorn Elaine had described in her last letter. He looked down at his wrists, at his incandescent fingers. The sun was annealing plates of copper light to his skin, dressing his arms and shoulders in a coronation armour. Time was condensing around him, a thousand replicas of himself from the past and future had invaded the present and clasped themselves to him.

Wings of light hung from his shoulders, feathered into a golden plumage drawn from the sun, the reborn ghosts of his once and future selves, conscripted to join him here in the streets of Cocoa Beach.

Startled by Sheppard, an old woman stared at him from the door of a shack beside the boat-house. Brittle hands felt her blue-rinsed hair, she found herself transformed from a shabby crone into a powdered beauty from the forgotten Versailles of her youth, her thousand younger selves from every day of her life gladly recruited to her side, flushing her withered cheeks and warming her sticklike hands. Her elderly husband gazed at her from his rocker chair, recognising her for the first time in decades, himself transformed into a conquistador half-asleep beside a magical sea.

Sheppard waved to them, and to the tramps and derelicts emerging into the sunlight from their cabins and motel rooms, drowsy angels each awaking to his own youth. The flow of light through the air had begun to slow, layers of time overlaid each other, laminae of past and future fused together. Soon the tide of photons would be still, space and time would set forever.

Eager to become part of this magnetic world, Sheppard raised his wings and turned to face the sun.

"Were you trying to fly?"

Sheppard sat against the wall beside his bed, arms held tight like crippled wings around his knees. Nearby in the darkened bedroom were the familiar pieces of furniture, the Marey and Magritte reproductions pinned to the dressing-table mirror, the projector ready to screen its black coil of film onto the wall above his head.

Yet the room seemed strange, a cabin allocated to him aboard a mysterious liner, with this concerned young psychologist sitting at the foot of the bed. He remembered her jeep in the dusty road, the loud-hailer blaring at the elderly couple and the other derelicts as they were all about to rise into the air, a flight of angels. Suddenly a humdrum world had returned, his past and future selves had fled from him, he found himself standing in a street of shabby bars and shacks, a scarecrow with an old dog. Stunned, the tramps and the old couple had pinched their dry cheeks and faded back to their dark bedrooms.

So this was present time. Without realising it, he had spent all his life in this grey teased-out zone. However, he still held the paperweight in his hand. Though inert now, raised to the light it began to glow again, summoning its brief past and limitless future to its own side.

Sheppard smiled at himself, remembering the translucent wings—an illusion, of course, that blur of multiple selves that shimmered from his arms and shoulders, like an immense electric plumage. But perhaps at some time in the future he became a winged man, a glass bird ready to be snared by Martinsen? He saw himself caged in the condor-traps, dreaming of the sun. . . .

Anne Godwin was shaking her head to herself. She had turned from Sheppard and was examining with evident distaste the pornographic photographs pinned to the wardrobe doors. The glossy prints were overlaid by geometric diagrams which this strange tenant of the motel had pencilled across the copulating women, a secondary anatomy.

"So this is your laboratory? We've been watching you for days. Who are you, anyway?"

Sheppard looked up from his wrists, remembering the golden fluid that had coursed through the now sombre veins.

"Roger Sheppard." On an impulse he added: "I'm an astronaut."

"Really?" Like a concerned nurse, she sat on the edge of the bed, tempted to touch Sheppard's forehead. "It's surprising how many of you come to Cape Kennedy—bearing in mind that the space programme ended thirty years ago."

"It hasn't ended." Quietly, Sheppard did his best to correct this attractive but confused young woman. He wanted her to leave, but already he saw that she might be useful. Besides, he was keen to help her, and set her free from this grey world. "In fact, there are thousands of people involved in a new programme—we're at the beginnings of the first true Space Age."

"Not the second? So the Apollo flights were . . . ?"

"Misconceived." Sheppard gestured at the Marey chronograms on the dressing-table mirror, the blurred time-lapse photos so like the images he had seen of himself before Anne Godwin's arrival. "Space exploration is a branch of applied geometry, with many affinities to pornography."

"That sounds sinister." She gave a small shudder. "These photographs of yours look like the recipe for a special kind of madness. You shouldn't go out during the day. Sunlight inflames the eyes—and the mind."

Sheppard pressed his face against the cool wall, wondering how to get rid of this overconcerned young psychologist. His eyes ran along the sills of light between the plastic blinds. He no longer feared the sun, and was eager to get away from this dark room. His real self belonged to the bright world outside. Sitting here, he felt like a static image in a single frame hanging from the coil of film in the projector on the bedside table. There was a sense of stop-frame about the whole of his past life—his childhood and schooldays, McGill and Cambridge, the junior partnership in Vancouver, his courtship of Elaine, together seemed like so many clips run at the wrong speed. The dreams and ambitions of everyday life, the small hopes and failures, were attempts to bring these separated elements into a single whole again. Emotions were the stress lines in this overstretched web of events.

"Are you all right? Poor man, can't you breathe?"

Sheppard became aware of Anne Godwin's hand on his shoulder. He had clenched his fingers so tightly around the paperweight that his fist was white. He relaxed his grip and showed her the glassy flower.

Casually, he said: "There's some curious architecture here—filling stations and laundromats like Siamese temples. Have you seen them?"

She avoided his gaze. "Yes, to the north of Cocoa Beach. But I keep away from there." She added reluctantly: "There's a strange light by the Space Centre, one doesn't know whether to believe one's eyes." She weighed the flower in her small hand, the fingers still bruised by Martinsen's wing-mirror. "That's where you found this? It's like a fossil of the future."

"It is." Sheppard reached out and took it back. He needed the security of the piece, it reminded him of the luminous world from which this young woman had disturbed him. Perhaps she would join him there? He looked up at her strong forehead and high-bridged nose, a cut-prow that could outstare the time-winds, and at her broad shoulders, strong enough to bear a gilded plumage. He felt a sudden urge to examine her, star her in a new video film, explore the planes of her body like a pilot touching the ailerons and fuselage of an unfamiliar aircraft.

He stood up and stepped to the wardrobe. Without thinking, he began to compare the naked figure of his wife with the anatomy of the young woman sitting on his bed, the contours of her breasts and thighs, the triangles of her neck and pubis.

"Look, do you mind?" She stood between Sheppard and the photographs. "I'm not going to be annexed into this experiment of yours. Anyway, the police are coming to search for that aircraft. Now, what is all this?"

"I'm sorry." Sheppard caught himself. Modestly, he pointed to the elements of his "kit," the film strips, chronograms, and pornographic photos, the Magritte reproduction. "It's a machine, of a kind. A time-machine. It's powered by that empty swimming-pool outside. I'm trying to construct a metaphor to bring my wife back to life."

"Your wife—when did she die?"

"Three months ago. But she's here, in the forest, somewhere near the Space Centre. That was her doctor you saw the other evening, he's trying to turn into a bird." Before Anne Godwin could protest, Sheppard took her arm and beckoned her to the door of the cabin. "Come on, I'll show you how the pool works. Don't worry, you'll be outside for only ten minutes—we've all been too frightened of the sun."

She held his elbow when they reached the edge of the empty pool, her face beginning to fret in the harsh light. The floor of the pool was strewn with leaves and discarded sunglasses, in which the diagram of a bird was clearly visible.

Sheppard breathed freely in the gold-lit air. There were no kites in the sky, but to the north of Cocoa Beach he could see the man-powered aircraft circling the forest, its flimsy wings floating on the thermals. He climbed down the chromium ladder into the shallow end of the pool, then helped the nervous young woman after him.

"This is the key to it all," he explained, as she watched him intently, eyes shielded from the terrifying glare. He felt almost light-headed as he gestured proudly at the angular geometry of white tile and shadow. "It's an engine, Anne, of a unique type. It's no coincidence that the Space Centre is surrounded by empty swimming-pools." Aware of a sudden intimacy with this young psychologist, and certain that she would not report him to the police, he decided to take her into his confidence. As they walked down the inclined floor to the deep end, he held her shoulders. Below their feet cracked the black lenses of dozens of discarded sunglasses, some of the thousands thrown into the drained swimming-pools of Cocoa Beach like coins into a Roman fountain.

"Anne, there's a door out of this pool, I'm trying to find it, a side-door for all of us to escape through. This space sickness—it's really about time, not space, like all the Apollo flights. We think of it as a kind of madness, but in fact it may be part of a contingency plan laid down millions of years ago, a real space programme, a chance to escape into a world beyond time. Thirty years ago we opened a door in the universe. . . ."

He was sitting on the floor of the drained pool among the broken sunglasses, his back to the high wall of the deep end, talking rapidly to himself as Anne Godwin ran up the sloping floor for the medical valise in her jeep. In his white hands he held the glass paperweight, his blood and the sun charging the flower into a red blaze.

Later, as he rested with her in his bedroom at the motel, and during their days together in the coming week, Sheppard explained to her his attempt to rescue his wife, to find a key to everything going on around them.

"Anne, throw away your watch. Fling back the blinds. Think of the universe as a simultaneous structure. Everything that's ever happened, all the events that *will* ever happen, are taking place together. We can die, and yet still live, at the same time. Our sense of our own identity, the stream of things going on around us, are a kind of optical illusion. Our eyes are too close together. Those strange temples in the forest, the marvellous birds and animals—you've seen them too. We've all got to embrace the sun, I want your children to live here, and Elaine. . . ."

"Roger—" Anne moved his hands from her left breast. For minutes, as he spoke, Sheppard had been obsessively feeling its curvatures, like a thief trying to crack a safe. She stared at the naked body of this obsessive man, the white skin alternating at the elbows and neck with areas of black sunburn, a geometry of light and shade as ambiguous as that of the drained swimming-pool.

"Roger, she died three months ago. You showed me a copy of the death certificate."

"Yes, she died," Sheppard agreed. "But only in a sense. She's here, somewhere, in the total time. No one who has ever lived can ever really die. I'm going to find her, I know she's waiting here for me to bring her back to life. . . ." He gestured modestly to the photographs around the bedroom. "It may not look much, but this is a metaphor that's going to work."

During that week, Anne Godwin did her best to help Sheppard construct his "machine." All day she submitted to the Polaroid camera, to the films of her body which Sheppard projected onto the wall above the bed, to the endless pornographic positions in which she arranged her thighs and pubis. Sheppard gazed for hours through his stop-frame focus, as if he would find among these images an anatomical door, one of the keys in a combination whose other tumblers were the Marey chronograms, the surrealist paintings, and the drained swimming-pool in the ever-brighter sunlight outside. In the evenings Sheppard would take her out into the dusk and pose her beside the empty pool, naked from the waist, a dream-woman in a Delvaux landscape.

Meanwhile, Sheppard's duel with Martinsen continued in the skies above Cape Kennedy. After a storm the drowned Cessna was washed up onto the beach, sections of the wing and tailplane, parts of the cabin and undercarriage. The reappearance of the aircraft drove both men into a frenzy of activity. The bird motifs multiplied around the streets of Cocoa Beach, aerosolled onto the flaking storefronts. The outlines of giant birds covered the beach, their talons gripping the fragments of the Cessna.

And all the while the light continued to grow brighter, radiating outwards from the gantries of the Space Centre, inflaming the trees and flowers and paving the dusty sidewalks with a carpet of diamonds. For Anne, this sinister halo that lay over Cocoa Beach seemed to try to sear itself into her retinas. Nervous of windows, she submitted herself to Sheppard during these last days. It was only when he tried to suffocate her, in a confused attempt to release her past and future selves from their prison, that she escaped from the motel and set off for the sheriff at Titusville.

As the siren of the police car faded through the forest, Sheppard rested against the steering wheel of the Plymouth. He had reached the old NASA causeway across the Banana River, barely in time to turn off onto a disused slip road. He unclenched his fists, uneasily aware that his hands still stung from his struggle with Anne Godwin. If only he had been given more time to warn the young woman that he was trying to help her, to free her from that transient time-locked flesh he had caressed so affectionately.

Restarting the engine, Sheppard drove along the slip road, already an uneven jungle path. Here on Merritt Island, almost within the sweeping shadows of the great gantries, the forest seemed ablaze with light, a submarine world in which each leaf and branch hung weightlessly around him. Relics of the first Space Age emerged from the undergrowth like overlit ghosts—a spherical fuel tank stitched into a jacket of flowering lianas, rocket launchers collapsed at the feet of derelict gantries, an immense tracked vehicle six storeys high like an iron hotel, whose unwound treads formed two notched metal roads through the forest.

Six hundred yards ahead, when the path petered out below a collapsed palisade of palm trunks, Sheppard switched off the engine and stepped from the car. Now that he was well within the perimeter of the Space Centre he found that the process of time-fusion was even more advanced. The rotting palms lay beside him, but alive again, the rich scrolls of their bark bright with the jade years of youth, glowing with the copper hues of their forest maturity, elegant in the grey marquetry of their declining age.

Through a break in the canopy Sheppard saw the *Apollo 12* gantry rising through the high oaks like the blade of a giant sundial. Its shadow lay across a silver inlet of the Banana River. Remembering his flight in the Cessna, Sheppard estimated that the nightclub was little more than a mile to the northwest. He set off on foot through the forest, stepping from one log to the next, avoiding the curtains of Spanish moss that hung out their beguiling frescoes. He crossed a small glade beside a shallow stream, where a large alligator basked contentedly in a glow of self-generated light, smiling to itself as its golden jaws nuzzled its past and future selves. Vivid ferns sprang from the damp humus, ornate leaves stamped from foil, layer upon layer of copper and verdigris annealed together. Even the modest ground-ivy seemed to have glutted itself on the corpses of long-vanished astronauts. This was a world nourished by time.

Bird-signs marked the trees, Picasso doves scrawled on every trunk as if some overworked removal manager was preparing the entire forest for flight. There were huge traps, set out in the narrow clearings and clearly designed to snare a prey other than birds. Standing by one of the trip-balanced hutches, Sheppard noticed that they all pointed towards the Apollo gantries. So Martinsen was now frightened, not of Sheppard, but of some aerial creature about to emerge from the heart of the Space Centre.

Sheppard tossed a loose branch onto the sensitive balance of the trap. There was a flicker of sprung bamboo, and the heavy hutch fell to the ground in a cloud of leaves, sending a glimmer of light reverberating among the trees. Almost at once there was a flurry of activity from a copse of glowing palmettos a hundred yards away. As Sheppard waited, hidden behind the trap, a running figure approached, a bearded man in a ragged bird costume, half-Crusoe, half-Indian brave, bright macaw feathers tied to his wrists and an aviator's goggles on his forehead.

He raced up to the trap and stared at it in a distraught way. Relieved to find it empty, he brushed the tattered feathers from his eyes and peered at the canopy overhead, as if expecting to see his quarry perched on a nearby branch.

"Elaine . . . !"

Martinsen's cry was a pathetic moan. Unsure how to calm the neurosurgeon, Sheppard stood up.

"Elaine isn't here, Doctor—"

Martinsen flinched back, his bearded face as small as a child's. He stared at Sheppard, barely managing to control himself. His eyes roved across the glowing ground and foliage, and he flicked nervously at the blurred edges of his fingers, clearly terrified of these ghosts of his other selves now clinging to him. He gestured warningly to Sheppard, pointing to the multiple outlines of his arms and legs that formed a glowing armour.

"Sheppard, keep moving. I heard a noise—have you seen Elaine?"

"She's dead, Doctor."

"Even the dead can dream!" Martinsen nodded to Sheppard, his body shaking as if with fever. He pointed to the bird-traps. "She dreams of flying. I've put these here, to catch her if she tries to escape."

"Doctor . . ." Sheppard approached the exhausted physician. "Let her fly, if she wants to, let her dream. And let her *wake. . . .*"

"Sheppard!" Martinsen stepped back, appalled by Sheppard's electric hand raised towards him. "She's trying to come back from the dead!"

Before Sheppard could reach him, the neurosurgeon turned away. He smoothed his feathers and darted through the palms, and with a hoot of pain and anger disappeared into the forest.

Sheppard let him go. He knew now why Martinsen had flown his kites, and filled the forest with the images of birds. He had been preparing the whole of the Space Centre for Elaine, transforming the jungle into an aviary where she might be at home. Terrified by the sight of this apparently winged woman waking from her deathbed, he hoped that somehow he could keep her within the magical realm of the Cape Kennedy forest.

Leaving the traps, Sheppard set off through the trees, his eyes fixed on the great gantries now only a few hundred yards away. He could feel the time-winds playing on his skin, annealing his other selves onto his arms and shoulders, the transformation of himself once again into that angelic being who strode through the shabby streets of Cocoa Beach. He crossed a concrete runway and entered an area of deeper forest, an emerald world furnished with extravagant frescoes, a palace without walls.

He had almost ceased to breathe. Here, at the centre of the space grounds, he could feel time rapidly engorging itself. The infinite pasts and future of the forest had fused together. A long-tailed parakeet paused among the branches over his head, an electric emblem of itself more magnificent than a peacock. A jewelled snake hung from a bough, gathering to it all the embroidered skins it had once shed.

An inlet of the Banana River slid through the trees, a silver tongue lying passively at his feet. On the bank fifty yards away was the nightclub he had seen from the Cessna, its luminous façade glowing against the foliage.

Sheppard hesitated by the water's edge, and then stepped onto its hard surface. He felt the brittle corrugations under his feet, as if he were walking across a floor of frosted glass. Without time, nothing could disturb the water. On the quartzlike grass below the nightclub a flock of orioles had begun to rise from the ground. They hung silently in the air, their golden fans lit by the sun.

Sheppard stepped ashore and walked up the slope towards them. A giant butterfly spread its harlequin wings against the air, halted in midflight. Avoiding it, Sheppard strode towards the entrance to the nightclub, where the man-powered glider sat on the grass, its propeller a bright sword. An unfamiliar bird crouched on the canopy, a rare species of quetzal or toucan, only recently a modest starling. It stared at its prey, a small lizard sitting on the steps, now a confident iguana armoured within all its selves. Like everything in the forest, both had become ornamental creatures drained of malice.

Through the crystal doors Sheppard peered into the glowing bower of the nightclub. Already he could see that this exotic pavilion had once been no more than a park-keeper's lodge, some bird-watcher's weekend hide transformed by the light of its gathering identities into this miniature casino. The magic casements revealed a small but opulent chamber, a circle of well-upholstered electric chairs beside a kitchen like the side-chapel of a chromium cathedral. Along the rear wall was a set of disused cages left here years earlier by a local ornithologist.

Sheppard unlatched the doors and stepped into the airless interior. A musty and unpleasant odour hung around him, not the spoor of birds but of some unclaimed carcass stored too long in the sun.

Behind the kitchen, and partly hidden in the shadows thrown by the heavy curtains, was a large cage of polished brass rods. It stood on a narrow platform, with a velvet drape across one end, as if some distracted conjuror had been about to perform an elaborate trick involving his assistant and a flock of doves.

Sheppard crossed the chamber, careful not to touch the glowing chairs. The cage enclosed a narrow hospital cot, its side-panels raised and tightly bolted. Lying on its bare mattress was an elderly woman in a bathrobe. She stared with weak eyes at the bars above her face, hair hidden inside a white towel wrapped securely around her forehead. One arthritic hand had seized the pillow, so that her chin jutted forward like a chisel. Her mouth was open in a dead gape, an ugly rictus that exposed her surprisingly even teeth.

Looking down at the waxy skin of this once familiar face, a part of his life for so many years, Sheppard at first thought that he was looking at the corpse of his mother. But as he pulled back the velvet drape the sunlight touched the porcelain caps of her teeth.

"Elaine . . ."

Already he accepted that she was dead, that he had come too late to this makeshift mausoleum where the grieving Martinsen had kept her body, locking it into this cage while he tried to draw Sheppard into the forest.

He reached through the bars and touched her forehead. His nervous hand dislodged the towel, exposing her bald scalp. But before he could replace the grey skull-cloth he felt something seize his wrist. Her right hand, a clutch of knobbly sticks from which all feeling had long expired, moved and took his own. Her weak eyes stared calmly at Sheppard, recognising this young husband without any surprise. Her blanched lips moved across her teeth, testing the polished cusps, as if she were cautiously identifying herself.

"Elaine . . . I've come. I'll take you—" Trying to warm her hand, Sheppard felt an enormous sense of relief, knowing that all the pain and uncertainty of the past months, his search for the secret door, had been worthwhile. He felt a race of affection for his wife, a need to give way to all the stored emotions he had been unable to express since her death. There were a thousand and one things to tell her, about his plans for the future, his uneven health, and above all, his long quest for her across the drained swimming-pools of Cape Kennedy.

He could see the glider outside, the strange bird that guarded the now glowing cockpit, a halo in which they could fly away together. He fumbled with the door to the cage, confused by the almost funereal glimmer that had begun to emanate from Elaine's body. But as she stirred and touched her face, a warm light suffused her grey skin. Her face was softening, the bony points of her forehead retreated into the smooth temples, her mouth lost its death-grimace and became the bright bow of the young student he had first seen twenty years ago, smiling at him across the tennis-club pool. She was a child again, her parched body flushed and irrigated by her previous selves, a lively schoolgirl animated by the images of her past and future.

She sat up, strong fingers releasing the death-cap around her head, and shook loose the damp tresses of silver hair. She reached her hands towards Sheppard, trying to embrace her husband through the bars. Already her arms and shoulders were sheathed in light, that electric plumage which he now wore himself, winged lover of this winged woman.

As he unlocked the cage, Sheppard saw the pavilion doors open to the sun. Martinsen stood in the entrance, staring at the bright air with the toneless expression of a sleepwalker woken from a dark dream. He had shed his feathers, and his body was now dressed in a dozen glimmering images of himself, refractions of past and present seen through the prism of time.

He gestured to Sheppard, trying to warn him away from his wife. Sheppard was certain now that the physician had been given a glimpse into the dream-time, as he mourned

Elaine in the hours after her death. He had seen her come alive from the dead, as the images of her past and youth came to her rescue, drawn here by the unseen powers of the Space Centre. He feared the open cage, and the spectre of this winged woman rising from her dreams at the grave's edge, summoning the legion of her past selves to resurrect her.

Confident that Martinsen would soon understand, Sheppard embraced his wife and lifted her from the bed, eager to let this young woman escape into the sunlight.

Could all this have been waiting for them, around the unseen corners of their past lives? Sheppard stood by the pavilion, looking out at the silent world. An almost tangible amber sea lay over the sand-bars of Cape Kennedy and Merritt Island. Hung from the Apollo gantries, a canopy of diamond air stretched across the forest.

There was a glimmer of movement from the river below. A young woman ran along the surface of the water, her silver hair flowing behind her like half-furled wings. Elaine was learning to fly. The light from her outstretched arms glowed on the water and dappled the leaves of the passing trees. She waved to Sheppard, beckoning him to join her, a child who was both his mother and his daughter.

Sheppard walked towards the water. He moved through the flock of orioles suspended above the grass. Each of the stationary birds had become a congested jewel dazzled by its own reflection. He took one of the birds from the air and smoothed its plumage, searching for that same key he had tried to find when he caressed Anne Godwin. He felt the fluttering aviary in his hands, a feathered universe that trembled around a single heart.

The bird shuddered and came to life, like a flower released from its capsules. It sprang from his fingers, a rush of images of itself between the branches. Glad to set it free, Sheppard lifted the orioles down from the air and caressed them one by one. He released the giant butterfly, the quetzal and the iguana, the moths and insects, the frozen time-locked ferns and palmettos by the water's edge.

Last of all, he released Martinsen. He embraced the helpless doctor, searching for the strong sinews of the young student and the wise bones of the elderly physician. In a sudden moment of recognition, Martinsen found himself, his youth, and his age merged in the open geometries of his face, this happy rendezvous of his past and future selves. He stepped back from Sheppard, hands raised in a generous salute, then ran across the grass towards the river, eager to see Elaine.

Content now, Sheppard set off to join them. Soon the forest would be alive again, and they could return to Cocoa Beach, to that motel where Anne Godwin lay in the darkened bedroom. From there they would move on, to the towns and cities of the south, to the sleepwalking children in the parks, to the dreaming mothers and fathers embalmed in their homes, waiting to be woken from the present into the infinite realm of their time-filled selves.

EPILOGUE: THE MAN WHO WALKED ON THE MOON

I, TOO, WAS ONCE AN ASTRONAUT. AS YOU SEE ME SITTING HERE, in this modest cafe with its distant glimpse of Copacabana Beach, you probably assume that I am a man of few achievements. The shabby briefcase between my worn heels, the stained suit with its frayed cuffs, the unsavoury hands ready to seize the first offer of a free drink, the whole air of failure . . . no doubt you think that I am a minor clerk who has missed promotion once too often, and that I amount to nothing, a person of no past and less future.

For many years I believed this myself. I had been abandoned by the authorities, who were glad to see me exiled to another continent, reduced to begging from the American tourists. I suffered from acute amnesia, and certain domestic problems with my wife and my mother. They now share my small apartment at Ipanema, while I am forced to live in a room above the projection booth of the Luxor Cinema, my thoughts drowned by the sound tracks of science-fiction films.

So many tragic events leave me unsure of myself. Nonetheless, my confidence is returning, and a sense of my true history and worth. Chapters of my life are still hidden from me, and seem as jumbled as the film extracts which the projectionists screen each morning as they focus their cameras. I have still forgotten my years of training, and my mind bars from me any memory of the actual spaceflights. But I am certain that I was once an astronaut.

Years ago, before I went into space, I followed many professions—free-lance journalist, translator, on one occasion even a war correspondent sent to a small war, which unfortunately was never declared. I was in and out of newspaper offices all day, hoping for that one assignment that would match my talents.

Sadly, all this effort failed to get me to the top, and after ten years I found myself displaced by a younger generation. A certain reticence in my character, a sharpness of manner, set me off from my fellow journalists. Even the editors would laugh at me behind my back. I was given trivial assignments —film reviewing, or writing reports on office-equipment fairs. When the circulation wars began, in a doomed response to the onward sweep of television, the editors openly took exception to my waspish style. I became a part-time translator, and taught for an hour each day at a language school, but my income plummeted. My mother, whom I had supported for many years, was forced to leave her home and join my wife and myself in our apartment at Ipanema.

At first my wife resented this, but soon she and my mother teamed up against me. They became impatient with the hours I spent delaying my unhappy visits to the single newspaper office that still held out hope—my journey to work was a transit between one door slammed on my heels and another slammed in my face.

My last friend at the newspaper commiserated with me, as I stood forlornly in the lobby. "For heaven's sake, find a human-interest story! Something tender and affecting, that's what they want upstairs—life isn't an avant-garde movie!"

Pondering this sensible advice, I wandered into the crowded streets. I dreaded the thought of returning home without an assignment. The two women had taken to opening the apartment door together. They would stare at me accusingly, almost barring me from my own home.

Around me were the million faces of the city. People strode past, so occupied with their own lives that they almost pushed me from the pavement. A million human-interest stories, of a banal and pointless kind, an encyclopaedia of mediocrity . . . Giving up, I left Copacabana Avenue and took refuge among the tables of a small cafe in a side-street.

It was there that I met the American astronaut, and began my own career in space.

The cafe terrace was almost deserted, as the office workers returned to their desks after lunch. Behind me, in the shade of the canvas awning, a fair-haired man in a threadbare tropical suit sat beside an empty glass. Guarding my coffee from the flies, I gazed at the small segment of sea visible beyond Copacabana Beach. Slowed by their midday meals, groups of American and European tourists strolled down from the hotels, waving away the jewellery salesmen and lottery touts. Perhaps I would visit Paris or New York, make a new life for myself as a literary critic. . . .

A tartan shirt blocked my view of the sea and its narrow dream of escape. An elderly American, camera slung from his heavy neck, leaned across the table, his grey-haired wife in a loose floral dress beside him.

"Are you the astronaut?" the woman asked in a friendly but sly way, as if about to broach an indiscretion. "The hotel said you would be at this cafe. . . ."

"An astronaut?"

"Yes, the astronaut Commander Scranton . . . ?"

"No, I regret that I'm not an astronaut." Then it occurred to me that this provincial couple, probably a dentist and his wife from the corn-belt, might benefit from a well-informed courier. Perhaps they imagined that their cruise ship had berthed at Miami? I stood up, managing a gallant smile. "Of course, I'm a qualified translator. If you—"

"No, no . . ." Dismissing me with a wave, they moved through the empty tables. "We came to see Mr. Scranton."

Baffled by this bizarre exchange, I watched them approach the man in the tropical suit. A nondescript fellow in his late forties, he had thinning blond hair and a strong-jawed American face from which all confidence had long been drained. He stared in a resigned way at his hands, which waited beside his empty glass, as if unable to explain to them that little refreshment would reach them that day. He was clearly undernourished, perhaps an ex-seaman who had jumped ship, one of thousands of down-and-outs trying to live by their wits on some of the hardest pavements in the world.

However, he looked up sharply enough as the elderly couple approached him. When they repeated their question about the astronaut, he beckoned them to a seat. To my surprise, the waiter was summoned, and drinks were brought to the table. The husband unpacked his camera, while a relaxed conversation took place between his wife and this seedy figure.

"Dear, don't forget Mr. Scranton. . . ."

"Oh, please forgive me."

The husband removed several banknotes from his wallet. His wife passed them across the table to Scranton, who then stood up. Photographs were taken, first of Scranton standing next to the smiling wife, then of the husband grinning broadly beside the gaunt American. The source of all this good humour eluded me, as it did Scranton, whose eyes stared gravely at the street with a degree of respect due to the surface of the moon. But already a second group of tourists had walked down from Copacabana Beach, and I heard more laughter when one called out: "There's the astronaut . . . !"

Quite mystified, I watched a further round of photographs being taken. The couples stood on either side of the American, grinning away as if he were a camel driver posing for pennies against a backdrop of thc pyramids.

I ordered a small brandy from the waiter. He had ignored all this, pocketing his tips with a straight face.

"This fellow . . . ?" I asked. "Who is he? An astronaut?"

"Of course . . ." The waiter flicked a bottle-top into the air and treated the sky to a knowing sneer. "Who else but the man in the moon?"

The tourists had gone, strolling past the leatherware and jewellery stores. Alone now after his brief fame, the American sat among the empty glasses, counting the money he had collected.

The man in the moon?

Then I remembered the newspaper headline, and the exposé I had read two years earlier of this impoverished American who claimed to have been an astronaut, and told his story to the tourists for the price of a drink. At first almost everyone believed him, and he had become a popular figure in the hotel lobbies along Copacabana Beach. Apparently he had flown on one of the Apollo missions from Cape Kennedy in the 1970s, and his long-jawed face and stoical pilot's eyes seemed vaguely familiar from the magazine photographs. He was properly reticent, but if pressed with a tourist dollar could talk convincingly about the early lunar flights. In its way it was deeply moving to sit at a cafe table with a man who had walked on the moon. . . .

Then an overcurious reporter exploded the whole pretence. No man named Scranton had ever flown in space, and the American authorities confirmed that his photograph was not that of any past or present astronaut. In fact he was a failed crop-duster from Florida who had lost his pilot's licence and whose knowledge of the Apollo flights had been mugged up from newspapers and television programmes.

Surprisingly, Scranton's career had not ended there and then, but moved on to a second tragicomical phase. Far from consigning him to oblivion, the exposure brought him a genuine small celebrity. Banished from the grand hotels of Copacabana, he hung about the cheaper cafes in the sidestreets, still claiming to have been an astronaut, ignoring those who derided him from their car windows. The dignified way in which he maintained his fraud tapped a certain good-humoured tolerance, much like the affection felt in the United States for those eccentric old men who falsely claimed to their deaths that they were veterans of the American Civil War.

So Scranton stayed on, willing to talk for a few dollars about his journey to the moon, quoting the same tired phrases that failed to convince the youngest schoolboy. Soon no one bothered to question him closely, and his chief function was to be photographed beside parties of visitors, an amusing oddity of the tourist trail.

But perhaps the American was more devious than he appeared, with his shabby suit and hangdog gaze? As I sat there, guarding the brandy I could barely afford, I resented Scranton's bogus celebrity, and the tourist revenue it brought him. For years I, too, had maintained a charade— the mask of good humour that I presented to my colleagues in the newspaper world—but it had brought me nothing. Scranton at least was left alone for most of his time, something I craved more than any celebrity. Comparing our situations, there was plainly a strong element of injustice—the notorious British criminal who made a comfortable living being photographed by the tourists in the more expensive Copacabana restaurants had at least robbed one of Her Majesty's mail-trains.

At the same time, was this the human-interest story that would help me to remake my career? Could I provide a final ironic twist by revealing that, thanks to his exposure, the bogus astronaut was now doubly successful?

During the next days I visited the cafe promptly at noon. Notebook at the ready, I kept a careful watch for Scranton. He usually appeared in the early afternoon, as soon as the clerks and secretaries had finished their coffee. In that brief lull, when the shadows crossed from one side of the street to the other, Scranton would materialise, as if from a trapdoor in the pavement. He was always alone, walking straight-backed in his faded suit, but with the uncertainty of someone who suspects that he is keeping an appointment on the wrong day. He would slip into his place under the cafe awning, order a glass of beer from the sceptical waiter, and then gaze across the street at the vistas of an invisible space.

It soon became clear that Scranton's celebrity was as threadbare as his shirt cuffs. Few tourists visited him, and often a whole afternoon passed without a single customer. Then the waiter would scrape the chairs around Scranton's table, trying to distract him from his reveries of an imaginary moon. Indeed, on the fourth day, within a few minutes of Scranton's arrival, the waiter slapped the tabletop with his towel, already cancelling the afternoon's performance.

"Away, away . . . it's impossible!" He seized the newspaper that Scranton had found on a nearby chair. "No more stories about the moon . . ."

Scranton stood up, head bowed beneath the awning. He seemed resigned to this abuse. "All right . . . I can take my trade down the street."

To forestall this, I left my seat and moved through the empty tables.

"Mr. Scranton? Perhaps we can speak? I'd like to buy you a drink."

"By all means." Scranton beckoned me to a chair. Ready for business, he sat upright, and with a conscious effort managed to bring the focus of his gaze from infinity to a distance of fifty feet away. He was poorly nourished, and his perfunctory shave revealed an almost tubercular pallor. Yet there was a certain resolute quality about this vagrant figure that I had not expected. Sitting beside him, I was aware of an intense and almost willful isolation, not just in this foreign city, but in the world at large.

I showed him my card. "I'm writing a book of criticism on the science-fiction cinema. It would be interesting to hear your opinions. You are Commander Scranton, the Apollo astronaut?"

"That is correct."

"Good. I wondered how you viewed the science-fiction film . . . how convincing you found the presentation of outer space, the lunar surface, and so on. . . ."

Scranton stared bleakly at the tabletop. A faint smile exposed his yellowing teeth, and I assumed that he had seen through my little ruse.

"I'll be happy to set you straight," he told me. "But I make a small charge."

"Of course." I searched in my pockets. "Your professional expertise, naturally . . ."

I placed some coins on the table, intending to hunt for a modest banknote. Scranton selected three of the coins, enough to pay for a loaf of bread, and pushed the rest towards me.

"Science-fiction films—? They're good. Very accurate. On the whole I'd say they do an excellent job."

"That's encouraging to hear. These Hollywood epics are not usually noted for their realism."

"Well . . . you have to understand that the Apollo teams brought back a lot of film footage."

"I'm sure." I tried to keep the amusement out of my voice. "The studios must have been grateful to you. After all, you could describe the actual moon-walks."

Scranton nodded sagely. "I acted as consultant to one of the Hollywood majors. All in all, you can take it from me that those pictures are pretty realistic."

"Fascinating . . . coming from you that has authority. As a matter of interest, what was being on the moon literally like?"

For the first time Scranton seemed to notice me. Had he glimpsed some shared strain in our characters? This care-worn American had all the refinement of an unemployed car mechanic, and yet he seemed almost tempted to befriend me.

"Being on the moon?" His tired gaze inspected the nar-row street of cheap jewellery stores, with its office messengers and lottery touts, the off-duty taxi-drivers lean-ing against their cars. "It was just like being here."

"So . . ." I put away my notebook. Any further subterfuge was unnecessary. I had treated our meeting as a joke, but Scranton was sincere, and anyway utterly indifferent to my opinion of him. The tourists and passing policemen, the middle-aged women sitting at a nearby table, together barely existed for him. They were no more than shadows on the screen of his mind, through which he could see the horizons of an almost planetary emptiness.

For the first time I was in the presence of someone who had nothing—even less than the beggars of Rio, for they at least were linked to the material world by their longings for it. Scranton embodied the absolute loneliness of the human being in space and time, a situation which in many ways I shared. Even the act of convincing himself that he was a former astronaut only emphasised his isolation.

"A remarkable story," I commented. "One can't help wondering if we were right to leave this planet. I'm reminded of the question posed by the Chilean painter Matta—'Why must we fear a disaster in space in order to understand our own times?' It's a pity you didn't bring back any memen-toes of your moon-walks."

Scranton's shoulders straightened. I could see him count-ing the coins on the table. "I do have certain materials. . . ."

I nearly laughed. "What? A piece of lunar rock? Some moon-dust?"

"Various photographic materials."

"Photographs?" Was it possible that Scranton had told the truth, and that he had indeed been an astronaut? If I could prove that the whole notion of his imposture was an error, an oversight by the journalist who had investigated the case, I would have the makings of a front-page scoop. . . . "Could I see them?—perhaps I could use them in my book . . . ?"

"Well . . ." Scranton felt for the coins in his pocket. He looked hungry, and obviously thought only of spending them on a loaf of bread.

"Of course," I added, "I'll provide an extra fee. As for my book, the publishers might well pay many hundreds of dollars."

"Hundreds . . ." Scranton seemed impressed. He shook his head, as if amused by the ways of the world. I expected him to be shy of revealing where he lived, but he stood up and gestured me to finish my drink. "I'm staying a few minutes' walk from here."

He waited among the tables, staring across the street. Seeing the passersby through his eyes, I was aware that they had begun to seem almost transparent, shadow players created by a frolic of the sun.

We soon arrived at Scranton's modest room behind the Luxor Cinema, a small theatre off Copacabana Avenue that had seen better days. Two former storerooms and an office above the projection booth had been let as apartments, which we reached after climbing a dank emergency stairway.

Exhausted by the effort, Scranton swayed against the door. He wiped the spit from his mouth onto the lapel of his jacket, and ushered me into the room. "Make yourself comfortable. . . ."

A dusty light fell across the narrow bed, reflected in the cold-water tap of a greasy handbasin supported from the wall by its waste-pipe. Sheets of newspaper were wrapped around a pillow, stained with sweat and some unsavoury mucus, perhaps after an attack of malarial or tubercular fever.

Eager to leave this infectious den, I drew out my wallet. "The photographs . . . ?"

Scranton sat on the bed, staring at the yellowing wall behind me as if he had forgotten that I was there. Once again I was aware of his ability to isolate himself from the surrounding world, a talent I envied him, if little else.

"Sure . . . they're over here." He stood up and went to the suitcase that lay on a card-table behind the door. Taking the money from me, he opened the lid and lifted out a bundle of magazines. Among them were loose pages torn from *Life*

and *Newsweek*, and special supplements of the Rio newspapers devoted to the Apollo spaceflights and the moon landings. The familiar images of Armstrong and the lunar
module, the space-walks and splashdowns, had been endlessly thumbed. The captions were marked with coloured
pencil, as if Scranton had spent hours memorising these
photographs brought back from the tideways of space.

I moved the magazines to one side, hoping to find some
documentary evidence of Scranton's own involvement in
the spaceflights, perhaps a close-up photograph taken by
a fellow astronaut.

"Is this it? There's nothing else?"

"That's it." Scranton gestured encouragingly. "They're
good pictures. Pretty well what it was like."

"I suppose that's true. I had hoped. . . ."

I peered at Scranton, expecting some small show of em-
barrassment. These faded pages, far from being the memen-
toes of a real astronaut, were obviously the prompt cards
of an imposter. However, there was not the slightest doubt
that Scranton was sincere.

I stood in the street below the portico of the Luxor Cinema,
whose garish posters, advertising some science-fiction spec-
tacular, seemed as inflamed as the mind of the American.
Despite all that I had suspected, I felt an intense disappoint-
ment. I had deluded myself, thinking that Scranton would
rescue my career. Now I was left with nothing but an empty
notebook and the tram journey back to the crowded apartment in Ipanema. I dreaded the prospect of seeing my wife
and my mother at the door, their eyes screwed to the same
accusing focus.

Nonetheless, as I walked down Copacabana Avenue to the
tram-stop, I felt a curious sense of release. The noisy
pavements, the arrogant pickpockets plucking at my
clothes, the traffic that aggravated the slightest tendency
to migraines, all seemed to have receded, as if a small
distance had opened between myself and the congested
world. My meeting with Scranton, my brief involvement
with this marooned man, allowed me to see everything in
a more detached way. The businessmen with their brief-
cases, the afternoon tarts swinging their shiny handbags,

the salesmen with their sheets of lottery tickets, almost deferred to me. Time and space had altered their perspectives, and the city was yielding to me. As I crossed the road to the tram-stop several minutes seemed to pass. But I was not run over.

This sense of a loosening air persisted as I rode back to Ipanema. My fellow passengers, who would usually have irritated me with their cheap scent and vulgar clothes, their look of bored animals in a menagerie, now scarcely intruded into my vision. I gazed down corridors of light that ran between them like the aisles of an open-air cathedral.

"You've found a story," my wife announced within a second of opening the door.

"They've commissioned an article," my mother confirmed. "I knew they would."

They stepped back and watched me as I made a leisurely tour of the cramped apartment. My changed demeanour clearly impressed them. They pestered me with questions, but even their presence was less bothersome. The universe, thanks to Scranton's example, had loosened its grip. Sitting at the dinner table, I silenced them with a raised finger.

"I am about to embark on a new career. . . ."

From then on I became ever more involved with Scranton. I had not intended to see the American again, but the germ of his loneliness had entered my blood. Within two days I returned to the cafe in the side-street, but the tables were deserted. I watched as two parties of tourists stopped to ask for "the astronaut." I then questioned the waiter, suspecting that he had banished the poor man. But, no, the American would be back the next day, he had been ill, or perhaps had secretly gone to the moon on business.

In fact, it was three days before Scranton at last appeared. Materialising from the afternoon heat, he entered the cafe and sat under the awning. At first he failed to notice that I was there, but Scranton's mere presence was enough to satisfy me. The crowds and traffic, which had begun once again to close around me, halted their clamour and withdrew. On the noisy street were imposed the silences of a lunar landscape.

However, it was all too clear that Scranton had been ill.

His face was sallow with fever, and the effort of sitting in his chair soon tired him. When the first American tourists stopped at his table he barely rose from his seat, and while the photographs were taken he held tightly to the awning above his head.

By the next afternoon his fever had subsided, but he was so strained and ill-kempt that the waiter at first refused to admit him to the cafe. A trio of Californian spinsters who approached his table were clearly unsure that this decaying figure was indeed the bogus astronaut, and would have left had I not ushered them back to Scranton.

"Yes, this is Commander Scranton, the famous astronaut. I am his associate—do let me hold your camera. . . ."

I waited impatiently for them to leave, and sat down at Scranton's table. Ill the American might be, but I needed him. After ordering a brandy, I helped Scranton to hold the glass. As I pressed the spinsters' banknote into his pocket I could feel that his suit was soaked with sweat.

"I'll walk you back to your room. Don't thank me, it's in my direction."

"Well, I could use an arm." Scranton stared at the street, as if its few yards encompassed a Grand Canyon of space. "It's getting to be a long way."

"A long way! Scranton, I understand that. . . ."

It took us half an hour to cover the few hundred yards to the Luxor Cinema. But already time was becoming an elastic dimension, and from then on most of my waking hours were spent with Scranton. Each morning I would visit the shabby room behind the cinema, bringing a paper bag of sweet-cakes and a flask of tea I had prepared in the apartment under my wife's suspicious gaze. Often the American had little idea who I was, but this no longer worried me. He lay in his narrow bed, letting me raise his head as I changed the sheets of newspaper that covered his pillow. When he spoke, his voice was too weak to be heard above the soundtracks of the science-fiction films that boomed through the crumbling walls.

Even in this moribund state, Scranton's example was a powerful tonic, and when I left him in the evening I would walk the crowded streets without any fear. Sometimes my former colleagues called to me from the steps of the newspaper office, but I was barely aware of them, as if they were planetary visitors hailing me from the edge of a remote crater.

Looking back on these exhilarating days, I regret only that I never called a doctor to see Scranton. Frequently, though, the American would recover his strength, and after I had shaved him we would go down into the street. I relished these outings with Scranton. Arm in arm, we moved through the afternoon crowds, which seemed to part around us. Our fellow pedestrians had become remote and fleeting figures, little more than tricks of the sun. Sometimes, I could no longer see their faces. It was then that I observed the world through Scranton's eyes, and knew what it was to be an astronaut.

Needless to say, the rest of my life had collapsed at my feet. Having given up my work as a translator, I soon ran out of money, and was forced to borrow from my mother. At my wife's instigation, the features editor of the newspaper called me to his office, and made it plain that as an immense concession (in fact he had always been intrigued by my wife) he would let me review a science-fiction film at the Luxor. Before walking out, I told him that I was already too familiar with the film, and my one hope was to see it banned from the city forever.

So ended my connection with the newspaper. Soon after, the two women evicted me from my apartment. I was happy to leave them, taking with me only the reclining sun-chair on which my wife passed most of her days in preparation for her new career as a model. The sun-chair became my bed when I moved into Scranton's room.

By then the decline in Scranton's health forced me to be with him constantly. Far from being an object of charity, Scranton was now my only source of income. Our needs for several days could be met by a single session with the American tourists. I did my best to care for Scranton, but during his final illness I was too immersed in that sense of an emptying world even to notice the young doctor whose alarmed presence filled the tiny room. By a last irony, towards the end even Scranton himself seemed barely visible to me. As he died I was reading the mucus-stained head-lines on his pillow.

After Scranton's death I remained in his room at the Luxor. Despite the fame he had once enjoyed, his burial at the Prot-estant cemetery was attended only by myself, but in a sense this was just, as he and I were the only real inhabitants of the city. Later I went through the few possessions in his suit-case, and found a faded pilot's logbook. Its pages confirmed that Scranton had worked as a pilot for a crop-spraying com-pany in Florida throughout the years of the Apollo pro-gramme.

Nonetheless, Scranton had travelled in space. He had known the loneliness of separation from all other human be-ings, he had gazed at the empty perspectives that I myself had seen. Curiously, the pages torn from the news maga-zines seemed more real than the pilot's logbook. The photographs of Armstrong and his fellow astronauts were really of Scranton and myself as we walked together on the moon of this world.

I reflected on this as I sat at the small cafe in the side-street. As a gesture to Scranton's memory, I had chosen his chair below the awning. I thought of the planetary land-scapes that Scranton had taught me to see, those empty vistas devoid of human beings. Already I was aware of a previous career, which my wife and the pressures of every-day life had hidden from me. There were the years of train-ing for a great voyage, and a coastline similar to that of Cape Kennedy receding below me. . . .

My reverie was interrupted by a pair of American tourists. A middle-aged man and his daughter, who held the family camera to her chin, approached the table.

"Excuse me," the man asked with an overready smile. "Are you the . . . the astronaut? We were told by the hotel that you might be here. . . ."

I stared at them without rancour, treating them to a glimpse of those eyes that had seen the void. I, too, had walked on the moon.

"Please sit down," I told them casually. "Yes, I am the astronaut."